In Loving Memory Of,

Kenny E. Davis III and Alex L. Turner

"Missed but never forgotten."

Dedicated to,

Johnte Harris and Sanya Gragg

The Secret to our wonderful Lives is Our Wives
Thank you both.

Published by
Books Brothers Publishing
5680 HWY 6 #329
Missouri City, TX 77459

Paperback ISBN: 1-4120-5087-1
Harris, Corey.
Secret Lives Of the Wives/by Corey Harris

Publisher Notice
This book is a work of fiction. Names, characters, places and incidents were created by the author and his imagination or are used fictitiously and any resemblance to actual persons, dead or alive, business establishments, events or locations is entirely coincidental.

"The ultimate measure of a man is not where he stands in moments of comfort and convenience, but where he stands at times of challenge and controversy...We must develop and maintain the capacity to forgive. He who is devoid of the power to forgive is devoid of the power to love. There is some good in the worst of us and some evil in the best of us...Love is the only force capable of transforming an enemy into a friend."

Martin Luther King

Prologue

Come explore with me, the professional football player's dilemma. The dilemma of maintaining the dominance and self-confidence that made NFL teams covet us and sports fans across the world love us - doing it in such a way that doesn't isolate or make our wives resent the very things that drew them to us. Think about it, so many Players don't know who to trust or who's being real. We just know what got us the money, fame, and prestige in the first place. Face it, a big part of why women love men in the League is because we're rich, athletic, respected and because of the life-style we can provide. How many times have you seen a drop dead gorgeous woman, with a drop dead ugly football player? Exactly, nine times out of ten, if that same guy was a school teacher, he wouldn't stand a chance.

Professional athletes are everything women "think" they want and need in a man. It's partially because we (players) know that only 1 in 500,000 men fit the above description, and that makes us *the winning lotto ticket.* And the admiration is unrestricted and void of racial barriers – we can have just about any woman we choose, but at what cost? It is this perception, on behalf of myself and other professional athletes, that has ruined so many high profile relationships. And, it is this arrogance that provides the backdrop for my personal experiences. Twelve years in the National Football League has inspired me with more material than I could possibly chronicle in one book.

The very reason that women fall in love with us many times ends up being the same reason they decide to get into the "GAME" in the first place. What game you might ask? You know the *game*. The one where lies, deceit, and selfish desires creep so far into our relationship, that by the time we realize what's at stake, we're either caught, about to get caught, don't care if we get caught or too infatuated with the "other" person to let go. And Players, we're so ignorant and full of ourselves, that often by the time we have a clue that our women are even in the game, it's too late to *right our wrongs*. We honestly feel that there is no way in hell that a woman would ever try to play us the way we play them. After all look how well we take care of them, right? *Look how well we take care of them.*

So ladies and gentlemen pay close attention because these are tales of beautiful, once faithful and devoted wives that got pushed into the "GAME" by the men they vowed to let only death part them. **S.L.O.W** (*S*ecret *L*ives *O*f the *W*ives): *"The Flip Side of the Coin."* Pro sports will never be the same and neither will *pro marriages*.

And yes there's a chance I could be describing your wife or the wife of your favorite player. It could happen to you if you're a player and if you're a player's wife, you might know exactly what I'm talking about.

So after you read this, I hope that you take it as a wake-up call, a wake-up call to the men who think that the things that their money and power can provide are the things that will keep their mates faithful and satisfied. Fellas it's clear to me that although we invented the *game*... the women have ultimately perfected it. Finally, let this book be a wake-up call to all the women who pursue Players for all the wrong reasons , if you're not careful, you might just get the "player" you wished for, and everything that comes with him, including the *game*.

There's nothing "slow" about the Secret Lives Of the Wives: "The Flip Side of the Coin." So, in the spirit of America's favorite game, *"What time is it?! Game Time!"*

Althea McQueen aka The W.I.N.N.E.R
Chapter 1

"Excuse me Miss...you can't sit there," a petite and attractive waitress interrupted.

Althea was instantly aggravated, "Why not?"

"Because these seats are reserved for *V.I.P* customers, you know the ones with money, not the ones waiting for the ones with the money.... So--"

"Excuse me?" Althea replied angrily with a roll of her neck.

"You're excused." the waitress snapped back.

"Sweetheart," Althea said with a patronizing sweetness, "Can you please do me a favor? Before you make a very big mistake, you need get the general manager for me."

Althea was so pissed she couldn't find the patience to wait, as she turned to her sister and best friend, "Fuck this. Let's go ya'll!"

Her sister Maia rolled her lips and face up as to say, *"Umm, we did just pay to get in here!"* Her girl Charlene was also visibly agitated.

"Althea, you are so high strung girl. Chill out! You know this is the place to be. Do you see all these fly brothas in here tonight? I'm not *trying* to be anywhere else girlfriend," Charlene said with attitude.

Althea didn't really care about what the other women wanted. "If ya'll think I'm going to stay in this place after that skank just disrespected me, then both of you have lost your damn minds. I'm not giving this raggedy ass club another dime! And you better believe my husband won't

4

be in this bitch again either. Althea noticed the women were no longer paying attention to her and blurted out, "I said let's go!" Althea screamed so loudly, the women damn near fell out of their seats. Charlene and Maia quickly grabbed their purses as they noticed Althea bolting towards the door. "As a matter of fact, they better give me the money back I spent getting into this sorry ass place. I hate it when these $1.50 an hour ass hoes pretend like they don't know who the hell I am. You just wait 'til--" Althea stopped mid sentence as she noticed two of the sexiest men she had ever laid eyes on approaching them. The women's thoughts were synchronized, *DAMN! These Brothers are FINE!*

"Honey, I did you one better," said the waitress upon her return, "I brought the general manager and owner too!" she said with a smirk.

"What seems to be the problem ladies? Oh I'm sorry... I'm Marcus Edwards, the general manager and this is Mr. Torey Franklin, the owner of the club.

"Now I *know* you three beautiful women aren't leaving so soon, are you?" Torey said as he cut his piercing brown eyes at the rude waitress. Charlene's mouth fell open as she gazed at the two good-looking, well-sculpted men. Both of them were over six feet tall with perfectly chiseled bodies. Torey's sheer black shirt showed off the sculpted muscles he spent years building as a pro ball player. Marcus was a bit taller than Torey and every bit as fine. Charlene's eyes caressed Marcus's entire body, ending at his crotch.

"Girl, close your mouth," Althea said emphatically under her breath to Charlene.

Torey knew he had seen two of these faces before. In fact, they were the wives of two well-known NFL football players. "Aren't you Charlene Johnson... and Althea McQueen?"

"YES, and we're leaving!" Althea quickly retorted. Although these men were absolutely gorgeous, Althea was entirely too pissed for it to matter. Her night had been ruined and not even two fine specimens like Marcus and Torey, could right this wrong. At this point, they could have been *Denzel* and *Taye Diggs* for all she cared.

"Ladies, at least give me a chance to make it right," said Torey. "Now ya'll know we don't tolerate anyone mistreating our patrons... especially our V.I.P's."

"I can't tell," Althea mumbled with a slight grin on her face.

"It might not seem like it tonight, but we do pride ourselves on great service. Besides, why wouldn't we want to make sure that the prettiest ladies in the building were taken care of, not to mention your husbands are associates of mine."

Unlike Althea, Charlene, the freak of the crew, was a lot more enthusiastic about the chance meeting. She was not about to let this "networking" opportunity go to waste. "Okay," Charlene said while flirtatiously biting her bottom lip and glancing at the men seductively. "Now, how can you gentlemen possibly make this up to us?"

"Well, I'm leaving town, but I'll leave you in very good hands with Marcus. And ladies, you have my personal guarantee that if he doesn't make it up to you – he'll have to answer to me. Better yet, Marcus I'm telling *you*." Marcus leaned in as Torey wrapped his arm tightly around his neck "Not only do I want you to fix this, but I want you to make sure that any ill feelings that Mrs. McQueen and her guests have about H-town Live disappear, period." Torey spoke loud enough so that the three women could overhear his instructions.

"You got it, boss!" Marcus said sarcastically.

The ladies recognized the good cop/bad cop routine, but were blushing nonetheless. How could they *not* be enamored by two suave Black men, dressed to the nines, and smelling just as sexy as they looked? These were the type of brothers that belonged on the cover of somebody's magazine: GQ, Black Enterprise, Playgirl, …something; they were definitely rare commodities.

"Nice meeting you ladies and I'm sorry for the inconvenience. Tell your husbands I took care of ya'll okay?" Torey said with the charisma that he was known for.

"Okay, ladies you heard the man. Your wish is my command," Marcus said charmingly. His voice reeked of sensuality.

Damn, this man knows he is too fine, Althea shamefully caught herself thinking. Conscious of her sinful thoughts, Althea quickly regained her composure.

By the look on Althea's face, there was not much more that Marcus could do – that night anyway. However, he would certainly continue to try. After all, his job was to make the club money, and letting Althea McQueen leave unhappy meant losing the thousands of dollars that she and her husband spent there regularly. Marcus recognized early on that Althea would be a challenge. But, his ability to read people was one of the things that made him a great general manager. He understood that if he was too persistent in his attempt to satisfy his V.I.P customers, he would come off as desperate. On the other hand, if he was too nonchalant, he would appear arrogant, possibly offending them even more. Marcus learned long ago, that V.I.P's were the most sensitive customers. So it was clear that he had to make these women feel important, yet expendable – sexy, but in a way that let them know they were only a few in a very elite class of good-looking , successful men and women who were afforded V.I.P treatment at H-Town Live.

There was a unique allure to H-Town Live - the hottest nightclub in Houston. It was definitely "The Spot." People didn't just want to get in, they *had* to get in. There were four different V.I.P areas in the club, all with their own "status" criteria. So Marcus was keen to the "ego blow" the women had suffered by being accosted by the waitress and in turn was willing to soak up some of their humiliation with a little of his own.

"Sorry Marcus. We appreciate *your* hospitality," Althea said as she rolled her eyes at the waitress once more, "but the night has already been ruined." *Damn Marcus, stop looking in my eyes like that,* she thought to herself.

"Okay ladies, I can see that tonight is not a good night. Please let me escort you out, but first let me give you my home number, cell, fax, pager, social security number… ya'll got a sidekick?" Althea managed to crack a smile while making eye contact with Marcus, who appeared genuine in his attempts to salvage the ladies' evening. She immediately realized that what started out as an inadvertent glance had turned into a full blown flirtatious stare.

"Nah, seriously ladies, here's my cell number," Marcus laughed. "We're having a huge concert next Friday. My man Musiq is performing. We're also trying to get the Roots to stop by and play a set. I am hoping you guys will do me the honor of being my special, V.I.P.A.P.W.D."

"What the hell is that?" Maia asked.

"Very Important Pretty Ass Players' Wives, Damn!" he said cleverly as he winked at Althea. The ladies burst into laughter. "So do we have a date?" he asked.

Charlene couldn't wait to put her sarcasm to the test. "Can you move the concert to next Saturday? I won't be back in town 'til then," she said humorously as she leaned in close to Marcus.

"I'll call you if we're coming," Althea cut in.

To Althea, Marcus' refreshing sense of humor made him even sexier. She felt a rare sense of excitement that no man had made her feel since Shawn during the "good ol' days." This had become unfamiliar territory for Althea. She was the type who thought a handshake between the opposite sexes should have a split second time limit in order to avoid mistaken sexual tension! But this brown-eyed god with lips like LL, beautiful white teeth and million dollar smile was making her giddy inside. It could've been the "playful, yet sexy Will Smith thing" he had going on that she liked so much. Whatever it was, it was doing something to her. She hadn't experienced lust like this, even in marriage, and she tried to convince herself that she wanted absolutely no part of it.

Marcus stepped towards Althea. As he whispered in her ear, she nearly broke into a cold sweat. Though she wanted to back away from him, he was simply too intoxicating. He reminded her of a potent drink that you know you should leave alone, but you just keep sipping on it anyway. And before long, you're not sipping anymore – you're *gulping* it down, and too drunk to know the difference. *I have got to get the hell out of here before this man gets us both killed,* she thought.

"Ladies let's go!" Althea said uneasily.

"Be good, and it was nice meeting all of you," Marcus said as he grabbed Althea's hand, kissed it gently, and acted as though he didn't want to let go. She nervously stumbled as she pulled her hand from him and walked away. As she strolled toward the exit, Marcus caught a serious glimpse of her backside. He got more than an eyeful of her generous calf muscles, long slender legs and well-proportioned derriere. *Hmmph,* he thought to himself, *so that's what a million dollar ass looks like huh? Niiiiccce, reallllll nice. Shawn got all that at home and he be up in here tryna' get on all these tack heads all the time? Dude is trippin'. If I had a woman like that, I wouldn't even go to FOOTBALL PRACTICE!* Marcus laughed at himself, and then headed straight to one of the V.I.P rooms, where all the musicians and rap stars hung out.

As Althea exited the club she could feel Marcus' eyes all over her. She tried to play it off, but that old "tingle" was coming back. And although the only man that had made her feel like that was Shawn, the only things she felt for him lately were anger, distrust and disappointment. Yet, despite Shawn McQueen's transgressions, she would always remain faithful to her husband, the man she loved more than anything.

***

Some men like to place women into categories, and Shawn "Halloween" McQueen was no different. In his time dating Althea she went from an "A.M." girl to "wifey" material. An "A.M. girl" is a woman that has enough right about her that if you hook up with her, you don't mind if she spends the night with you and leaves in the morning, hence the "A.M." prefix. Now, a "P.M. girl" is the exact opposite. She has enough right about her that you still might want to bring her back to the crib, but she must be gone before daybreak! P.M. girls are *never* allowed to spend the night. Then there are "Outback girls." These are the ones you take outback to your ride or a nearby park, who don't even know your zip code.

Then there's what you call "wifey" material. Of course a wifey is someone you could see yourself marrying – the whole 'til death do you part bit. Thus, one girl could be an A.M., P.M. or even an outback girl, while wifeys are always A.M. girls. Got it?

When Shawn McQueen met Althea he knew she was wifey material. She was gorgeous, with smooth chocolate skin that reminded people of Naomi Campbell. She even had the figure to match. She was the type of woman that would walk into a room and could be greeted by stares of lust, admiration, or pure envy. But her beauty wasn't her most attractive quality. It was her down to earth demeanor and old school ways. She was just like her momma and her grandmomma. She had always believed in the sanctity of marriage and in keeping the family together no matter what. She was faithful and traditional in every sense of the word. But for Althea, it was a daunting task to take on a traditional role while being married to one of the most celebrated athletes in the world.

Although she was a traditional woman, Althea was fiercely independent. After earning her undergraduate degree from Southern Tech University in Psychology, she became a licensed massage therapist and enrolled in courses for a Master's Degree in Physical Therapy. She had everything going for her and knew that one day she would surely become "Mrs. Althea 'Halloween' McQueen."

Shawn McQueen was the 1st pick of the 1996 draft and was touted as the fastest, toughest, and most versatile player in football since "Neon" Deion aka "Prime Time". And the hype was not unwarranted; he had backed it up throughout his entire career. He quickly became the face of "the league," and had been for the last six years. Hell, he got his nickname, "Halloween" because he was so good, so strong, and so fast that it was downright "scary." His skills were far superior to others his size and position. Shawn was also a very charming, charismatic guy that everyone seemed to fall in love with instantly. Such a personality, coupled with good looks, freaky athletic skills, and of course a multi-million dollar contract, made him irresistible to most of the ladies he came into contact with. And oh, did he love the ladies. An indiscriminant lover, Shawn didn't like to choose just one color; he wanted the whole box of crayons so to speak. Black, white, brown, cream, red, beige, yellow…it didn't matter to him. He'd go after a blue woman if she was fine enough. But Althea seemed to have a different effect on him. She was different from the chicken heads that constantly pursued him. He had grown tired of the women who "bumped into him," claiming that they didn't know he was a big-time football star. He could read those types of women a mile away. Althea, on the other hand, didn't chase at all. Instead, he chased *her*. Better yet, he begged and pleaded with her. He pulled out all the stops to get her attention, but Althea refused to be like any other woman in Shawn's life.

By no means was their relationship love at first sight. Althea certainly didn't feel any bells and whistles go off in her head when he pushed up on her on campus during the summer of their sophomore year in college.

"Man, who is *that*?" Shawn whispered to his teammate Ronny. The two stared intently as they watched the slim goddess glide past them on her way to the cafeteria for lunch.

"Man, don't even try that smooth brotha mack daddy shit with her S-Dog, she's wayyyy out your league," Ronny whispered back.

"Please, I'm 'Halloween' McQueen baby, watch me work!" he said as he turned to follow Althea.

"Hey baby, you mean to tell me you're going somewhere without *me*?" Shawn said as hurried to catch up with her.

Althea whirled around 100 miles per hour to face Shawn as if to say, *I know you're not talking to me?* "Did I just hear you call me *baby*?" Althea snapped back.
The sudden burst of female attitude took Shawn aback, and stopped him dead in his tracks. As he stood there frozen, all the confidence and charisma he usually exuded

13

disappeared. He was used to women automatically falling at his feet. *Damn!*, he thought.

"Ahem!" she cleared her throat while working her neck like only a true sista could. "Hellooo…you did hear me, right?"

Shawn could not understand why his heart was beating so fast. Was it embarrassment? Why couldn't he think of anything to say? Or was it that sexy dark skin of hers? Shawn hadn't felt this nervous since the first game of his freshman year at Tech when he threw up twice right before kickoff. "Uh, I'm uh, I'm sorry. I didn't mean to disrespect you," Shawn said.

"Hmmph, you could have fooled me," she quipped. "Is that how our Black men approach sistas these days?" Her style was so "in your face" that Shawn nearly answered her with a swift "No ma'am."

"Miss… I don't know your name, but again, I apologize if I offended you."

Although Althea's first impression of Shawn wasn't positive, she couldn't help but notice how beautiful his skin and teeth were. Althea was a serious academic, and had little time outside her studies to keep up with the latest sports news. She was completely oblivious to his "star" status, however, his 6'3, 220 pound, frame had "jock" written all over it. *Damn, this boy is so cute* she thought, *But, I sure hope he can put a complete sentence together.*

As a 'totally humiliated' Shawn turned away to begin walking back towards his boy Ron (who was standing nearby pretending to ignore the exchange), he heard Althea's voice.

"It's Althea... Althea Jefferson. Sorry, I don't remember your name, but I do remember that you missed plenty of freshman English last year."

Damn, this chick just won't let up one bit, will she? Shawn thought to himself. He had certainly had enough, so he decided to keep walking instead of turning back to engage Althea in any more conversation. As he walked back with his tail between his legs, his boy Ronny didn't cut him any slack.

"You did say you were 'Halloween' McQueen right? Well, you looked more like *Hallow-weenie* McQueen back there my brotha!" Ron said as he doubled over with laughter. "I told you not to step to her with that pimp shit man. As you learned first hand, she don't play that. A babe like that is different from most of the freaks here at Tech bruh. She's got style, class, and a good upbringing. I bet she didn't even know who you were, did she?"

"Well, she knew of me, sort of," Shawn admitted sheepishly. "She reminded me that during our freshman year I skipped most of our English 101 classes. I don't even remember taking that class with her."

"Well, remembering who was in your class would require you to actually *attend* class S-Dog," Ronny kidded while playfully punching Shawn in the stomach.

"Yeah, I hear you, but I didn't have to go class to get her name playa!" Shawn said with a laugh.

Truth be told, Shawn had skipped more than half of his classes during his first two years at Tech. After all, he was a *big time athlete*, so who needed school. *All I need is to know, is how to sign a check and how to count my money. I came to college to get to the pros, and English damn sure ain't gonna get me there, or out of the ghetto,* he'd often say to himself.

That night Shawn couldn't get her, off his mind. *Althea Jefferson, now she's definitely a winner,* Shawn thought. But could he really pull a woman who had it together the way Althea did? Shawn had always been extremely self-confident, yet when it came to Althea he began to doubt himself a bit. Was he smart enough for her? Would she really give him the time of day? Would she always think of him as another dumb jock? Shawn was never the type to back down from a challenge, so he made up his mind that Althea would be the one for him. And so, the chase began.

Shawn was one of the most attractive, eligible bachelors at Southern Tech, but he still had to *work* to get Althea. He knew the only way he was going to have any chance with Althea was if he got serious about school. After nearly a year of rejecting Shawn's advances, Althea finally began taking him seriously. She noticed that he was actually beginning to take his education seriously. And although he didn't stop skipping classes entirely, he was improving. Shawn and Althea began a classic courtship, dating throughout the remainder of college and eventually marrying during Shawn's third year in the NFL.

Althea was born and raised in Pennsylvania, so when the Pennsylvania Steel Cats drafted Shawn, she knew it was fate. The first couple of years of their marriage were magical. Their first major purchase (after the Mercedes Benz Shawn just had to have) was a beautiful 7,000 square foot home in one of Pittsburgh's most exclusive suburban neighborhoods. A year later they were able to move her mother and sister into a three-bedroom condominium near their home. Life couldn't have been better. Shawn made the money and Althea handled all their business affairs. Paradise was short-lived after Althea gave birth to their first son. Shawn's star status in the NFL was rising mercurially and he soon became a household name across the country. Companies loved his famous moniker "Halloween McQueen" and competed heavily to get his name on endorsement contracts. Soon there were Halloween McQueen dolls, commercials and of course the black and orange "Halloween" sneaker. October 31st had become an unofficial national holiday where NFL fans paid homage to the greatest wide receiver in the game. The producers of *Monday Night Football* even got in on the act, by making sure that the Steel Cats were one of the teams that played on Halloween night. Everyone wanted a piece of him, including the major television networks. Instead of getting celebrities outside of the NFL to ask, "Are you ready for some football?!" during Monday night football, the producers used Shawn to ask the famous question instead. Like many young ballers, Shawn began enjoying the good life a little too much, neglecting the woman he married, and opting to stay out until the wee hours with his boys. Not only was everyone who could even say the word 'football' feeling "Halloween," but he was feeling *himself.*

Little by little, Althea began to notice that her husband was gradually changing back into that arrogant young man she once had to put in his place at Tech. Money started disappearing from the checking account in larger amounts, and Shawn began hanging out late with his teammates more and more. Even more disturbing were the number of so-called "friends" that came out of the woodwork once he signed his NFL contract.

Althea learned that Shawn had planned to uproot their family and move to his hometown of Houston, Texas without so much as asking her opinion. But, he assured her that it was the best thing for the family while he continued to play football in Pennsylvania. Althea was furious, but her mother convinced her that she needed to follow and support her husband, no matter what. Shawn was the man of the house and the bread-winner, which by her mother's standards, meant that he was the head of the household. Hence, she needed to support the decisions her husband made, especially those made in the best interest of his family.

Since *Black Professional* magazine had named Houston as one of the top 10 cities for African-American families to prosper, Althea became less skeptical. She trusted that her husband had taken the time to do some homework, and decided to embrace the idea of moving to a new city. She did, however, *strongly suggest* that her sister Maia would benefit if she were to move to Houston as well. Maia had been struggling to find her way for some time, and moving in with her big sister would provide the security she needed to jump-start her new career. Shawn didn't put up much of a fuss. He knew that the $20 million signing bonus he was about to receive from his contract extension with the Steel would pay for a house big enough for an army. So having Maia in the house wouldn't be too bad. If he was lucky he'd be able to avoid her altogether by putting her in the basement or in a separate wing of the house.

The more money Shawn made, the more his mentality towards women and money changed. In the beginning, he was a little more open-minded, adopting the old school mantra: "The man makes the money and the wife makes the home." But like a lot of big-time NFL players, his maxim quickly transformed into, "The husband makes the money, spends it at will, and the wife makes the home with what I say she can spend."

Although Althea was a loving and devoted wife and mother, she was not without flaws of her own. Despite her strong sense of family, she had never really experienced a healthy relationship. Before Shawn, she had an abusive high school sweetheart that ended up stalking her when she went off to Tech. Her first college boyfriend was no different. Althea always thought that she could change the person she was with, so she often stayed in dead end relationships far too long. Sadly, her relationship with Shawn was starting to feel like the others, minus all the physical bruises.

Married for over 6 years, Althea McQueen had it all – wealth, beauty, family, and a celebrity lifestyle. But amazingly, *she* viewed her situation quite differently. She felt unhappy, unattractive, overweight and inadequate. Additionally, Shawn was doing little to boost her self-esteem. She would soon realize that the woman she saw in the mirror was not who she was, but rather the woman her *husband* had created, and she simply accepted as true. Althea had become the classic example of a **W.I.N.N.E.R**, a wife that *W*alked *I*nto a *N*ightmare & *N*ever *E*ven

*R*ealized it. What began as a fairytale filled with wealth, security, and most importantly, love, had transformed into a nightmare.

On the way home from H-Town Live, Althea couldn't stop herself from thinking about Marcus. And she couldn't dare bring him up to her girls. Thanks to Maia though, she didn't have to. "Did ya'll see that fine ass man? Lord, have mercy! Y'all better be glad we were at the club, because I might have had to give him some!" teased Maia as she jumped up and down in the back seat of Althea's Range Rover, and waived her hands in the air like she was holding a winning lottery ticket. Of course they had seen Marcus. How could they *not* notice a man of his stature?

"Shittttt, I don't know what the two of you were looking at, but I saw *both* of them fly ass niggas, and I can tell ya'll that the other one…. Ooh wee, 'D'boy be wurkin' dat ting wit at least 8 eenchess!!' Charlene spat out in the worst Jamaican imitation imaginable. "And you best believe by that swagger, the brother *knows* how to twerk it. What's his name? Tony? Torey? Oh right, Torey. That boy got me moist! Whew!" Although she was extremely sophisticated, Charlene was quick to revert to Ebonics when talking about fine men. Even a degree from Cornell couldn't mask the wild and freaky side of Charlene.

Althea nearly wrecked the luxury SUV as she laughed hysterically.

Maia chimed in, "I thought I was the only one with an "Instantaneous Dick-Analysis Degree?""

Charlene was laughing so hard she choked on the clove she was smoking. "Don't be re-dick-ulous, I was a child prodigy girlfriend!" she added with a quick sista-girl snap of her fingers.

The joke had gone on long enough, and Althea sensed it might be a perfect segway to share her thoughts. "Yeah, Marcus was kinda sexy too. Ya'll remember when he whispered in my ear after I told him that I would call him if I was coming?"

"What girl? What? Jinx!" The two ladies demanded simultaneously.

Althea was almost too embarrassed to say it. "He said...umm, remember when he leaned over to say something to me."

"You said that already... quit stalling and spit it out girl!!!" Charlene was getting impatient.

"He said, "Don't call me if you're *cumming*, bite me instead.""

"WHATTTTT?!! AAAAHHH!!!" Charlene and Maia said screaming out of control. "Girl, you are LYING!" Maia exclaimed.

"I swear, that's what he said," Althea said wishing she had not opened up her big mouth. After all, she was always the one with the conscious, the one always under control, and the one everyone else relied on to steer them clear of trouble. And now here she was, talking about another man and sex in the same sentence. She hadn't even been alone with another man since her freshman year in college.

Charlene caught her breath and added, "Ooooooh, Althea I wasn't gonna say anything, but I saw the way ya'll was staring at each other. You know he was feeling you girl."

"I know, but-" Althea started.

21

"Ooooh girl, he's feeling you, and pretty soon he's going to be feeling *on* you...." Maia playfully interrupted. High-pitched laughter quickly consumed the SUV.

Althea decided that she had revealed enough. There was absolutely no way she could tell them what else Marcus had done. They would never let her live it down. But her mind wandered to the moment when his tongue delicately stroked her ear as he erotically whispered to her. He stood behind her so close that she felt his half-erect penis brush against her backside. It took everything she had not to push her sex deprived body back against it. Mid way through the thought she realized that she was becoming aroused. And even though she usually told Maia and Charlene everything, this was top-secret, highly classified, "take to the grave" material.

Althea could not believe what had transpired that night. There was no way *she* was having these feelings. Not the all-American wife; not "Mrs. Faithful," and definitely not "Mrs. Girl You Shouldn't Do That You're Married!" *What's going on with me?* She thought to herself, as the women continued to cackle hysterically.

As they pulled into the driveway of the luxurious McQueen Estate, the ladies noticed Michael's truck pulling out of the driveway. Michael was both Shawn's teammate and roommate in college, turned best friend. They had vowed to "take over the world together," so despite the fact that Michael suffered a career-ending injury in college and would never play ball in the NFL, Shawn made him his business partner. And although Shawn got all the athletic accolades and admiration, he believed Michael was the strongest person he knew. Shawn never told him directly, but he loved and respected Michael more than his own brothers. He remembered how Michael lay motionless on the practice field after being tackled during an intrasquad scrimmage game. The entire team, including the players, coaching staff, and trainers all knelt down simultaneously to pray for Michael, as the paramedics strapped him onto a gurney and hoisted him into the ambulance. The remainder of practice was solemn for obvious reasons. It was also a humbling experience for Shawn. It was probably the first time he gave serious thought to the notion that his football career was only one lethal hit away from being over.

The team dedicated the remainder of the season to Michael. He was one of their best players and team leader. His absence left a gaping hole in the backfield and Tech simply didn't have anyone who could come close to filling his shoes. And to Shawn, Michael was just as indispensable as a friend, which is why they vowed to always look out for one another.

2

Shawn and Michael spent countless hours together, so Althea was not surprised to see Michael backing out of the driveway. However, it was still awfully late for him to be leaving the house –especially if it was the same Michael that kept 2-3 hoochies with him at all times. Althea wanted to second guess herself, but there was no mistaking Michael's souped up, candy apple red, Lincoln Navigator. She was 100% certain it was him.

"Were there females in the truck with Michael?" Althea asked naively.

"Nah, it looked like three other guys to me," Maia said nervously. It was obvious Maia had seen the three women in the car and was attempting to protect her sister.

Althea looked down at her ringing phone to see that it was her husband. *Shawn calling at this hour could only mean one thing: damage control,* she thought.

"Hello!"

"Hey baby!" Shawn replied with an unusual enthusiasm for this time of night.

"Where are you Shawn?"

"Oh, um, me and Michael bout to go grab something to eat and pick up something from his crib…"

"You were in the truck with him?

"HUH?"

"You heard me! If you saw me driving up, why in the hell didn't you stop and speak to me? And why didn't he bring that something with him when he brought his ass over here? Shawn its 1 o'clock in the morning, what-"

"Look Althea, please don't start, "Lil Man" is over momma's. Was I calling you all night while you were out? Damn, can't I chill with my fuckin boy if that's what I want to do? Since when do I have a curfew?"

"Shawn this is the only weekend you have off this season. I wanted us to spend at least a few hours together before you head back to Pittsburgh. You need to be resting anyway. You're about to make a playoff run and you need all your strength right? Althea said in her best "Shawn" voice. "At least that's what you've been telling me."

"You should've thought about that before you took your ass to the club!"

"But I asked you if…"

"Baby, look I said I was going to get something to eat." Shawn interrupted. "Damn, now stop naggin' like somebody's damn mama all the time. I'll be back in a minute, I love you, bye." *CLICK.*

After a few seconds of silence Michael composedly asked, "Do I need to take you back home dog?"

"Nigga please, let's do this!" Shawn said grinning as he turned up the music to full blast, and launched into a free style rap over a hypnotic Carlos "Six July" Broady beat. It was clear that the party was just getting started.

Meanwhile, back at the McQueen estate, Althea continued to talk on the phone as though Shawn was still on the other end. "Yeah, I know you're sorry Shawn– you should be! I'll talk to you later… Nah, I don't want shit to eat and I don't want to talk anymore now – bye!" she said acting as though she hung up in *his* face.

"Althea I've told you a billion times - that nigga ain't shit. It's bad enough that he's bought cars for other women and shit, but now he's blatantly disrespecting you. Okay, it's one thing to do that bullshit behind your back, but in your face?! And I know I don't usually say nothing but --"

"Then don't start now! … I'm sorry, I know Charlene, I know. Look, I'm tired. I'm going to bed, but I'll straighten this out later - as soon as he gets back. I'll see you two hoes in the morning, goodnight." Althea didn't look back as Charlene and Maia watched her storm up the regal staircase to the Master bedroom.

"Girl, you know what? I'm hungry. Let's go to Taco Bell, you know they stay open all night," Maia said to Charlene. "She's not going to talk to us anymore about this tonight anyway, so let's eat."

"Girl, we'll be back!" Charlene yelled up the stairs to Althea.

Althea's mind was way too preoccupied for her to respond. As the car pulled back, the automatic garage door began to close. Ironically as the garage door was shutting them out, in an entirely different way, the woman who had no secrets was now building a wall that not even her sister and best girlfriend could penetrate.

Althea took the blame for the deterioration of her marriage. If only she had not let their problems compound without discussing them, or if she had just communicated her needs to Shawn, maybe things would be different. But it wasn't in her nature anymore. She had somehow lost that fiery, "no nonsense" attitude that had made her so attractive. Instead, she coped with the pain and learned to put her feelings aside for the sake of her family. But after a long shower, she decided that tonight was going be different. Tonight she was going give Shawn the night of his life- making love to him all night long. Then, over breakfast in bed, they would talk. No, they would communicate. She would ask him if there were things he needed from her that she wasn't giving him, and she would finally tell him some of the things that she needed from him.

The scenario was clear in her mind. He would see her on the stairway in her devil-red crotchless panties, matching garter belt and 6-inch pumps, and nothing else would matter. Their son was visiting Shawn's mother, Maia's room was on the opposite wing of the house and Charlene, in town for her husband DJ's game against the Houston Oil, would be sound asleep in the guest suite.

Althea exited the shower, massaged moisturizing oil all over her wet skin, then lightly dabbed her neck and stomach with "Infatuation," an intoxicating fragrance that drove Shawn crazy. After she slinked out of her silk robe, she put on her sexiest lingerie, admiring her voluptuous curves in the opulent, floor length mirror of her dressing room. She was stunning and she knew it. Hell, she was turning *herself* on. As she moved back into the sitting area of the massive suite, she lit a few candles around the fireplace, poured herself a glass of red wine and lay seductively across the bed. *Shawn should be home in about an hour*, she thought to herself as she allowed one hand to caress the front of her panties. "Ummmm," she hissed. "Damn, I can't wait 'til Shawn gets home." she said softly. She imagined that her husband was there watching her. Oh how he loved to watch. As she continued to please herself, she fell deeper and deeper into fantasy. "Oooh, yeah," she

27

moaned "I can't wait to feel you inside me." She imagined Shawn licking all the spots she was touching. Althea's back began to arch as she felt her wetness overwhelming her fingers. She was dripping wet by now and needed some attention. "Oh baby, give it to me," she said as if Shawn was right there. "Uuuuhhhhh, uuhhhhh, uhhhhhh, yeahhhh…" she wailed as her head thrashed from side to side. Her orgasm was more than satisfying, but she was anxious for more. As she lay in the center of the sumptuous bed, she realized that Shawn had not made love to her in over a month. *We're long overdue honey, don't keep me waiting,* she thought to herself before drifting off to sleep.

<hr>

Althea jumped up suddenly from her slumber. *What's that?* She could hear commotion coming from outside. *What time is it? Damn, I must have dozed off* she thought. She looked out the window just in time to see Shawn's truck driving off. "What in the --" she started as she looked at the clock and it read 7:00 AM. *I know he didn't just…"* she said to herself as she reached for the phone and dialed furiously.

"Shawn, where have you been?" she screamed into the phone. "I waited for you all night!"

"Baby I got in 'bout 3:30 in the morning. I didn't want to wake you so I slept on the couch. I tried to --" Althea hung up. "Hello, Althea, Althea!? Fuck it then!" Shawn shouted to the heavens as he continued to drive.

Althea knew he wouldn't call back. Hell, she might not see him again until it was time to go to bed that night. That was his pattern. He'd stay out all night, and the moment Althea complained, he'd make it seem like her nagging was the reason he didn't come home in the first instance. His transgressions were always her fault. Althea couldn't believe she had tolerated his bullshit for this long.

"I can't take it, God why me?!" she wailed before throwing the phone across the room with all the strength she could muster. Her beautiful almond shaped eyes, usually the fixation of any admirer, now overflowed with tears of frustration and unbearable pain. Her pitiful cries soon turned to rage as she began obliterating everything in the room.

Maia heard the commotion and rushed to Althea's room. "What's wrong Althea?" Maia could hear Althea crying and screaming out of control. "Are you o.k. Althea?" Maia yelled while running up the stairs. By the time she reached her sister's room, Althea was balled up, still crying and so stressed that her muscles were spasming. "Oh my God Althea, you need a doctor."

"No, I'm fine. DON'T call anyone," Althea demanded.

"Well, you need to take something," Maia said as she quickly ran to the medicine cabinet in the nearby master bathroom. "Here take this, you'll feel better when you wake up," she said as she handed Althea one of Shawn's muscle relaxers. Althea gazed lovingly at her sister as to say "Thank you," but instead she said nothing, laying motionless, almost paralyzed in her sister's arms.

"I know sis, I love you, girl." Maia kissed her sister's forehead, and held her until she fell asleep.

On his way to the stadium, Torey felt a little more excited than usual. He was considered one of the better strong safeties in the league and the match-up between him and Darryl Ray "DJ" Johnson was going to be a great one. They were playing the Baltimore Rage, one of the biggest and baddest teams in the NFL. He knew that everyone in the country would be watching and they were about to see how Torey put it down. His phone rang suddenly but he hesitated to answer because the caller I.D. displayed *"private caller."* He picked it up anyway realizing that there was a strong chance it was his mother. She adored her baby boy and called him before every single game.

"Hello?" Torey said with a curious look on his face.

"What's up boy? This is Marcus."

"Oh, what's up playboy? Where are you calling me from? How did we do last night?"

Marcus proudly boasted, "Bout thirty-thousand on the bar and another fifteen grand on the door. And don't you know not to ask playas where they are calling from?" he asked with a chuckle.

"Man, you are doing your thang down there, huh? Keep this up and I may have to give you a fat raise. PSYCHE! Look man, I'm headed to the stadium, you coming to the game, right?"

"Yeah dog of course. I actually called to ask you something," Marcus said as he cleared his throat. "Tell me something... What's up with Althea?"

"Althea who?" asked Torey.

"Althea McQueen, nigga! How many Altheas do you know? You know who I'm talking about!"

Between chuckles Torey responded, "I can only tell you the OBVIOUS, and what everyone else already knows: Her husband is one of the best players in pro football; every woman in the country would love to have him and every man in the country would love to be him, annndd -you're not him! I also know that Althea is fine as hell! But, she is also faithful as hell. Besides, you don't make NEARLY enough money to *even* ask me about her. So why *are* you asking?"

"Well you told me to take good care of her and that's exactly what I intend to do," Marcus replied with a grin.

"NEGRO, did you hear anything I just said? Have you seen the car that woman drives? I know you seen they house on "Cribs?" You know, the huge house on the hill with like 10 bedrooms, a waterfall, and a guesthouse bigger than your condo. Dude, they interviewed that babe, her monthly spending budget was over $20,000, and that ain't including bills and shit. Do I even pay you that much in a year?" Torey said laughing.

"Ha Ha, very funny. Look, whatever man, good luck today, and I will fill you in on my progress with Ms. McQueen. Trust me brotha, Marcus Edwards and Althea McQueen are about to crash into each other *real* hard."

"Get it right, that's *MRS.* Althea McQueen. Marcus you're playing with fire. You do know the top two reasons for murder, don't you?" asked Torey. "Money and women, Mr. Gigolo, so watch yourself man. I'll see you after the game."

"Whatever choirboy, I'm cool. I can handle mine. You just worry about the game. And try not to intercept too many passes. You get all happy when you have a good game and end up giving out too many free drinks at the club, fucking with my sales bonuses and shit!"

That cat is crazy. Torey couldn't help but grin as his hung up the phone.

3

"Charlene your ass better hurry up, you know DJ don't like it when you're late to his games" Maia yelled. "And Althea you gon' make me hurt you if I miss my man, Lewis Raymond coming through the tunnel. Girl, you know I almost got pregnant by him last week, watching the football highlights on EPSN (Everybody's Pro Sports News)!"

Charlene and Althea both broke into laughter.

"Don't forget the liquor," Charlene reminded. "Pour it in the juice bottles 'cause you know them groupie hoes will be all in our business. Girl I'm so glad my husband don't play for Houston anymore. I hope we beat their asses."

Trying not to crack a smile Althea said, "Girl you know the Rage ain't gonna' beat the Oil, so stop dreaming and keep drinking. Let's go! The limo is waiting."

As usual, the ladies were dressed to impress. After all, they were NFL wives, except for Maia, and they knew everyone and their mother would be critiquing them from head to toe as soon as they walked into the stadium. Charlene decided to go "ghetto classy" by donning a pair of tight Dolce & Gabana jeans that were at least two sizes too small, a baby blue halter that showed her diamond belly ring, and matching Jimmy Choo stilettos. She didn't want to look too much like the groupies that regularly chased the NFL players, but she also didn't want to look like their mothers. Charlene knew she was playing with fire by wearing the outfit. Her husband DJ, who played running back for the Baltimore Rage, wasn't like a lot of the players who enjoyed seeing their women dressed provocatively. DJ was a relatively conservative Christian that did not involve himself with the proverbial "hoochies." But his wife, Charlene wasn't far from one. She may as well have been a man in a woman's body. She did what she wanted, when she wanted, and with whomever she wanted.

Like always, Maia was dressed in the skimpiest outfit she could find. She was dressed appropriate for amateur night at the strip club, but for a football game she looked...well, ...like the freak she was. Her tight black top was busting at the seams with her ample bosom spilling out from her Vicky Secrets push up bra. *Damn I look good*, she thought as she took one last look at herself in the mirror. She just *knew* she'd be going home with some high profile baller at the end of the night.

Althea was dressed atypically – almost as though she knew that today would be a special day. Even though she was still very upset with Shawn, she wasn't going to let him spoil her day out with her girls. *Hell, if he doesn't want all this, I may as well show it off to the rest of the men out there*, she thought as she pulled on a pair of tight, black, low-rise Gucci pants that made her matching thong noticeably visible. *Eat your heart out Shawn. Too bad you won't be around to see me today. I bet Marcus would like the way I look in these pants*, she caught herself thinking. *Oh Lord, what am I doing?*

The chiming doorbell meant it was time for the ladies to head to the stadium. Althea and Charlene always rented a limo to travel to games just in case they wanted to get a little tipsy.

"Are you ready ladies?" the driver asked. "I'm Vegas, I used to drive for Charlene when her and her husband lived here, so I'm quite familiar with the level of treatment you're accustomed to. Just buzz me if you need anything," he said as the women settled into the back seats.

"Vegas is cool as hell. You know, I'm the one that nick-named him Vegas," Charlene bragged.

"Why?" Maia asked.

"'Cause just like Sin City, what happens in Vegas' limo stays in Vegas' limo."

"Girl you are so stupid." Althea quipped.

"Girl for real, ...if this limo's windows could talk, ooohh wee!" Charlene had a brief flash of some of her wild excursions that had taken place in that very limousine.

"You remember Torey Franklin? He plays for Houston?" Charlene asked the ladies.

"Torey who?" Maia asked.

"Torey, the owner of H-Town, the guy we met last night."

"Oh yeah girl," Maia said, "How could I forget his fine ass? What about him?"

Althea was unusually quiet. Rather than thinking about Torey, she was too busy contemplating a chance reunion with Marcus.

It was obvious that Maia was wondering the same thing as she asked, "I wonder if ol' boy Marcus is going to be there?" Althea was always amazed at how her sister could nearly read her mind.

Without hesitation Charlene answered, "I hope so, 'cause that shit that Shawn pulled last night was BS girlfriend! Besides you need to be romanced by a brotha that can remind you how it feels to get that --"

"Charlene will you shut....up!" Althea said, trying not to blush.

Vegas had to drive at top speed to get them to the game in time. But it didn't matter to the ladies – they were too busy sippin' on their drinks and bumpin' Usher's new CD.

"That's right Usher! Let it burn baby! Let it burn!" Maia sang out of tune to the beat.

"Shitttt," interrupted Charlene over the loud music, "You need to let us burn your ass up!" The women cackled loudly as the Ciroc vodka martinis they were drinking began to kick in.

"Sang 'Ursha'! You go head and sing that song boy!" Maia continued.

They reached the stadium just in time to hear a horrible version of the national anthem by an equally bad high school band. It wasn't long before the Rage proved why they were one of the most dominant teams in the NFL. The Rage's explosive kick returner ran back the opening kick for a touchdown and the rout was on. DJ scored three touchdowns in the first half. He even tossed one of the footballs into the stands to his wife Charlene. In true Charlene spirit, she acted the part of the devout wife that didn't miss a single play of the game, when in actuality she had just gotten back from the bar a few seconds earlier. She blew him a kiss and winked at him as he ran into the arms of his celebrating teammates. The only bright spot for Houston came right before halftime when Torey Franklin got an interception and ran it back for a touchdown as the clock expired. Maia jumped up and down like it was her man, while Charlene and Althea cracked up laughing.

"Now ya'll know ol' boy intercepted that one for me right? Let's go get some food and more drinks," Maia suggested.

"Yeah, since somebody only brought back one drink to their seat," Althea quipped while staring at Charlene who had just reappeared.

"Whatever!" Charlene looked up from sipping her martini – disguised in a Coke cup. "Ya'll know where the bar is!"

The section that the ladies were seated in was full of irony. It was symbolic of all the contradictions that infested pro sports. The section was full of wives, children, strippers, girlfriends, mother-in-laws, mistresses, baby mamas, and various others. It was amazing how jealous mistresses were of the wives. If looks could kill, mistresses would become one step closer to their ultimate goal – becoming a player's wife. Althea had grown tired of this scene early on in Shawn's career and now it weighed on her more heavily than in the past. She would often find herself fantasizing about being elsewhere. But now, she was not only fantasizing about being somewhere else, she was visualizing being with someone else.

The ladies were headed to the bar when they were surprised to see none other than Althea's husband Shawn McQueen. He was with Michael and two of Michael's female friends. As Althea began approaching the foursome, Shawn hurriedly moved to meet her halfway.

"Hey baby!" Shawn said, as he tried to give Althea a friendly kiss on the cheek.

"So that's why you sped off this morning, huh?" Althea said as she looked at the two women standing a few feet away.

"Nah baby, Mike called me while I was getting rehab on my ankle, and asked if I wanted to come to the game. I didn't plan it. I didn't know ya'll were coming to the game."

"You wouldn't know... Your phone hasn't been on much since last night, remember? And why in the hell do you think Charlene came to town anyway? Exactly, ...to see her husband play today, Shawn."

"Oh, yeah, I'm sorry baby I forgot," Shawn offered.

"Hey Althea," Mike said delicately as he approached the obviously upset spouse of his best friend. "This is my cousin Tracey and her girl Tangie."

As embarrassed and hurt as Althea was, she was not about to let Shawn get the best of her. To make things worst, Shawn didn't even have his wedding ring on. *Keep it together girlfriend. Don't go off – yet,* she said to herself while glancing down at his naked left ring finger.

Althea proceeded to walk over to one of the girls, who appeared to be Shawn's muse, and whispered into her ear, "Be careful girl, I saw his wife here earlier and I heard that bitch *loves* some drama."

"For real, 'preciate it," Tangie said thanking Althea while cutting her eyes at Shawn.

"Alright Shawn, call me later on," Althea said with a wink as she turned to walk back to her friends.

Althea played Shawn that way because it was obvious those women didn't know he was married. And they *surely* didn't know he was married to her. But Tangie's high-pitched, "Shawn, you didn't tell me you had a wife! And don't lie nigga, cause that woman just said she saw her here earlier!" was enough to keep her from breaking down.

Before Shawn could wipe that perplexed look off his face to say anything, the three women disappeared into the crowd. For the first time, Althea controlled her emotions and she was proud of herself. This time she didn't just sit there and take it. She turned the tables and made Shawn look like the ass he was - and she loved every minute of it. She even managed to smile as Tangie continued to berate her husband.

After busting Shawn, the remainder of half time became a sort of liberated mini-celebration for the ladies.

"Drinks are on me until the end of the third quarter!" Althea yelled to all the fans that were at the bar.

"Shitttt, I may not even go back out to my seat then!" a random fan responded.

"Drink up baby," Althea said to the man, "It's on Halloween McQueen."

"In that case, I'll take a Hennessey and Coke," responded another patron.

"Why have just one?" Althea asked, "Get another one. Take one to your friend in the stands too."

"Althea...Althea!" Maia called out.

"What girl?"

"Look behind you..."

As Althea turned around, her heart skipped a beat.

"Hey ladies," Marcus said. He looked just as surprised to run into them.

"Heeyyyy," Maia replied flirtatiously rushing to stand directly in front of Marcus. Her ample cleavage was intoxicating, but Marcus had his sights set on an even bigger prize.

"This must be my lucky day…Oh but I forgot. DJ's *your* husband, right Charlene?" asked Marcus.

"Yes, he is," she replied. Maia continued under her breath, "But you could most certainly be my *man*."

"DJ does it all out there. He's definitely one of the top players in the league," offered Marcus.

"Your friend Torey is doing his thing, too," Charlene replied as she tried to divert the conversation from her husband.

"Would you ladies like to sit with me after halftime? Torey rents a skybox for all home games and since his little girl is out of town, I'm the only person in the box so far. Two of my partners might be joining me later."

"Uh, that would be a yes." Maia replied without hesitation.

Althea would not normally put herself in this type of situation but she was fed up with Shawn and it didn't help that she was seriously attracted to Marcus. The chemistry between them was apparent, yet neither seemed to be concerned with the dangerous path they were on. As they walked toward the suite, Maia began quizzing Marcus.

"So how did you meet Torey," Maia inquired.

"We played college ball together at Houston A&M.

"Houston? Do they even *have* a football team there?" Maia asked jokingly. Since she had always been an avid football fan, she knew that Houston A&M was known for its academic programs and not its lowly football program.

"Well, at least that's what the coaches told us when we were playing. But when you only win two games a year, you begin to wonder. Fortunately, my man Torey was able to make first team all-conference his last two seasons at safety. He left the rest of the stiffs on our team behind to play some *real* football at the college level." Marcus' tone was riddled with sarcasm. "Yeah, we've been super tight for a long time."

"So, how did ya'll start working together?"

"Oh, well like I said, we were already close from football. So when he opened H-Town Live he needed somebody that he could trust to manage the place. It wasn't much of a surprise when he asked me to come run the club with him."

"Is he married?" Maia asked, cutting to the chase.

"He is, but he's going through a pretty bad divorce. Damn, 50 Cent, what's up with the 21 questions?"

Maia burst into laughter, not only was Marcus' exterior amazing, but he was also cool as hell. Althea looked over her shoulder curious as to what they were laughing about. Marcus caught Althea's glance and moved towards her to speak to her exclusively.

Althea was accustomed to all the things money could buy, from D-colored, flawless diamonds to lavish vacations in St. Tropez. Her husband was so popular that hanging out with celebrities was a common occurrence. So when Marcus played his "P Diddy" card by inviting her to the luxury suite, she wasn't overly impressed. But like most women, she noticed he was an intelligent brother that had access, and access was half the battle when it came to making things happen.

"So I saw your husband downstairs," Marcus said to Althea. Marcus had no idea how close he was to making

Althea shut him down for good until she noticed his sincerity. "I didn't know he was that big. I mean, I got his autograph for my nephew. That brotha is the truth."

More like "The Lie" she thought to herself. "Yeah, he's okay I suppose," she said sarcastically.

"So ya'll coming to the concert next week?"

"I thought you said to bite you if I was coming?" Althea teased back.

They both just about died laughing. For the next two hours Althea felt like Marcus had gotten to know her more than Shawn had in the last 2 years. She felt comfortable with Marcus instantly. They didn't even notice what was going on in the background, too busy flirting and playing around. What scared her most was that she realized that even at her high point in her relationship with Shawn she had never felt this free. The two drank and talked the game away. Marcus had all the ingredients of a great friend –in every way a man could be a friend to a woman – but it was feeling a bit too close to home.

Marcus was a good man but he operated primarily on instinct and his heart. He had difficulty focusing on real responsibilities such as his career. The primary source of most of his problems, was his inability to pass a sexy brown sister without completely losing his mind.

"So I'll see you and Maia Friday at the club, right?" Marcus asked.

"Look Marcus, I don't think this is a good idea," Althea said reluctantly.

"What's not a good idea - you and your sister coming to the club?" Marcus said sarcastically.

"Don't play with me Marcus... you know what I'm talking about."

"Look beautiful, you are definitely worth anything your man gives you, and it is obvious that I'm not him. I'm just trying to make up for what happened in the club the other night. My boss told me to make your ill-feelings disappear, and that it is what I intend to do...if you let me."

If a man ever said the right thing to a woman, Marcus Edwards did just then. Althea wasn't going to say it, but if Marcus was even close to the man he portrayed himself to be, their "friendship" was about to make 'Sex in the City' look like an after school special.

After the game, Althea, Maia, Charlene and Marcus headed to the team tunnel, which is where the buses picked up the players from the opposing team. It was also where the home team players met their families. They all moved hastily through the crowd to avoid the rush of people exiting the stadium. Charlene didn't want to miss DJ. She knew he would be in a great mood after scoring four touchdowns including the game winner. Although the visiting Rage were up by three scores at halftime, the home team gave their fans something to cheer about during the final 30 minutes of the ballgame. Houston had rallied back to tie the game. But it was DJ's last second plunge into the end zone that sealed a victory for Baltimore.

While waiting for DJ, the ladies couldn't help but notice being stared at by groupies who were no doubt wondering whose wives they were. In turn, the groupies were now being stared at by other wives who were wondering which players the groupies "belonged to."

Marcus noticed Torey looking for him as he walked out of the locker room area and shouted to get his attention.

"Yo' T! Torey, over here man!"

"What's up playboy?" Torey said while giving Marcus the standard masculine hug.

"You did your thing as usual 'T,' I must admit. And of course I was doin' my thang too. Guess who I had in the suite during the second half." Marcus's sneaky grin spoke volumes.

"Let me guess…" Torey replied as he glanced towards Althea, Maia and Charlene.

Meanwhile, Althea curiously watched the two of them wondering what was being said. Charlene, who was also eyeing the two men, was too busy trying to figure out a way to get her legs around Torey's neck by the end of her visit. And as usual, Maia was looking for some poor, unsuspecting rookie to take advantage of.

"Ladies, you remember Torey," Marcus politely introduced his friend.

"Hey Torey," Maia replied. "You got any single friends?"

Torey tried to keep a straight face but couldn't help but crack a smile. "Yeah, I got a few that are coming to the concert Friday at the club. I'm going to see you guys there, right?"

Before they could answer, DJ walked up and greeted Charlene with his usual win or lose, bear hug and sensual kiss.

"Did you enjoy the game beautiful?" DJ asked blissfully.

"I sure did. You played a great game baby! Oh, I'm sorry baby, this is Torey Franklin and his friend Marcus."

"What's up man? You played a hell of a game," Torey said as he reached out to shake DJ's hand.

"Thanks man. You looked great yourself. You're a free agent after this season right?"

"I sure am, and I'm definitely going to explore my options. The legs are getting a little older, so it's time for me to really get paid before I get that pink slip," Torey answered.

"You know we need a strong safety," said DJ, "Man you need to stop trippin' and come win this thing with us next year." Both of them laughed, but they both knew it was a serious thought.

The two players clicked as if they had known each other for years. They had played against each other at least 10 times in their respective college and pro careers. And being Psi Kappa brothers didn't hurt. After all, the league was one big fraternity in a way. The NFL was an elite class in and of itself, and competition was like quality time to its members. And although players wanted to be touted as the best in the league, they also wanted to play with and line up against the best in order to prove it. Thus, DJ's inquiry about Torey's free agent status was much more than just idol chatter.

The team bus horn blew 3 times, alarming everyone except for the players, who were used to it.

"Well baby, you know what that means...I gotta go." said DJ. "Coach wouldn't let me fly back on my own, so I will see you when you get back tomorrow. Be safe...oh, and I'm sorry Althea." DJ apologized for not speaking to her as he leaned over to give her a hug and kiss on the cheek. "I'm trippin, you know how I get when I see this fine wife of mine," he said while staring into Charlene's eyes.

She has the perfect man, Althea thought to herself as she smiled pleasantly and hugged DJ goodbye.

"Okay, I love you baby. I'll call you when we land. Good to see you Torey. See ya'll," DJ said as he hopped onto the bus.

"DJ, my flight gets in at six tomorrow night. Call me if you won't be able to pick me up," Charlene said to her husband before the bus door closed.

"I will baby!" he yelled, knowing there was no way he would ever let her catch a cab while he was in town.

"See Charlene, you have a great husband. That man knows he loves your dirty draws and I swear I don't know why," Althea said with admiration and a hint of envy.

"Whatever. Girl, you know why he loves me. It ain't the draws, it's what's *in them* my dear," Charlene said as Maia joined her in a high five. "But you know, sometimes he's way too square. No wine, no R-rated movies, no hip-hop. And Lord, if I ever suggested a porno flick, the boy would surely have a heart attack," Charlene said cracking herself up.

Marcus and Torey said goodbye to the ladies and headed to Torey's car. Marcus had no intention on waiting until Friday to see Althea again. "Hey Maia, here's my cell, call me tonight. Maybe you and your buddies can meet me tomorrow night. I'm hosting a private dinner."

"Okay, I'll give you a call later and we'll see if something can be arranged," Maia said sneakily.

46

"You do that," Marcus said as he smiled and waved goodbye to the ladies.

On the way back to the house the ladies tried to figure out what they would do for the rest of the night. Charlene was ready to get buck-wild. DJ was gone and she was horny as hell. She was in the mood for what she called "real deal sex" and not the ordinary Christian-boy missionary thing DJ liked so much. Althea, on the other hand, figured she would just lay low in case Shawn wanted to do something with her. Her sister Maia was always ready to go out, and tonight was no different. She was just as eager as Charlene to explore the opportunities of the evening. She knew several players from the Houston Oil would be looking for someone to play with, despite their heartbreaking loss.

"So I know we're getting out tonight, right?" Charlene asked her two friends.

"Girl you know I'm down," Maia responded.

"Well, I don't know. Shawn may want to do something," Althea said. Even *she* didn't really believe what she was saying. Shawn rarely wanted to do anything with her these days. Even before their one month drought, they were rarely intimate, except for an occasional quickie right before he'd rush out to be with his best friend Michael.

"Well, me and Maia are burning Houston down tonight baby," Charlene said while stooping in the limo and giving her version of Beyonce's booty shake.

"Girl, I swear, for someone who graduated from Cornell you sure can be ghetto fabulous!" Althea joked. Through the laughter Althea heard her phone ring.

"Hello," she said while signaling Vegas to turn down the music.

"What's up baby?"

The look on her face said it was Shawn. "Whose phone are you on Shawn?" she asked.

"Oh, my battery is dead so I used Michael's. Where are you headed?"

"Home," she said dryly. "Shawn, if you're calling from Michael's phone, why is the number blocked out?"

"Do I look like Sprint to you? How the hell would I know! Anyway, look, ..um, me and Michael are 'bout to go to his crib and go over some business since I'm leaving in the morning. So, umm, don't wait up for me okay?" *CLICK...*

Not wanting to hear Charlene's mouth again, Althea said, "Oh, Okay, I'll see you at home. I love you too baby." She hoped the two women wouldn't realize that Shawn had already hung up.

"I can't hang out with ya'll. Shawn said he'll be home in a little and he just wants to watch a movie."

"Well that's cool. Do yo' thang girl, do yo thang," a tipsy Charlene said as she reached for the cognac. Maia knew Althea wasn't being truthful, but Shawn's routine was getting old, and she knew Althea was getting tired of everyone blasting her about putting up with him.

By the time the limo made it back to the house, the three of them were riding on a new high from all the alcohol they had consumed. Althea proceeded up the stairs to shower and change clothes, in order to give the appearance that she was waiting for Shawn. Charlene and Maia both escaped to their respective parts of the house to don their best "baller" catching clothes. In other words, they looked like they were about to step on the set of the latest rap video. Charlene knew DJ would kill her if he knew what she was wearing. But since he was on a plane heading back to their home in Baltimore, she didn't have to worry about him. Besides, she knew most of the NFL men wouldn't kiss and tell, especially the married ones that had just as much to lose as she did.

Just as Charlene and Maia were leaving, Althea surprisingly asked, "Hey Maia, what's Marcus' phone number? He gave you his number right?"

"I'm one step ahead of you big sis. I saved it in your cell phone under the name Marcia," Maia said grinning. "Althea, you need to think about *you* for once... I love you."

"Girl, please, you know I'm not going to do anything crazy. I just wanted to thank him for sharing the suite with us. Ok, ok....I know you know Shawn's not coming home...I just need some male conversation this evening. It's only a *phone call* okay? I just want someone interesting to talk to on the *phone* tonight. Got it?"

"Got it," Maia replied tickled to death. "Tell Mr. Telephone Man I said hello when you talk to him," Maia said as she did an impromptu Bobby Brown/New Edition dance move. "And don't wait up!" she said as she hurried out the door to join Charlene in the limo.

4

Althea knew that Shawn would not be home anytime soon, if at all that night. She had grown numb to his antics and tired of being ignored. She also couldn't get Marcus Edwards off of her mind. She sat looking at her cell phone, seriously contemplating whether she should call him. She dialed the number a few times, but would stop short of hitting the "send" button. She began questioning herself. What would she say to him, and what would he think of her? She decided to pour herself a glass of her favorite wine, a Robert Mondavi Reserve Merlot. The more she sipped, the more she relaxed. After two full glasses she was halfway there, she was also feeling quite sensual. After changing into her sexy boy-shorts and a fitted sheer top, (and not to mention another half glass of wine), her mind was made up. *Liquid courage* she thought to herself, *works every time. What the hell, I'm calling him. 5-8-2-1-0-2-5* she mumbled aloud while dialing the number. *Maybe he won't pick up and I can just leave him a nice little message.*

"Hello… Hello" a sexy deep voice answered.

Oh shit, he picked up! Althea thought to herself as she sat in silence on her bed. *"CLICK,"* the phone sounded as she instinctively hung up the phone.

"Hello! Hello…" Marcus continued.

Get it together girl, call him back, she said in a self-rousing pep talk. *5-8-2-1-0-2-5.*

"Hello," Marcus answered again.

"May I speak to Marcus?"

"This is Marcus. Who's calling?"

It was obvious the wine was talking for her, "Who do you want it to be?" she teased, not believing she had uttered those words.

"I know this isn't who I think it is? Could it be? Is this the one and only.... Halle Berry?" he said breaking into hearty laugh. "I'm just playing, this sounds like the beautiful Althea McQueen. Am I correct?" he asked smiling to himself.

"Yes silly, this is Althea, how are you doing?"

I'm sitting here thinking about you, Marcus said to himself. "Well, I was hoping that you were calling to tell me you're coming to the dinner tomorrow."

"What exactly is this dinner you keep mentioning?" she asked.

"Well, it was supposed to be a business meeting but Torey had to cancel. So, instead of letting the deposit go to waste, I was just going to have a friend or two join me for a nice little get together."

"Sounds nice, but I'm not a fan of strangers. I can't trust just anybody with my business, and I can't really afford to be out in public with another man," Althea responded.

"I understand...Well, how about this, ...?"

"Marcus, may I ask you a question?" she interrupted.

"Of course you can."

"What exactly do you want from me?"

"Well, what I think I want, I can't have because you're already taken. So, at least for now, despite your situation, I want to make you smile. You look like a woman who could use one. You're too beautiful to be so angry and sad. So let's just say, I'd like to be your friend. Is that cool?"

"So you're telling me that pussy isn't a factor at all, huh?" She couldn't believe she just said the word "pussy" as she put her hand over her mouth. She almost dropped the phone. *I knew I shouldn't have drunk all that wine!*

Marcus laughed, then nearly choked as he spit out the water he was drinking. Her question obviously caught him off guard. "Girl you are a trip. What are you doing over there?" Marcus said, trying to change the subject.

"I'm drinking a glass of my favorite wine. My wonderfully attentive husband left me home alone once again, but it's cool."

Marcus could picture Althea's beautiful slender body, lying picturesque across her bed, sipping wine to escape her loneliness. He could sense how vulnerable she was by the sound of her voice. *I wonder what she has on*, he caught himself thinking as he felt his nature rising in his briefs. *Down Moby* he said quietly while glancing at his bulging crotch.

The two new friends conversed for what seemed like an eternity, covering a plethora of topics including their families, college life, and the events that led them both to Houston. Althea felt tears well up in her eyes when Marcus spoke of lying in the hospital unable to move after bruising his spine in football practice. She realized that she had not had meaningful conversation like this in years. Marcus was such a great listener. He made her feel like she could talk for hours without interruption.

"May I ask you a personal question Althea?" Marcus asked.

"Sure, go ahead," she responded while taking another sip of wine.

"Have you ever cheated on your husband?"

"Not even close. You're the first guy I've even talked on the phone with since I got married."

"So what's up? Are you going to take me up on my offer? All bullshit aside, I'm feeling you Althea, and this is not about sex, ...well not *totally*. Just come to dinner with the intention of having a great time and go with the flow."

"Marcus... I, I, just can't do that. Maybe if my situation was different. I hope you understand. Good night Mr. Edwards." *CLICK...*

After hanging up, Althea realized that she had been on the phone for hours. Not surprisingly, Shawn was still not home, but this time it really didn't matter to her. She deleted Marcus' number from her phone, washed her Tiffany's wine glass, and prepared to go to bed alone, again. As she wrapped her hair in a Louis Vuitton silk scarf, the reflection in the mirror looked familiar. She couldn't remember the last time a man had made her feel beautiful. Now, if only it were Shawn who made her feel that way.

While rushing to pack for his trip back to the Steel City, Shawn nudged Althea to wake her.

Barely coherent, Althea asked, "Shawn what are you doing?"

"Hey, good morning baby. I'm heading to the airport, remember? I fly back today. Baby, don't forget to pick Lil' Man up from Mama's tomorrow."

"Well, can I at least take you to the airport?"

"Nah, I'm good. Michael is outside waiting. You just rest," Shawn said as he reached out to caress her shoulder a bit.

"Shawn… Where is your wedding ring?" Althea asked glancing at the hand on her shoulder.

"Oh, I was working out earlier and forgot to put it back on."

"Why do you always say that when I ask you why you're not wearing your ring?"

"Because, it's always the truth. Look baby, I gotta go. I love you. I'll call you later tonight okay?"

Althea felt an agonizing tug at her heart. Once again, Shawn had spent the night out and didn't come home until sunrise. And yet again, he had a very noticeable passion mark on his neck. *He doesn't even try to hide them anymore*, Althea thought while glancing at the quarter-sized hickey on Shawn's neck.

"Have a safe flight baby. Call me when you get a chance," Althea said as she turned over to conceal her tears from Shawn. Hell, if he had a better attitude, and was a bit more respectful, she just might have dealt with his bullshit the rest of her life. She definitely would have never looked at another man. She had tolerated the groupies because she felt that they were only temporary. She had also tolerated the long nights alone, but now she growing more and more tired of his blatant disrespect.

After Shawn left with Michael, Althea took a quick shower and got dressed. She was starving and felt a slight hang over coming on from the drinks at the game and the wine she drank during her late night conversation with Marcus. She thought it would be nice to cook a big breakfast for her and the girls. However, after going downstairs to rouse the women, she realized that they were nowhere to be found.

They are definitely some hoes, she thought aloud, and wondered what category *she* would be in if she hooked up with Marcus. The door opened suddenly, and Maia walked in smiling from ear to ear.

Althea looked concerned, "Where's Charlene?"

"She caught an early flight. She was off the hook last night."

"What did she do? Or should I say *who* did she do?" Althea asked.

"Nobody, but she spent the entire night trying to get that fine ass Torey Franklin to bite. He must be gay. Cause every man in the club was trying to get at her, but she was *throwing* the pussy at him. He's gotta be gay."

"Umm, why is it that when a brotha doesn't sleep with a woman the first time he meets her, he's gay? Maybe Torey just didn't want her like that. Plus, I heard he was going through a divorce. Anyway, guess who's going to an extravagant spa to get some good ol' fashioned pampering today?"

"Where?"

"Hotel Riviera."

"Oooh, girl, you know that's supposed to be the *spot*! But you know Shawn isn't going to let you spend that kind of money for a place like that," Maia said.

"Fuck him, we're going. So go on upstairs and get ready lil' sis."

"I thought they had a waiting list anyway?"

"You must have forgotten who I am… I'm Mrs. Halloween McQueen," she said imitating her husband's raspy voice. "Now are you going or not?"

"Well, I did have plans for the evening. I was supposed to be hooking up with that new rookie sensation Jerron Williams. You know I like 'em young. But I'm not about to miss out on this, …and you're treating too! Give me 20 minutes."

As the two ladies pulled up to the Hotel Rivera, in the brand new convertible 650 BMW Shawn had bought Althea (a make up present for forgetting her last birthday), they grew more and more excited. They had experienced many of the finer things life had to offer, but there was nothing like living the good life on someone else's dime.

"Good afternoon ladies. Would you like to valet your car?" a uniformed hotel employee asked.

"Yes, thank you?" Althea replied.

"Last name?"

"McQueen," Althea said.

"McQueen? You look familiar," said the valet, trying to place her face. "You're Halloween McQueen's wife aren't you?"

"Yes," Althea answered flatly; obviously not nearly as excited as she once was to be recognized as THE Mrs. Shawn McQueen.

The Riviera was known world wide for its spa treatments and exclusive services, and the ladies would not be disappointed. Immediately after checking in for their appointment, two handsome men carrying plush robes approached the ladies asking them their drink preference. Each guest was assigned to a personal attendant before their designated spa services were rendered. The attendants were expected to be at the beck and call of the guests, some who paid up to thousands of dollars a day to stay at the hotel. The ladies asked for their "sweetest" Sauvignon Blanc, then were guided to the "Chateau," a lavish waiting area decorated with marble floors, priceless tapestry, majestic columns and gold trimmed crystal chandeliers fit for the Royal family. The area was accented with fresh fruits, candles, and an array of posh hors d'oeuvres. But as grand as the entrance was, its splendor was no match to the statuesque waterfall in the center of the room. As well traveled as they were, this was still unlike any place they had been.

"Madame," said one of the attendants to the ladies, "Would you like your wine poolside?"

"Actually, we'll be in the whirlpool instead," Maia replied.

After the ladies found their way out of their respective changing rooms, they disrobed and slinked into the soothing hot water. Their attendants wrapped their hair in towels and brought spa pillows for them to relax on. The infinity pool and sauna had its own attendants who greeted patrons with their personal favorites – drinks, warm towels, or a light massage. They had found paradise. Shortly thereafter, the ladies were being called for their massages.

"This way, madams" the attendant said politely while pointing the way to the massage area. As they moved towards the massage area, the ladies noticed a handsome man approaching them. He was shirtless and glistening with what was seemingly massage oil. As the he came closer Althea's heart began to race. *Oh my God*, she thought, *it's Marcus!*

"Girl, that's Marcus!" Maia said through her teeth with quiet enthusiasm.

"I know who it is Maia," Althea said bumping her sister lightly as if to say "Shut the hell up!"

"Ladies! What a surprise. But I guess I should have known that you two would be regulars at such an exclusive spa. I'm almost ashamed to be here myself, but what can I say, I like being treated like a king every now and then," Marcus said while shyly covering his upper body.

"Marcus, what a nice surprise," Althea said blushing. Maia was too busy looking at his chiseled abdomen and perfectly sculpted pecs to speak.

"Had I known the two of you were coming, I would have had a bottle of champagne waiting for you in your room," Marcus said.

"That's very sweet of you, but we don't have a room here. We're just doing the "girls' spa day" thing. Wait, I thought you were planning some dinner for the evening," Althea inquired.

"Right, well it was supposed to be here at the Riviera, but since everyone cancelled on me, I'm having dinner solo …unless of course, you two lovely ladies wouldn't mind joining me.. I'm in the Grande Suite on the 30th floor, room 3000." Marcus knew that Maia would jump at the chance to join him for dinner. Hopefully that would be enough to convince her big sister to tag along as well.

"We'll definitely be there Marcus," Maia replied while winking at her sister. "What time should we come up?"

"7:00 pm would be ideal."

5

"Girl, what are you going to wear tonight for dinner," Althea asked her sister.

"Please, I'm not going to dinner with you two and be a third wheel! I gotta booty call to make. No way am I wasting this night watching Marcus make googly eyes at you. No ma'am. I'm calling Jerron," said Maia.

"Maia! Maia!"

"Talk to the hand big sis, I'm calling Jerron," she said while dialing Jerron's number.

Shit, I can't go back to a hotel by myself. What am I going to do? Althea thought. *Well, I guess it's only dinner. But nothing else! Dinner, conversation, and then back to this house for bed.* Althea had an idea.

"Okay, I'm out...I'm meeting Jerron in a few. Call me- I love you, bye." Maia said abruptly as she grabbed her overnight bag and bolted towards the door.

"Hey baby sis. Why don't I just get you and Jerron a room at The Hotel Riviera for the night? I hear the rooms are really nice. I'd just feel better with you being in a hotel versus being at his house. You know how athletes can be."

"Bitch you think you're slick, but that's cool. Hell, if I'm going to give up the panties I may as well do it in style. And yes I plan to give the up the draws so close your mouth and make the reservation, whore." Maia said jokingly.

It was all set. Althea would see Marcus and she had an alibi for being in the hotel, done like a *true player*.

As the two arrived at the hotel Althea realized that there was no turning back.

"Althea, call me about 30 minutes before you're ready to go tomorrow so I can put my company out and meet you downstairs to check out."

"Okay," said an obviously nervous Althea. "I'll see you tomorrow sis."

Damn these panties are irritating me Althea thought to herself. *That damn Brazilian bikini wax. I should have known better.* On the elevator she kept squirming and fighting with her thong. "Oh the hell with it," she said aloud. She quickly glanced around to make sure no one was in the hallway and slid her lacy thong panties off and shoved them in her purse. As Althea moved closer to Marcus' room she became even more nervous. *Girl, what are you doing here? You know this is crazy. And what would Shawn think?* A voice in her head said. *Shawn?! To hell with Shawn* another voice in her head echoed. *If Shawn was taking care of business you wouldn't be here in the first place!* Althea took one last deep breath to calm her nerves right before pressing the doorbell to the room.

"Who is it?" Marcus asked jokingly.

"Boy, open the door and stop playing."

"Who is it?"

"Don't make me leave Marcus. It's Althea! Now open this door!"

Marcus opened the door and couldn't believe how sexy Althea looked. She was breathtaking. She had on a strapless, ivory sundress with matching Gucci lace up stilettos.

Marcus had the table set up for both ladies, but he was quite pleased that Althea had arrived alone. The silky sound of Prince's "Adore" was playing in the background. There were also dozens of pink and ivory roses spread throughout the lavish hotel suite. The large dining room table was set for three, but he quickly removed the third place setting to make the mood even more intimate. The smell of scented candles filled the room. The whole scene was quite intoxicating, from the tray of smoked oysters and the stuffed mushrooms to the rare bottles of wines and champagne. As she strolled toward the dining room table to sit down for dinner, Marcus gently grabbed her arm and gracefully whisked her to the center of the room. He took her purse to the bedroom, then led her to the living room where they began to slow dance. Althea's heart was melting. She fell limp in his strong, muscular arms. He wasn't a professional athlete, but he was surely built like one. He breathed softly on her neck, inhaling her essence. Marcus had Althea feeling weak at the knees.

"Marcus, I came here to eat," she said gathering herself.

"That's right, you sure did, didn't you?" he replied with a smile.

The two new friends spent the next couple of hours eating, laughing, and talking as if they had known each other for years. Althea's nervousness eventually subsided during dinner and she felt more comfortable with Marcus than she ever could have imagined.

"Let me get you some more wine Ms. Lady," said Marcus.

"Marcus, are you trying to get me drunk?" she inquired.

"Hellll yeahhhhh I'm trying to get you drunk," he responded as they both laughed. After finishing the glass of wine, Althea began gathering herself for a quick exit. *I better get out of here now, and fast* she thought. "Marcus, what did you do with my purse? It's time for me to go."

"Are you leaving so soon?" he asked.

"Yes, it's time for me to get some beauty rest. Thank you for a wonderful evening. I haven't had such a good time in ages. I really, really appreciate you taking time out to entertain me," she said. Althea took her purse from Marcus's outstretched hand and headed for the door.

"Oh," Marcus said, "There's something I forgot to give you."

"What's that?" she asked.

"This," he said as he placed a deep, sensual kiss on her lips. Her only response was a faint moan. She glanced into his eyes and felt the hair on her neck stand on end. This man wanted her. She wasn't accustomed to this, especially since Shawn had basically ignored her for the past three years. All at once her entire body was overwhelmed by passion and she could no longer resist him, even if she wanted to. He pulled her closer to kiss her again. This time their tongues found one another as he rubbed her back and caressed her legs under her dress. As his hands helped themselves to her naturally toned ass, Marcus noticed that Althea wasn't wearing any panties. The bulge in his pants grew even more.

"I thought you were leaving," he said with a smile as he began kissing her neck. "I am leaving... tomorrow."

After entering the bedroom of the suite, Marcus' kisses began drifting from her neck, to her breasts, and down to her thighs until his lips found the spot that set her entire body on fire. They hadn't taken the time to remove her dress, but she didn't care. While tasting her, his hands brushed over every inch of her two beautiful breasts. And she wasn't about to stop him. She hadn't had this kind of intimacy in a long, long time and she was on fire. As Marcus slipped off her dress, he walked around to the front of her.

When did he take his shirt off? she wondered. He slid out of his pants and showed her she wasn't the only one who wasn't wearing underwear. His penis was fully erect now, stretching towards her begging for her touch. They both smiled as he began caressing her shoulders. He was a man of patience, and he especially wanted to take his time with Althea. While massaging her shoulders he allowed his tongue to taste her beautiful chocolate skin. His tongue worked its way down the small of her back over her firm buttocks. She clutched the sheets as he teased her with gentle strokes of his tongue from the small of her back to the top of her vagina, careful to not miss a spot. As he plunged his tongue deep inside her, she knew she wouldn't regret this decision. *Damn, this man loves to eat pussy* she thought as she grinded against his tongue.

"Oh Marcus, I'm going to cum baby, don't stop, please don't stop! Uhh, uhh, ooohhh, ooohhh!!" *Okay, we can fuck now!"* she thought. She definitely wasn't going to get any wetter. Or was she?

"Turn over," he said.

Damn, he's gonna kill me, she thought. Marcus knew that there was a chance this would be his only encounter with Althea, so he wanted to do any and everything to please her. She was in ecstasy from her first orgasm. The room began to spin. "Marcus, please, fuck me! Please?!"

Marcus gladly obliged and slowly penetrated her throbbing opening. But this wasn't just a fuck to Marcus. He had every intention of letting her know just how bad he wanted her. As he went in and out of her vagina with just the head of his penis, he questioned Althea's desire, "I don't think you want it?"

"Oh baby, please fuck me. I do want you baby please put it in." she squealed.

"Beg me."

The silence was a sign that Althea was slightly embarrassed.

"I said beg for it. If you really want it… then I want you to beg…."

Althea was about to explode. If just the head of his penis felt this good she had to have the rest of it, "Please Marcus fuck me. Please. I want you inside of me. Please fuck me now."

The involuntary slap to Marcus' chest turned him on even more. He raised her ass off the bed, and while lying pelvis to pelvis, he gave her every inch of him.

"Oooohhh, I'm soooo tight."

"Yes you are baby girl and it feels soooo good," he replied as he plunged deeper insider her. She dug her nails into his shoulders and held on for dear life. Each climax was even more amazing than the one before. Her entire body quivered. Simply put, he was fucking her better than she expected him to, melting more each time he re-entered her. "Ooooh Marcus, it's so goooood. Damn!"

"You think so huh?" he asked as he placed her legs over his shoulders and gently navigated every inch of her pussy while sucking her freshly pedicured toes. The deeper he went, the louder she got; and luckily for her, the louder she got, the harder he pumped. Althea loved his forcefulness and his animal-like response to her, as he pounded her into submission. "Give it to me," she screamed. "More daddy, oh please more!!! Uhh, uuh, yeahhh, yeahhh, Ohhhhh yesssss!!!" Althea couldn't believe that Marcus had made her feel this good. *This man is possessed,* she thought to herself. There was no way she could allow *him* to go unsatisfied. "Let me get on top," she said while gazing deeply into his eyes. Althea wanted to "thank" Marcus the right way for what he was giving her that night. She slowly slid up and down on his long, thick penis. She took every inch deeper and deeper.

"How does it feel? Do you like the way I ride you?" she breathed.

"Yes, baby I love it," he replied as she continued to ride him unmercifully.

"Is it good to you daddy? Is this pussy good? Tell me it's good!"

"Oh, it's good, it's so good! Oh Althea," he said as he reached to grab her ass cheeks. He held out for as long as he could. He had reached the point of no return. Althea was now riding him at a ferocious pace, her hair swaying amongst the candle lit backdrop. Marcus' orgasm was building. "I'm about to cum Althea."

"Tell me when," she demanded. "You better say when."

"Now! Althea, I'm about to cum!"

Just before Marcus reached his peek Althea dismounted from her position and decided to try a little trick that Charlene had suggested. Marcus wondered what was going on. Althea clamped her hand tightly around his testicles with one hand and vigorously stroked his rock hard penis with the other. She was driving him wild and she enjoyed every second of it. Anxious to share his ecstasy, Althea again straddle him. Marcus shook uncontrollably as he exploded deep inside his new lover, experiencing the most intense orgasm he ever had.

RINGGGGGGGGGGGGG... "Hello, hello," a groggy Marcus said into the phone. "Mr. Edwards this is your 7:00 a.m. wake up call sir. Have a pleasant morning and a great day!" a friendly voice said. "Thank you," Marcus answered. He had forgotten about his 9:30 a.m. meeting downtown. Thank goodness he had set the wake-up call before Althea arrived.

"Hey you," he said while lightly stroking Althea's shoulder, "I have a meeting downtown in a couple of hours. I'm about to jump in the shower. You can just sleep in and go back to your room whenever you decide to get up okay?" *Damn his hand feels good,* she thought pretending to be asleep.

"I had a wonderful time last night. But before you jump in the shower..." she whispered while stroking his already rising penis, "Do you think you have a few minutes to spare?"

"It's about damn time," Maia said as she unlocked the suite door to let her big sister enter the room. "I was about to leave your ass," she said with a fake attitude.

"Girl please, how are you going to leave me when we came in MY car?" Althea responded with a girlish giggle.

"Oooooh, you little HOE!" exclaimed Maia. "You did it didn't you?"

"Okay let's go." Althea responded.

Give me the valet ticket," Maia demanded. "Alright, you have 24 hours to bask in the glow, but tomorrow, you're gonna tell me what happened!"

6

Althea slept the entire evening. She woke up the next morning wondering if the night with Marcus ever even happened. It was the most amazing sexual experience she ever had. She wanted to savor the sensual moments between them but knew Maia would soon be questioning her, so she was already prepared to tell her a little white lie. As she searched for clothes to put on, she remembered that she needed to call her mother-in-law to make arrangements to pick up her son.

"Mama I will pickup Lil' Man in about 30 minutes."

"Okay baby," her mother-in-law responded. "We'll see you in a few minutes."

"Yes ma'am. Just put his blue Sean John outfit on. And Mama, do you think you can baby-sit for me Friday? I want to go to out with the girls, you know, have a little me time." Althea was already thinking about seeing Marcus again.

"Althea, I will baby sit anytime you want me to." Mama McQueen was old school and believed you stay with your man through whatever. But she also didn't approve of how Shawn treated Althea. She knew about her son's antics. After all, she raised him. She also knew that Althea was a good woman, a magnificent mother, and Shawn's main supporter even before the NFL. So if it was going to help take some stress off of Althea, Mama McQueen would help out any way she could.

Althea wondered why Maia hadn't already barged into her room and grilled her. But she remembered Maia had to be at work early. She felt relieved. Althea fixed breakfast and rushed off to pick up her son. *I haven't seen my baby all weekend; I miss him so much,* she thought as she pulled out of the driveway. However, Althea's thoughts were not only on her son. Her mind soon drifted to Marcus, who she would get to see again later that week.

When Friday morning arrived, the nostalgia of their rendezvous had not faded one bit. Althea was still terribly excited. She had gotten her stylist to come to her home to style her hair, then she was off to get her weekly manicure and pedicure. The dress she picked out was even sexier than the one she wore to the Hotel Riviera. She wanted to have a great time at the concert, and maybe even spend some quality time with her new friend Marcus. Althea danced around to music in her room as she began to dress for the concert. While dancing, she noticed that her message light on her phone was flashing was flashing. *Who called me from a private number?* she wondered. *Probably Shawn calling me from some other woman's phone.*

As she picked it up, it rang once again. "Hello."

"Hey you, its Marcus...I've been really missing you. I just got back from Nashville. I just wanted to make sure you were still coming to the concert.

"I wouldn't miss it for the world."

"Okay, then I will leave Maia's name at the door. She can have a guest, and your table will be already set up. I'll see you tonight."

Althea was giddy beyond belief. She had a feeling tonight would be just as exciting as the last time they were together.

"Maia are you ready yet?!" Althea screamed.

As soon as Mama McQueen got to the house the ladies sped off in Althea's burgundy, Maybach Benz, the latest *"baby I'm really sorry this time"* gift from Shawn. The women looked liked superstars, and justifiably so, considering they might actually get to meet Musiq after the concert. There was a line around the club, but the ladies weren't concerned. They were on "the list." Security quickly escorted them to the front of the V.I.P line as if they had been waiting on them.

A large man in a black suit approached them. "Welcome ladies. The hostess will take you to your table."

The ladies had a fabulous evening. Musiq and free drinks hit the spot. Since Musiq had recently divorced his wife (not that it mattered to her), Maia tried her damn-dest to get back stage to see him, to no avail.

"Girl where the hell is Marcus? He needs to get me back stage," Maia said to her sister.

"I think that's him right there," Althea said while eyeing her new friend.

"Yea, that's him. How could I miss that tall specimen? Althea, I think he just saw you."

"Hey pretty ladies. Are you all enjoying yourselves?" Marcus inquired.

"We most certainly are stranger," Althea replied.

"Well do me a favor. In five minutes, meet me in that hallway by the second V.I.P area, I want to show you something," Marcus requested.

As she made her way toward the hallway Marcus mentioned, Althea saw several familiar faces. Mostly women she had run-ins with about her husband Shawn.

She smiled with a fake grin and kept moving, because this was not about them or Shawn, it was about what Marcus wanted her to do.

As Marcus walked by her, he motioned for her to follow him. They went through a mirror-covered door that led to a stairwell, and got into the elevator. After exiting the elevator, the two climbed a short flight of stairs to reach the roof of the club. Without saying a word Marcus signaled for Althea to come to him. Althea moved in quickly, invading his personal space, standing nearly nose-to-nose with him.

"I want to give you something," Althea breathed seductively into his ear. "Here…" she said while taking off her panties and handing them to him. "I wanted to give them to you before I ruined them." It was obvious that she could not resist the sexual trance Marcus put her in when she got close to him; she was already soaking wet.

It was clear that Althea had her own agenda, as she forcefully pushed Marcus against the door. Her hands quickly found their way down his pants. "Damn your dick is amazing!" she said as she stooped down to put all of it into her mouth. Althea sucked his dick like her life depended on it. She wanted him to feel what she had felt earlier that week at the hotel. And he did. Marcus quickly came as he uncharacteristically lost all *dick control.* She had made him do something he had never done before, have an orgasm from oral sex. Now they were even. She neatly tucked his shirt back into his pants and zipped him up.

As Althea stepped out of the elevator she looked back smiling and said, "I had a wonderful time. I'll see you

Sunday at the game!" Marcus showed her an alternate route to get back into the club, and eventually eased himself back into the flow.

"Oooooh Althea where in the hell have you been?" Maia inquired teasingly as Althea approached the table.

"I had to give Marcus something."

"Girl, now I *know* you didn't fuck that man in this club!" Maia exclaimed.

"Girl nah, I didn't do all that. But I did go down on him on the roof. Now let's go," Althea quickly threw in with a devilish grin.

Maia nearly fell over the balcony. This was definitely not the prim and proper sister she knew. Althea was acting like *her!* On the way home, Althea was blasting the Musiq CD she received at the club. The girls laughed the entire time as Althea described the things that had happened between her and Marcus. But her feelings for him were real. She didn't feel like this was just a "sex thing." Her feelings were real…even for a married woman.

When the ladies arrived back at the McQueen estate, Lil' Man and Mama McQueen were already sleep.

"Sis, do you think what I'm doing is bad. Do you think I'm a hoe?" Althea asked.

"Althea let me stop you there. Girl I have never seen you smile like you've been smiling this last week. I just want you to be happy. I just want to see that smile. And you know how I feel about your husband anyway. So, no I don't think you're a hoe. Besides you got too much money to be a hoe girlfriend, you're a whore," she said with a British accent.

7

RINGGGGGGGGGGG… "Damn, where is the phone? " Althea mumbled while scurrying to find the cordless house phone. "Maia, answer the phone!"

"Okay! Hello? Shawn, what's up?" Maia asked.

"Who is this?" Shawn inquired.

"Maia, fool," she snapped. *Damn, this nigga has so many women he doesn't even know MY voice.*

"Oh, what's up sis. Where's Thea?"

"Hold on. Althea, Shawn's on the phone!" Maia yelled up the stairs.

"Hello, hey sweetie," she said in an unusually excited and flirtatious voice.

"Hey, don't be mad but I'm not going to be able to have dinner when the team gets in town. But you can come to the hotel for an hour before curfew."

"That's cool. You ready to play?" Althea asked.

"Come on girl. It's October and I am Halloween McQueen, ain't I?"

"Alright Mr. Man. And Shawn, please don't you have any of those other bitches at this game. This is our hometown. Please don't embarrass me, okay?"

"Don't start Thea. You know I do a lot of business with women and men. Look, I'll call you after our team meetings and you can just come to the hotel. The meetings may be running late so wait until I call you. I don't want you to be in the lobby just waiting."

"He is so full of shit…" she said to Maia while covering the phone receiver with her hand. "O.k. Lil Man wants to talk to you. I love you," she said flatly. "If your meetings run late and I can't see you tonight I'll just see you tomorrow." It was obvious she probably wouldn't see Shawn until after the game.

It was already 11:00 pm, Shawn's team curfew time, and he still had not called. She found her mind drifting from Shawn to her new friend, who she wanted more than ever to *accidentally* bump into at the game the next day. She just didn't feel like dealing with all the pre-game tailgating, the in-laws, and the rest of the bullshit that accompanied Shawn playing in town.

As the morning sun peeked through her massive bedroom window, Althea began devising her master plan for the day. She would play sick, stay home, and then go to the game late by herself and find Marcus. *Besides, why should I go support that no good ass nigga? He couldn't even call to say goodnight to his wife and child?* she thought. As her mother walked into the room she delivered her best performance. "Mama, I'm not feeling too good. I already threw up twice. I'm just gonna stay here, but if I feel better, then me and the Lil' Man will just drive by ourselves," Althea sickly stated.

"Well, maybe I should take him with me so he can see the whole game?" her mother-in-law suggested.

"Okay, that's fine. I'll text message Shawn after the game starts so he won't be worried." *Yeah, like he's ever worried about me,* she thought.

"And I'll fix you a hot toddy to go with the soup I made for later. I bet that will make you feel better."

"Thank you so much Mama."

"You're welcome baby. Oh my, the limo driver is blowing. I'll leave the soup in the microwave. And you stay home if you're not feeling better, you hear me?"

"Yes, Ma'am," she said weakly. *Damn, maybe I should take this act to Hollywood,* she thought.

RINNNNGGGGGGGGGGG… Althea finally answered her phone. It had been ringing off the hook.

"Hello."

"Althea?"

"Speaking."

"Hey beautiful, it's Marcus.

"Hey you."

"I figured since your husband is playing in town today that I wouldn't see you. So, I was just calling to say hello."

"Oh, don't worry Marcus, you *will* see me today."

"Is that right?"

"Yes, I'm coming to the game late. I'm not that pressed to see the game, but I intend to see you. Is that ok with you?"

"That's perfect. Just call me on my cell when you get to the stadium. I'll be in suite 325, the same as last time."

Althea hurried to get dressed. Her BCBG mini skirt would be perfect for the occasion, with no panties of course.

———————————

After pulling into the reserved parking, located by the player's entrance to the stadium, she pulled her hat down a little lower than usual then entered the stadium. "323, 324, 325 here it is," she said as she arrived at the suite where Marcus was waiting.

Marcus was his usual, good-looking and irresistible self. There were only 10 minutes left in the fourth quarter when she reached the suite. Before she could apologize for taking so long, Marcus snatched Althea into the suite restroom, and turned the volume of the television, which was mounted overhead, to full blast. Foreplay was not an option. He pushed her against the door, standing firmly behind her and slid every inch of his thick penis inside her. It was as if he knew she was still wet from the club on Friday. Marcus was fucking Althea like he was trying to get even with her for making him lose control on the roof of the club. Every time she made a sound he slapped her on her ass to remind her that they were surrounded by fans who occupied the suites next to them. He was driving her crazy; his dick pounding into her forcefully from the back, his tongue tickling her ear lobe, and his hands gripping her waist tightly. The scene was almost more than she could stand. She turned her head trying to bite any part of his body to muffle the sounds of an unsatisfied wife being fucked the right way. The two lovers could hear the crowd roaring. Althea wanted to let out screams of her own. She simply couldn't hold it anymore. She was about to burst as they both glanced upward at the television. The two scenes played out simultaneously, nearly synchronized.

Shawn caught a pass and was running up the sideline just as Marcus was running up in his wife. The faster Shawn ran, the harder Marcus stroked. *Go baby,* Althea thought as she glanced up and let out quietly, "Oh yeah baby, you know I love this." Shawn darted down the sidelines as Marcus' tongue raced up and down Althea's neck. The crowd was going wild and so was Althea. The two could hear the sounds of the commentator overhead:

"It's McQueen to the 50," as Althea bit her lip to keep from screaming. "He's at the 40," as she scratched the door. "The 35," just as she grabbed the sink to brace herself for the explosion. "The 10! McQueen is gonna score!" "TOUCHDOWN!" Althea and the commentator screamed together in unison, "Yes! Yes! Oh my God Yes!!" Just as Shawn leapt into the end zone, Marcus exploded into the player's wife. The Pennsylvania fans were going crazy and Althea's screams blended in like a perfectly harmonized symphony. She was cumming so hard that it seemed to last forever. Marcus grabbed her by the neck and went as deep as he could one last stroke. Althea felt like there was a waterfall between her thighs and was tickled by the mess she made. The two were just as exhausted as Shawn, who had caught a pass to run 85 yards for a touchdown to win the game in the final seconds. Like the players on the field, the lovers had given all they had.

"Damn, I better get down to the tunnel!" Althea exclaimed while trying to catch her breath. Althea knew she was pushing it, but she still knew she could still beat their family to the team tunnel. She washed off as quickly as she could, straightened her hair, and then jogged briskly to the area that led to the tunnel. Luckily she arrived just before their family members. She told them that she sat in the club area to watch the game because she didn't want to chance making anyone sick, especially her son.

Shawn was being interviewed by Sports World News' top anchor when Marcus and Torey walked by. Marcus and Althea caught themselves staring at one another a bit too long. Just as Torey and Marcus strolled by, Shawn walked up.

"Hey baby I got your page. Are you okay?" Shawn asked Althea.

"I'm better now," she said.

"You look pretty tired," Shawn looked concerned.

"Yeah, I feel like I've been working out," she responded.

"Did you see my touchdown?" he asked.

She whispered in his ear. "Shawn, believe it or not, I could've had an orgasm watching that play. It was amazing."

"Damn, I might have to start playing my highlights, if touchdowns are getting you off like that," Shawn joked. "Well, you make sure you get some medicine for that little bug you have okay? Me and the fellaz will probably go out to celebrate when we get back to P.A. So, I'll just call you tomorrow okay?"

"Okay Mr. Touchdown, you be careful. I should be celebrating that fourth quarter too but I'm exhausted. I'm just going to go home and go to bed."

"Althea, baby, where's your ring?" Shawn asked while glancing at her left hand.

"Oh, it's in my purse. I took it off when I was working out," she responded.

Shawn was too consumed with how great he played to realize that if his wife was sick she probably wouldn't have worked out. "Oh, okay. Well be sure and tape EPSN for me. I'll call you tomorrow after practice. I love you."

"I LOVE YOU TOO!" Althea mouthed as she waved good-bye. Oddly enough from where she was standing, Althea could see both Shawn *and* Marcus. Shawn was boarding the team bus and Marcus was a few feet behind him getting into Torey's car. Shawn and Marcus both waved back to her simultaneously, neither man noticing the other. Although the Steel had claimed victory on the field that day, Althea turned out to be the true W.I.N.N.E.R. Hell, from where she was standing, she was the game's MVP, deserving of her *own* nickname. *Althea "the Dream" McQueen...No Althea "the Diva" McQueen; nah...*Althea cracked herself up as she made her way through the crowd.

From then on, she pledged to play to win and not to lose.

Keisha Franklin aka The M.I.D Wife
Chapter 8

"You're a damn liar Ivy! Now you *know* you've thought about being with another woman!" Keisha screamed, almost spilling her shot of Patron.

"Ohhh, so just because you're a freak means I'm one too?" Ivy replied.

"Puh-lease Ivy. You *are* a freak! Remember, I'm the one who's been around for your little escapades. You may be able to lie to Danielle and Jewel, but I know the truth girlfriend," Keisha said with a snap of her fingers. "Don't you get me started on your list of antics young lady. Remember Brian in your mother's bed? What about when you did Sidney while we were in college while your real boyfriend was passed out drunk in the same room? And, who could ever forget Paul..."

"Alright Miss Thang, that's enough of *my* business," Ivy replied. "Don't hate me because you ain't me!" she said as the women burst into laughter.

For Keisha, Ivy, Danielle, and Jewel their monthly pamper party was the glue that kept them tight. These parties were like counseling without the $150 an hour counselor's fee. The ladies could relax, have drinks, get massages, talk about whatever came to mind and be listened to without the sound of EPSN drowning out their voices. The ladies had deemed the event, *The Sistas Sanctuary.* It had become the official spot for their *souls* to unwind after a long few weeks of work, kids and husbands. Nothing was off limits at the gatherings and what made the parties more special was the only rule of the event, which was known as the *Sista Act.* The *Sista Act* simply stated that whatever issues any of them had before arriving had to be left at the door, even if they had conflicts with each other. There were no problems, conflicts or issues allowed at *The Sistas Sanctuary.*

If only the walls could talk. These ladies had mastered the art of letting it all hang out. It was Keisha's idea that as a hard working housewife she deserved a day a month in which she could go and do whatever it was she wanted with her girls. She felt she deserved a day that called for no responsibility, her day of rest. And when her husband Torey agreed, she called her girlfriends and it was official. Thus, on the last Friday of every month the four friends rented the most impressive stretch limo and largest hotel suite in Houston.

_____

"Ugghh Keisha...you've been with a woman before?" Jewel seemed semi-disgusted or at least ignorantly curious.

"First of all, my husband is Torey Franklin. So if you ain't freaky then you can't be a Franklin my dear. The bottom line is, me and my husband do whatever makes us happy. But honestly ladies, I was with a woman once even before I met Torey. Quiet as is kept, my most intense orgasm *came* from a woman, no pun intended. Shhhh, don't tell nobody!" she said with a wink.

As Ivy continued to practice her stripper routine, Jewel seemed even more intrigued. "I'm sorry girl, but there is absolutely nothing a woman can do for me!" shouted Ivy as she shimmied in front of the full-length mirror near the door of the enormous suite.

Dannielle, or Danni as she was affectionately known,

quickly intercepted Keisha's response. "Jewel let me ask you a couple of questions. Number one, in general are men as detailed as women?"

"No, not generally."

"Okay, number two, have you ever tried to tell your husband something or tried to get him to do something without actually saying exactly what it was you needed for him to do? And not just sexually...around the house, in the yard...you know?"

"Girl, what woman hasn't?" Jewel quickly responded.

"Number three, who can find your hot spot faster, you or your husband?"

"Bitch, who do you think? Me, now what's your point?"

"Well, simply put...You can give an American a map of Africa with every road and tree in Africa on it. But when its all said and done ain't no American gon' navigate his way through Africa better than an African. I don't care what kind a directions you give him or how many times he's been there!" The women burst into an uncontrollable laughter.

"Ivy, will you sit your drunk ass down? Gerald don't want to see your non-dancing ass strip, so stop practicing. You look like Jel-lo, not J-Lo!" Keisha yelled through the laughter.

"Forget you hoe. I'm not even thinking about Gerald. I'm 'bout to quit my job, go to the A.T.L, and make me some change. And for the record, I'm not drunk, I'm high, thank you very much. Watch me make my booty clap ya'll." Ivy could barely dance on beat from the hydro Keisha had brought.

"Seriously though Jewel, the first time I did it I felt a little weird, but there's just something different about being with a woman. I mean, don't get me wrong a woman could never take the place of a man, at least not for me, because I love me some *magic stick*. But, the curves of a woman's hips, the softness of her breasts, a woman's ass... It's something you can't get from a man. I can't explain it. Sex with a woman is just, different. I'm not saying it's better, but it is definitely different. Take kissing for instance. Most men don't realize, that kissing is very intimate and turns a lot of women on, which is why they usually don't want to kiss or at least kiss on you, that long. They don't realize that staring deep into our eyes can be foreplay. I can't remember the last time Torey just played with my hair... Imagine making love to yourself..."

"Ugghh you nasty!" One of the women blurted out while sipping wine.

"I mean look at it this way. You know where all of your spots are. You know when to rub hard and when to rub soft. You know when to use one finger, two or even three fingers. And don't be frontin', because I know you use that little silver bullet I gave you to get off. I used to think the next best thing to some good down and dirty sex with a man, was masturbating. But I am now a witness that getting your *cat* licked by an experienced female is a *very* close second to a nice fat penis."

"Damnnnn Keisha, you make it sound like it's better than some McDonald's french fries, after a week of fasting," Danielle said jokingly.

"I don't know about all of that but what I do know is that when I realized that Torey was a voyeur, I felt like I had just hit the *Licky Licky Lotto*. So now, all he has to do is just say the word and I give my man, correction, my husband the show he wants to see. Hell, if I don't, one of those groupie hoes will. So I ask you ladies, *If not me, who?* If you're not freaky for your husband in the end...he'll surely find, a freaky friend." Ivy high-fived Keisha as the group once again broke into laughter.

"Oh shit, I think that's security. Girl put that weed out." As Danielle ran to answer the hotel door the ladies quickly sprayed the room with air freshner.

Dressed in her see through boy-shorts and half t-shirt Danielle tried disguising her high level of intoxication. As she opened the door an unavoidable back draft of marijuana smoke escaped the room. "Oh good, it's our food."

"Yes ma'am Mrs. Franklin." The room service waiter politely responded. "I smell... I mean, I see you ladies are having a pretty good time."

Danielle could barely contain her giddiness. "Yeah, you could say that."

The other ladies teased the waiter and put $10 and $20 dollar tips in his pants as he set up the food. "Oooh, you're a cutie," Ivy said flirting with the obviously embarrassed youngster.

"Thank you," he replied as Ivy grabbed a handful of his backside.

As he completed setting up the food Danielle gave him a $100 bill. "Now if security heads up here or anything like that give us the heads up and call the room sexy."

"Thanks ladies. I got you. Ya'll have a good night and call me if you need *anything*," he said while watching

Ivy's ass cheeks sway as she continued her dance routine.

"Bye cutie," Ivy said with a wink.

"Okay girls, we're going to play a game. I call it, "Don't Lie Bitch". We draw names and we can ask the person we draw any question we want. It's truth or dare without the dare." Just like Keisha figured the ladies were hyped about the idea. "Alright everybody write your name on a piece of paper and put it in this bowl. Danielle you're the youngest so you draw last. So it's me, Jewel, Ivy, and then Danni. But Danni who ever has your name gets to ask you the first question."

"Now, why do I have to draw last, and ask first?" Danni said playfully rolling her eyes.

"Heffa, because I wrote the rules." Keisha snapped.

Ivy was more than willing to pop the first question. "Danni, if you could lick yourself, would you? And if so, how often?"

"Damn, how did you come up with that one? The answer is easy though. I most certainly would. Now as for how often, just put it this way, I would drop protein and carbs from my diet and replace them with pussy, the other white meat. I'm talkin' breakfast, lunch, and dinner." It was clear that Dannielle was just as drunk as she was high.

"Danni you are a crazy. I know you did not say pussy, the other white meat. Oh my God! I'm next to answer, who has my name?" Ivy was curious as to what she would be asked.

"That would be me," Jewel excitedly chirped. "Okay, Ivy would you ever have sex with two men?"

"Oh no you didn't! You must think I'm some dumb hoe that would let two men have their way with me.

You've been waiting to ask me that shit, haven't you Jewel? If you think I'm a hoe then say it. Because you have got to be out of you damn mind if you think I would sleep with two men... Hell no, I sure wouldn't...Not without condoms!" Ivy winked. Security was sure to come after their latest outburst.

Keisha caught in mid pull, coughed out a cloud of smoke. "Girl, does your husband know what he has at home? You are a nut. Now it's my turn. Now we gon' get to the dirt. Jewel, what's a fantasy you have that you've never told your husband about?"

"Umm, Umm, Oh...And you hookers better not ever tell nobody. Well, I have this fantasy where I'm supposed to be meeting Emory at a nice hotel room, a penthouse I'm thinking. But somehow I accidentally sent the email to this guy that works with me name Miles. Well, the email had the time, what hotel and the room number on it. I told him not to worry about bringing anything just come to the room and the door would be unlocked. So, I get this response email saying cool he would love too. So when I saw the return email address I was excited, even though I thought it was weird because it wasn't Emory's usual email. And you know how much Emory likes to role-play, so I didn't trip. Well, to make a long story short in my fantasy I'm in the shower and it's all steamed up and this muscular dark-skinned frame opens the shower, quickly spins me around and puts this blindfold on me. And although I kind of know it's not Emory, I never make the guy stop. I mean he is doing me so good from the back... and kissing all over my neck, playing with my breasts and squeezing my hips and massaging my clit. After of few minutes of the best sex I ever had, I can tell he's about to cum because he starts fucking me harder and faster. So before he cums, I turn around and I'm feeling so freaky and so turned on by everything; the steam, his body, the shower spraying our bodies that I kneel down, take off the blind fold, and even after I see it's not Emory I still suck his dick until he cums."

"In your mouth?" Danni questioned.

"Yes in my mouth, where else?"

"I knew you were a freak."

"He bathes me and then leaves," Jewel concludes with a long sigh...

Keisha hadn't realized that she wasn't the only woman with a strong sex drive and strong imagination. "Diz-amn girl, like I always say, if you gon' go, then go hard! That sounds like some shit I would do." The other women praised Jewel for the thought. They were feeling her fantasy one hundred percent.

"I need a cold shower after that one." Danni joked. "J, are you trying to tell us you fucked Miles on the sly?"

"Girl, hell no. Miles is fine as hell but I heard he has a *donkey dick*! You know, one so big that when he puts it in, *you* sound like a donkey! And I heard he wasn't circumcised. And I needs my penis with a helmet on it, you feel me!" Not surprising chuckles consumed the suite.

Keisha was antsy for her question. "Come on Danni, give it to me. Give me you best shot."

"Now we can ask anything?"

"Yes, anything!" the three ladies chimed in unison.

"Okay, here it is... If you could do anything with your husband Torey, what would it be?"

87

After the other women's answers to questions, the tone had been set for one of her off the wall sexual responses. The women sat on the edge of their seats for her response. Her answer was something Keisha had been hoping would come true for the past two years. Keisha answered the question with two words. "Start over. I would start over. I would start over so I could be a better wife. And I would start over so I could tell Torey everything he needed to know about me to be a better husband."

Keisha had almost broken the *Sista Act,* but her friends knew that it was just a matter of time before her situation broke her down. But they didn't care. After all, *The Sistas Sanctuary was* the place where your soul could unwind. Jewel quickly killed the silence, "Let's make a toast. Everybody get some champagne. Okay, to another wonderful weekend with my sisters. To Keisha Franklin, for coming up with one of the greatest ideas ever, The Sistas Sanctuary, it has definitely helped me keep my sanity many a night. But most importantly, here's to unconditional love and eternal friendship. Ya'll my girls and I love all of you."

As the ladies sipped their champagne they turned the music up, lit another blunt and continued like teenage girls at a sleepover, Keisha dazed into the thick cloud of smoke. She seemed to be in deep thought. For Keisha, life had been a terrible roller coaster ride and she was ready to get off, for good.

9

Keisha and Torey Franklin were known for the lavish cookouts and parties they hosted at their 6.5-acre estate. Torey was the proverbial professional athlete, a millionaire who never hesitated to roll out the red carpet to family, friends, associates, and even strangers. He wanted everything first class. The lavish spread was set out in grand fashion – steak, seafood, ribs, burgers, and all the alcohol you could drink. The top DJs in the city vied for the opportunity to spin on the 1's and 2's at the barbeques. The Franklin estate instantly became an adult playground for those lucky enough to get an invitation. Some of Houston's most eligible bachelors attended because they could count on the ratio being at least 3:1 women to men. And the women who showed up weren't ordinary by any stretch of the imagination. The finest women west of the Mississippi River managed to not only show up but turn heads all night long at the fabulous soirees. Of course, most of the women assumed that they would meet some of Torey's football buddies. Hell, even the "Ordinary Joes" (called OJs by the pro ballers) sometimes got lucky.

Simply put, Keisha and Torey made a stunning couple. Heads turned anytime they went anywhere together. Keisha's long, naturally curly hair was a product of being the offspring of a white father and black mother. It was also one of the things that made her the envy of several other players' wives. Her golden brown eyes were spectacular, especially in the sunlight, and her body came second only to her sexual nature. Had she been a little taller, she'd probably be walking the runways of Paris and

Milan. Torey himself was the epitome of rugged masculinity. His boyish good looks and unpredictable hairstyles made him a stand-out off the field, as much as his speed in the 40 yard dash did, on the field. The handsome couple became intertwined in what could only be described as a relationship choreographed by destiny.

Torey first met Keisha when she was in town visiting a girlfriend for the Houston State University homecoming, which was always one of the city's largest events. As with many black college homecomings, the main focus was not on the football game, but what everyone, especially the ladies, were wearing at the game, the halftime shows, and on the post-game parties. As fate would have it, Torey, who played for Houston's pro football squad, was in town and not with his team because he had injured his knee in a game a few weeks earlier. Therefore, he was forced to stay in town to receive medical treatment. Torey was a warrior on the field, so the mere thought of not traveling with his comrades drove him crazy crazy. But he was determined to make the best of a bad situation.

After the Houston State game, Torey decided to attend his fraternity's party with his good friend and frat brother Aaron Townsend. Aaron loved Psi Kappa with all his heart and spent much of his time with his fraternity brothers. If anyone could bring Torey out of his mama's boy/preacher's son personality it was Aaron Townsend. Aaron was outgoing, witty, and intelligent. The best thing about him was that he could sell a polar bear a fur coat. He had attended college with Torey, but never graduated because he longed to start his own business. He often made money in college by getting rich White boys on campus to finance his pipe dreams, some of which actually worked. While his boys were driving their parents' beat up hoopties, Aaron was cruising in his brand new, drop top Mustang 5.0. Aaron's entrepreneurial spirit was matched only by his passion for the opposite sex. If he wasn't selling something, he was chasing skirts.

Psi Kappa had a reputation for throwing the best parties and this one was no different. All women of age received free champagne all night and were later treated to an "all male revue" hosted by the fraternity and members of the Houston State football team. The all male revues had become legendary. Men flocked to the revues as well, because they knew that every fine honey in Houston would be on hand to see the college boys shake their thangs.

"Hey Frat, did you see the ass on that one?" Aaron yelled to Torey above the loud sounds of DJ Jazz.

"Did I see it? I think Stevie could have seen that ass. Her friend isn't bad either," Torey replied. "Man, I think I'm going to have to scoop that one up."

"Nah playa, I saw her first. And since I pledged the frat the year before you did, I'm going to have to ask for a little deference on this one," said Aaron.

"Damn A.T., your ass is always hollering that deference shit when it comes to the ladies."

"Hey baby boy, I don't make the rules, I just follow them," Aaron replied with a wink.

"Hello my beautiful Black sisters, I'm Aaron Townsend and this is my man Torey. We'd love to buy you ladies a drink."

"Oh my, a couple of gentlemen huh? I'm Keisha and this is my girl Tia." Keisha stared intently at Torey trying to remember where she had seen him before.

"I thought you Kappa boys were more into having the ladies buy *you* drinks," said Tia.

"Now who in the world told you that?" asked Aaron with his beaming smile and perfect teeth gleaming. "The Psi Kappas always cater to the ladies. Ain't that right T?"

"That's right Frat," answered Torey while staring back at Keisha. Torey was speechless. He wasn't blessed with the "mouth piece" his boy Aaron had. His strict upbringing didn't leave room for him to develop his "game" or the art of wooing women. All he could do was stare blankly into Keisha's heavenly eyes, and pray for the right things to say. Unfortunately for Torey, Aaron knew exactly what to say on every occasion, in fact, flattery was his specialty. He hadn't become known as the "panty wetter" for nothing. Although the eye contact between Keisha and Torey was electric, Torey's boyish shyness all but spoiled the moment. And like clockwork, Aaron began to seize the moment.

"Hey beautiful, would you like to dance?" Aaron asked Keisha while caressing her hand. "Your hand is so soft. What do you use on them?" Keisha couldn't help being mesmerized by Aaron's charisma and charm. As usual, by the end of the night Torey was saying good night to Keisha, Tia, and to his boy Aaron, who was going home with Keisha. Aaron always went home with the flyest woman at the party. Meanwhile Torey went home alone, using the back streets of the city to dodge cops who would surely love to bust a pro ball player with alcohol on his breath.

Although he had not seen or heard from Keisha since the Psi Kappa party, she crossed his mind constantly. He wanted to reach out to her, but he didn't know how. He thought about asking A.T. for Keisha's number, but didn't want to step on his boy's toes. As should be expected of a close friend, A.T. sensed the chemistry between Keisha and Torey. But he only went after Keisha because she was the best looking girl at the party, nothing more, nothing less. That was just the type of guy Aaron was.

Two weeks later, during lunch between the two friends, Torey decided to swallow his pride and ask Aaron for her number.

"Yo A.T., remember that girl you met at the Houston State after-party?"

"Shhhhhitttt man, you know your boy A.T., I met plenty of women at the party that night playboy. You need to be more specific," Aaron replied.

"Keisha, the redbone sista. Fly. Real classy?"

"Man, do you know that you just described nearly half the females I met that night?"

"The girl you went home with man. Do you know how to get in contact with her?"

"Ahhh, yessss, baby girl. Man, I had to stay up until 5:30 in the morning working on that. I was about to bounce, but you know ain't too many women that can withstand the "M.G.M," but I can't blame you for wanting to tag that."

"What in the hell is M.G.M?"

"Marvin Gaye and Marijuana!" A.T. said laughing.

"Nah man, it's not that. I was actually kind of feeling her. For real," Torey replied trying to play the whole thing off.

"Man, are you serious? You were really feelin' her? Damn, that's a new one on me. You do realize that I got with her the other night, right?"

"Yeah, I figured that, but it doesn't really matter. Hell, it's not like this is the first time we've been diggin' the same woman. Remember Yvette? Sondra? Tina?"

"Man, do I? You're going to make me get out my lil' black book and call those freaks up right now!" Aaron said with a laugh. Even through the laughter, he could still see that Torey was serious. "Alrighty then. I'll tell you what. I'll give ol' girl your number. That way she won't be pissed at me for giving out hers. Cool?"

"Cool," Torey replied.

"By the way, I have something to tell you my man," Aaron said.

"Oh Lord, I guess now you want to tell me which positions you had Keisha in that night huh?" Torey asked half jokingly.

"Nah man, nothing like that. I'm shutting it down playboy. I'm givin' up my pimp card forever. I'm going to marry Kenyetta."

"Shut your damn mouth A.T.! Stop bullshitting man. Didn't you just sleep with that Marci chick from Yonkers the other day?"

"Yeah man, but I'm telling you, I'm done with all that. I need to settle down. Kenyetta has been patient with a nigga man. And, I think she's the one who can help me take my business to another level. I'm moving back to

Memphis my man. I'm going to marry her and run the business proper like."

Torey was caught off guard by Aaron's sudden announcement, but not completely surprised. After all, like Aaron said, Kenyetta had been more than patient with him over the years. He and Kenyetta began dating steadily during their sophomore year in high school. And while Aaron loved her, the temptations of college got to him on more than one occasion. Actually, the temptations of college got to him more than a couple of hundred times. But this time, his mind was made up. He loved Kenyetta with all his heart and soul, and that was enough.

Keisha and Torey began talking on the phone regularly, and on a whim, they decided to attend Aaron and Kenyetta's wedding together in Memphis. Ironically, they didn't immediately hit it off. Keisha even insisted that they get separate rooms at the hotel where they were staying. The attraction between Keisha and Torey was very strong and quite mutual, but Keisha was more mature than Torey. She was young, sexy and ready to be loved exclusively.

Keisha grew up in East Chicago raised by a single mother who had never been married to her father, a white man who was all "brotha" on the inside. She often wished she had siblings, but the benefits of being an only child were plentiful, including being more like her mother's sister or best friend rather than her daughter. Keisha, like many young Black women, grew up with the baggage and issues of not having a male figure in her life, and being "mixed" didn't help either. She had to grow up fast, and it wasn't easy without the love and attention of her father.

Because of this, she was convinced that a woman had to take care of *herself,* no matter the cost.

Torey on the other hand, had just been drafted into the NFL a year earlier, and was enjoying his new celebrity status to the max. He wasn't serious, because he did not have to be. Marriage was certainly the furthest thing from his mind. He had finally broken away from his father, the Reverend, and his saintly mother who raised him. He was becoming the stereotypical, buck wild, preacher's son. He did however, love and adore his parents who had been married for over 40 years. He often referred to their relationship as that "old school love." Unlike Keisha, Torey was raised in a very stable environment. He hoped that he would some day have the same type of relationship with a woman that his father had with his mother. Growing up, Keisha had much more freedom than Torey. He wasn't even allowed to stay at home by himself until he was almost 14 years old. Torey had three brothers and two sisters, one of which was the product of an affair on his father's behalf, and that's probably why he admired his parents so much. They had made it through something that most people would kill each other over. Torey was their baby boy, and his athletic talent made him the "star" of the family. Naturally, he was spoiled rotten by the time he went off to college.

While Torey was consuming the pleasures of being a star athlete and enjoying the college life, Keisha was educating herself on the ways of the real world, doing what she had to do to survive. She had been working since she was sixteen and had developed a sense of urgency when it came to finding ways to get what she wanted. She grew up with cousins, aunts and uncles all around. As dysfunctional as her family and home environment were at times, she loved them dearly and never put anyone before them.

Once Keisha and Torey started dating, what they didn't have in common didn't seem to matter much. They were in a mutually open relationship for a couple of years and then nature took its course. After living together for another two years "in sin," as Torey's father deemed it, marriage seemed to be the obvious next step. And though they loved each other, they both secretly questioned the timing of their marriage. And as much as she felt it wasn't the right time, Keisha still said yes when he asked her to marry him. Besides, when a handsome superstar like Torey Franklin asks a woman to marry him, "Let's wait" probably isn't the best answer. Keisha knew that Torey could have any woman he wanted, and besides loving him, she had invested too much in the relationship not to reap the benefits of being married to a rising star.

Keisha was somewhat of a complex woman. She wanted much out of life, but she wasn't necessarily willing to work for it, kind of like in pro football. Every player wants to win but every player isn't willing to put in all the strenuous physical and mental work that it takes to win. She always took short cuts, never wanting to go the extra mile for success. Despite the fact that she felt she didn't *need* a man; she always wanted one who could support her rich taste. Keisha was what one would call a M.I.D Wife aka **M**s. **I**ndependent **D**ependant. She was like the women you meet that you think have it going on, but in actuality, they're only independent because of their dependency on their mate - the one who's *actually* financing their "balling" ways. More than anything, Keisha was a survivor and being married to a man like Torey Franklin was the perfect scenario. He didn't believe in divorce and he was a team player. He believed that sometimes role players had to carry the team, but most of the time stars had to carry the load. But what he didn't want to accept was that most of the time, he was *both* on this team. He was the star and the role player, and Keisha was the teammate with all the potential in the world, playing for the pay check and not for the *love of the game.*

10

While marinating a rack of ribs for their 5th annual "NFL Summer Splash," Keisha began thinking about how things were between her and her husband. Keisha loved Torey, but there were still things that she wanted that were missing. Marriage to a pro athlete hadn't been what she expected. It had been nearly eight years and they still hadn't had children of their own. Torey seemed to be too simple for her at times, content with life as it was, but she still wasn't about to leave him. After all, she didn't have to work outside the home and though he often nagged her about being more responsible with their money, it was worth the lifestyle and security that came along with being Mrs. Torey Franklin.

While Keisha was enjoying the lifestyle she lived as an NFL player's wife, Torey was dealing with his own issues. He had been through many drama-filled moments with women during the past, and because of that, Torey found it hard to fully trust any woman besides his mother and sisters. He wanted to trust Keisha with everything, but his suspicious nature and her sometimes shady behavior, often caused him to question her loyalty to him. As a preacher's son, Torey learned at an early age that there were certain things that he had no control over, and those things he left up to God. He felt that God had put him and Keisha together, and like the *Good Book* says concerning marriage, "What God hath wrought, let no man put asunder." Torey was committed to making his marriage last, even though he felt that his mate did not appreciate such commitment at times.

DING DONGGGGG, the chimes of the Franklin estate rang throughout the home.

"I'll get it!" yelled Torey while walking up the stairs from the basement.

"Hey boy, you better get back on that grill, it's my job to answer the door, remember?" Keisha replied, shooing Torey away from the door.

"Yeah, you're right, I'm about to burn up the burgers!" he said while sprinting back down the stairs. "I still need to fix the guests downstairs some more drinks."

"Torey, I swear I don't know why you just don't hire someone to cook and tend the bar each year."

See there she goes with that, thought Torey, *Always trying to spend some more of a brotha's money!*

As the huge front door crept open, Keisha's eyes lit up. It was D'Angelo Hampton. D'Angelo was the neighborhood wannabe, who would do just about anything to be the center of attention. He was a street-wise smooth-talker that Torey had introduced to Keisha when they moved in together. D'Angelo, a Houston native, was a former local high-school football star turned savvy hustler, that Torey met while in college. Torey and D'Angelo interacted as if they were best friends. They had known each other almost seven years before Torey and Keisha met. Torey considered him trustworthy and often relied on D'Angelo and his best female friend Sharice, to look after Keisha when he traveled for countless football commitments. D'Angelo was always one of the first people invited to anything the Franklins had at their home.

Despite his obvious shady demeanor, people loved D'Angelo. He was an unadulterated ladies man who surrounded himself with beautiful women as often as he could. He still had the body of an athlete and his deep hazel eyes made the ladies swoon on sight. In addition to his good looks, D'Angelo was a non-judgmental, understanding, super cool cat that knew when to listen and when to talk. Thus, he was notorious for his penchant to draw married and unsuspecting women.

"Heyyyy D," Keisha said as she embraced D'Angelo.

"Sup girlfriend?

"Baby where's the Patron?" Torey asked as he shuffled through the liquor cabinet downstairs in the basement.

"Damn! Baby, I'm sorry. I forgot to pick it up," Keisha shouted back.

"Baby, I asked you two days ago to make sure you got it. Could you please go get some?" Torey yelled from the basement.

"Sure baby."

"Hey, who was that at the door?" Torey asked.

"Oh, it was those damn Jehovah's Witnesses again. I told them we're about to have a huge orgy, so they split," she said as she covered D'Angelo's mouth to keep him from laughing loudly. "I'm heading to the liquor store. I'll be back okay?"

Keisha was feeling *really nice*. After she and Torey had their quickie in one of the upstairs bathrooms (their ritual when guests were in their home), she smoked the remainder of a blunt, another habit the couple had picked up. You could see that the "Mary Jane" had taken full effect as a devilish smirk appeared on Keisha's face. She had tuned Torey out, reducing him to a faint voice in the background. And, it didn't matter that she could barely hear him as he reprimanded her, yet again, for forgetting his favorite liquor. She had reached her high, and not even *her husband,* was going to ruin her buzz.

Since all the guests were downstairs playing cards, slamming down dominos or mingling poolside, Keisha and D'Angelo were about to slip out of the house unnoticed. Keisha knew the only liquor store that carried his favorite tequila was 20 minutes away. So, she figured she had at least 45 minutes to disappear from the party without causing suspicion. Like always, the weed made Keisha feel like doing something wild and adventurous, and besides fucking in their bathroom amongst a house full of people, she and Torey hadn't done anything even close to wild or adventurous, in quite some time.

As Keisha and D'Angelo exited the house, Keisha noticed a gorgeous Hispanic woman sitting on D'Angelo's purple and chrome sport motorcycle. Keisha caught herself being somewhat jealous. This had to be one of the finest redbones in Houston staring back at her and the *bitch* was sitting on D's motorcycle.

"Oh, I'm sorry. Keisha this is Antoinette. Antoinette this is Keisha. Antoinette is a good friend of *MAY's,*" said D'Angelo. When Keisha heard the word MAY she knew it was all good. It was their little code word for "me and you" or "mine and yours". They used it for anything that they intended to share with one another. She smiled and quickly hopped into her convertible Lexus while D'Angelo and their new friend followed on his motorcycle.

11

As Keisha pulled back into the driveway she noticed Sharice standing on the porch.

"Keisha where in the hell have you been? Torey has been calling your phone for the last 20 minutes," Sharice exclaimed.

"I went to get the liquor and forgot to take my phone," answered Keisha.

"Where in the hell have you been Keisha?" snapped Torey as he approached the women.

"First of all, who are you talking to? Second of all, I had to go to the ATM to get money. Damn what's wrong? Who drowned?" Keisha snapped defensively.

"You've been gone a whole hour, that's what's wrong," Torey said as he snatched the bag and walked back into the kitchen. Torey stormed into the kitchen without even noticing D'Angelo's arrival. As D'Angelo slowly parked the bike, Sharice felt that something wasn't right. She was good friends with Keisha, Torey and D'Angelo, but she was more loyal to Torey by far. Torey trusted Sharice like a sister and even allowed her to serve as the general manager at his sports bar.

"Keisha, I'm not telling you what to do, but if you're doing something you shouldn't be doing, you need to be careful. You know…"

"Look Sharice, I'm grown. I got this. So save your speech and come on and help me with these other bags," Keisha interrupted.

Sharice saw the situation as a train wreck waiting to happen. D'Angelo was not known for being discreet and he always told the wrong people all his business, and Sharice knew that if Torey heard the wrong things about his wife, it could spell disaster.

"Okay, I'm just telling you. Don't mess up a good thing for a good time," Sharice warned.

"Are you finished? Now get your big booty over here and help me with these bags." The ladies' laughs broke the tension between them.

What ever happened between D'Angelo, Keisha and their new friend "May" must have been something special because Keisha was grinning and glowing as though she had just returned from a long vacation in the Bahamas. She was even talking to a couple of Torey's female friends that she couldn't stand. Keisha's peculiar behavior did not go unnoticed. Torey observed her sweet demeanor towards the women he knew his wife detested, and knew something was up. He knew his wife well, well enough to know she could be a real bitch when it came to his female friends. But something else felt strange to Torey. He had not seen D'Angelo, who always made a grand entrance with three or four ladies on his arms. D'Angelo was always one of the first guests to arrive at their get-togethers.

Torey just blew it off and figured he was being paranoid. *Damn, I knew I shouldn't have smoked that blunt,* Torey thought to himself. *My mind is playing tricks on my ass like Scarface and the Ghetto Boys,* he thought as he chuckled to himself. He was obviously still a little high. However, while discarding the paper bags containing the food and liquor his wife had just purchased, Torey noticed something that caused him to sober up a great deal.

"Sharice will you come here for a minute?" he said through his kitchen window.

"What do you want man? You see a sista is out here trying to get her eat on!" Sharice joked.

"Let me show you something. Why do the grocery store receipts have today's date on them, but the Patron receipt has yesterday's date?" he asked while holding the receipts up to Sharice's face.

Sharice knew exactly why the receipts did not have the same date on them. But even though she was closer to Torey than Keisha, she would never tell him anything or even offer an opinion that could destroy his marriage.

"I don't know Torey, that's a good question.... Maybe the store register was wrong."

Torey's paranoia began to surface once again, however, he wasn't about to air his family's potential dirty laundry in front of a house full of guests. So, like times past, he pushed the issue to the back of his mind.

Nah, I'm just trippin', she'd never play me like that, Torey thought to himself as he and Sharice glanced at one another, all the while, keeping their true feelings to themselves.

———————

Keisha was ecstatic when Torey told her that the team was leaving two days early, for their San Diego game, the weekend after the cookout. But, she caught herself, and adjusted herself to appear heartbroken. After all, her husband would be gone for four days, and she needed to make him feel like she would miss him in order to spend time with D'Angelo. D'Angelo's birthday was quickly approaching, so the timing of the team's early departure couldn't have been better.

Keisha thought Thursday would never come. D'Angelo's birthday was the next day and she had planned a special evening just for him. To make things appear normal, Keisha made sure that she and Torey had their usual wild and passionate love-making session before he left town. Early on in their relationship, she had always made sure to satisfy his sexual appetite before he left her for an extended amount of time. Of course, this was mainly to deter him from having another woman to satisfy his needs on the road. But now, sex was feeling much more like a chore; a monotonous routine that no longer satisfied her. She only kept up the charade so that Torey wouldn't become suspicious.

Yes! I am going to kick it this weekend, she thought to herself with a smile. Keisha snapped back to reality as Torey forcefully grabbed her from behind.

"Boy, you know how slow you drive. You're going to miss your flight," Keisha murmured as her husband's hands eased underneath her sheer black bra.

"Umm, you smell good baby," Torey replied as his penis began to grow. "You know I love these," he said as his right hand traveled from Keisha's nipple to touch the thin fabric of her matching thong.

"No, you love what's IN these," Keisha replied while grinding her backside into Torey's crotch. "Go on now before you mess up my hair. You're also going to miss the team charter if you keep this up." Keisha managed as Torey's fingers crept beneath the fabric to touch her already swollen clit.

"I won't mess up your hair baby," Torey answered.

"Oooh, see, there you go starting something we don't have time to finish," Keisha breathily answered as her husband's fingers traveled inside her wetness.

"Oh, I'm going to finish baby, trust me," he said as he lifted Keisha onto the granite vanity. "You are SO sexy, you know you make me crazy right?" Torey asked as he forcefully tore the thong from his wife's body.

"Torey! That's a hundred dollar thong you just... Ohhh... Ummm... Oh yeah baby, like that," Keisha said as Torey's probing tongue darted in and out of slit.
RINGGGGGG!!!

"Torey, your cell phone..."

"Let it ring," he said as he entered his wife from behind as she braced herself against the vanity. She could see the lust in her husband's eyes in the mirror as he pounded away like a wild man. Although their sex life was lacking some of the spontaneity of earlier days, Keisha did enjoy the fact that Torey could not resist her at times. She didn't even protest when he grabbed a fistful of her hair as he raced against time to finish.

"Damn baby, you still got that bomb don't you?" Torey asked with a smile as he pulled on his jacket and picked up his team bag.

"That's right. And don't you ever forget it," Keisha winked.

"How can I? I hope I get there on time."

"You better get there on time. We gotta get that money baby."

"Oh, most definitely. I'm about to jet," said Torey as he whizzed out of the house.

"Torey, you'd better hurry up or you're going to miss the team bus!" Keisha yelled anxiously, while glancing at her diamond-crusted Chopard watch.

"Yeah baby, I'm ready to roll. I love you. I'll see you when we get back. Make sure you watch the game. What you got planned for the weekend?" Torey asked as he hopped in his trendy sports car.

"Nothing much, D'Angelo's birthday is tomorrow, so I might go have a drink with him, Sharice, and a couple of his female friends. If we do much more than that, I'll let you know. Call me when you get into the hotel."

"I will. And why don't you buy D'Angelo a bottle of champagne for his birthday from us, and see if he wants to hook up Sunday night when I get back. Oh yea, baby, make sure that you call Marcus tonight if you're going to the club so that he can have a table for ya'll. You know it's going to be crowded."

"Okay baby, now get out of here and go make us some more money," Keisha said jokingly. "I love you."

"I love you too."

After Torey left the house, Keisha called Sharice to plan out her weekend surprise for D'Angelo. She needed a co-conspirator to pull off such a caper. A third wheel was a must in Houston, since there was no way she could chance being seen alone in public with D'Angelo.

"Hello," Sharice answered while driving 80 miles an hour to the bar. She was running late and certainly didn't want Torey on her case, or worse, docking her pay.

"Sharice, this is Keisha. What are you doing girl?"

"Nothing, driving to the bar. You know if I'm not at the sports bar on time your husband will be trying to fire my ass."

"You know he is not going to fire you. Hell, he'd fire me before he'd fire you. Anyway, the team is leaving today for this weekend's game, and it's D's birthday, so you know what that means." Keisha sounded as giddy as a teenage girl who just got a date to the prom with the star, high school quarterback.

"Girl I told you, you're playing with fire," Sharice warned.

"Sharice, can't friends celebrate a birthday and have a drink?"

"Now if the answer to that question was yes, you wouldn't be asking me to tag along, now would you?"

"Smart ass. Look, just call me when you finish at the bar so we can meet up. See you later."

"Keisha, I really don't think we should do this. Keisha... Keisha... Damn," Sharice said realizing that Keisha had hung up the phone. *This is not going to be good,* she thought to herself as she pulled into her reserved parking spot at the bar.

12

On Friday, Keisha could hardly contain herself. She and Sharice met D'Angelo at a trendy bar in Midtown called Veragio's. The upscale Veragio's had quickly become a popular spot frequented by the affluent. The music and drinks were always good, and the food was also a hit amongst the locals. However, the good music, food and drinks were not the only attractions at the trendy establishment. Sharice had never been to the club, but had heard a lot about it. She was very curious to find out if the rumors she had heard were true. One of them being something about a members only floor and V.I.P suites where "anything" goes. Keisha on the other hand, used the club to curtail her own curiosity, but not about the club. Tonight would be the night that Sharice revealed with *whom* her loyalty ultimately lied; Torey or Keisha.

As they entered the member's only section of the bar, a beautiful, exotic looking hostess approached the trio.

"Hello, may I help you this evening?" the hostess asked.

"Yes," answered D'Angelo who had been a member of the club since its inception. "I've made arrangements for my usual suite. Seclusion is a must for this evening."

Sharice was lost. "What is he talking about?" she asked Keisha. Keisha's only response was a wink and a wicked smile.

"Right this way Mr. Hampton. And happy birthday sir...We reserved the special Hedonism booth for you," said the hostess.

"Why they call it the Hedonism booth? What kind of club is this?" Sharice was dumbfounded.

"Because you can do what you want to do here girl. Membership certainly has its privileges. Is this too much for you Sharice? If so, I can get the limo driver to take you home if you like," asked Keisha.

"Hell no, I'm not going home you freak, but I am going to have another shot of tequila!" Sharice wailed giddily as the alcohol began to take its toll. "I came to have a good time and that's what I plan to do. I can't believe ya'll have been keeping this all to yourselves."

Sharice simply could not believe her eyes. The place was spectacular, surrounded by double-sided mirrors, so customers in the secluded areas could see those around them, but no one could see them. Their booth also had a surround sound stereo system, flat screen television and the entire floor was padded like a huge bed. Sharice had seen most of the nice places in Houston but this was on another level.

"Damn, this is so nice. You could really get your freak on in here," Sharice joked.

"We sure could," D'Angelo responded. "Unless you're scared of course?"

As Sharice looked out of the double-sided mirror, she saw the servers walking around half naked. But Keisha still could not tell if her girlfriend was game or not.

D'Angelo was even more ready for trouble than usual, an obvious side-effect of the ecstasy he had taken while he visited the plush men's room. He turned the music on, took off his shirt, lit a blunt and poured everyone a double shot of Patron. He raised his glass to make a toast, "To us,

111

friends just making friends happy... To us ya'll." The ladies drank the shots and D'Angelo passed the blunt.

"Damn, you can even smoke weed in here?" Sharice asked. They knew Sharice wasn't a true weed smoker and that with one hit of the *hydro* her inhibitions would soon disappear.

After smoking nearly a whole blunt herself, Keisha was as high as a kite – her favorite past time.

"So what do you want for you birthday, Mr. Hampton?" Keisha asked flirtatiously while sliding her hand onto D'Angelo's crotch.

"I don't know. What are ya'll going to give me?"

"Whatever you want, ain't that right Sharice?"

Sharice looked baffled, but as they planned, the weed and the shots of tequila had Sharice in another world, making her down for just about anything.

"Yep, whatever you want daddy." Both women giggled uncontrollably.

"I know what he wants," Keisha said as she worked her hands on D'Angelo's rising erection while sliding closer to him. Keisha leaned in slowly, their tongues met and D'Angelo wasted no time, as he gently caressed Keisha's breasts.

As Sharice looked on, Keisha seductively turned her attention to Sharice, sliding in close to kiss her. Although Sharice had fantasized about beautiful women at times, she had never had a woman invade her personal space in this way. She was somewhat shocked at first, but her nervousness subsided as she felt Keisha's hand slip under her skirt. Keisha's tongue was softer than anything Sharice had imagined and her hands were just as supple.

"Ummm," Sharice moaned as Keisha's hands found their way underneath Sharice's thong to find her soaking wet. "Ooh, deeper," Sharice said as Keisha pushed one then two fingers deep into her friend. D'Angelo then joined them in a three-way kiss. He grabbed Keisha's hand and slowly licked her fingers, knowing full well they were just inside of Sharice.

"Damn, ya'll are soooo nasty," Sharice said somewhat embarrassed.

"Oh it gets better, trust me." D'Angelo opened the door and signaled for the hostess. "Miss, please put this on my tab, we're about to leave," D'Angelo instructed. "Let's get the hell out of here ladies."

The sexual escapade reached a fever pitch after they made it back into the limousine. Sharice had barely made it inside before she noticed Keisha going into D'Angelo's pants. A few seconds later she was witnessing her best friend's wife sucking another man's dick right in front of her. To make matters worse, she too would take her turn getting D'Angelo off in the same way.

Damn, what am I doing here? She thought as she felt Keisha's head between her legs. Sharice had only planned to tag along so that she could report back to Torey. Now she was not only a participant in the ménage a trios, she was actually *enjoying* it. As wrong as she felt, the sight of Keisha returning to D'Angelo to kiss his big, beautiful, caramel colored penis again, sent her over the edge. Sharice stopped counting the orgasms she had from riding D'Angelo while watching Keisha masturbate. Now Sharice had a secret of her own, and that's exactly what Keisha had hoped for.

Torey arrived back in town nearly three hours early. The team's charter plane actually arrived on time, but the team secretary made a mistake on the travel itinerary. Torey attempted to call Keisha to tell her he would be arriving earlier but she never answered.

"Sexy lady!" Torey bellowed, "Daddy's home! Where are you? Keisha!" *She must be out running errands or something,* he thought to himself. Torey was a little disappointed that his wife wasn't there. Although they weren't as connected as they had been in years past, he still loved her a great deal. He thought about her the entire time he was away and returned home with a new attitude, vowing to pay more attention to her. As he placed his bags in their bedroom, he noticed that Keisha had failed to log off her lap top computer.

That girl always forgets to shut down the computer, Torey chuckled to himself. His demeanor quickly changed when he noticed that Keisha had been chatting with someone on the instant messenger. *Scorpio1108?* He mumbled to himself. Torey scrolled up to view the previous instant messages between his wife and Scorpio 1108.

"Hey beautiful, do you miss me?" he read.

"Of course, I wish I was with you right now."

"Ummmm, this weekend wasn't enough for me either."

"I know we spent the past 48 hours together, but I'm still missing you!"

"I'm missing you too. Well hopefully I'll see you sooner than later."

Torey's blood began to boil as his heart raced a thousand miles a minute. *Man if this bitch is...*, he thought. Hoping that whoever was on the other end of the computer was still there, he sent another instant message:

I'm back, but I only have a few minutes, the big bad wolf will be back soon. What are you doing? A few seconds later, he got a response.

Nothing, just sitting here thinking about the sexiest woman in Houston... I didn't think I would hear from you again today, Scorpio 1108 replied.

I know but I started missing you and...I have to go, my husband is driving up. I'll get at you later. Till next time.

I can't wait till next time Scorpio 1108 replied to conclude the conversation.

Torey abruptly printed out all the previous messages that Keisha had sent and then permanently deleted them. He knew that his wife was clever but he never thought she was stupid enough to have any type of affair in Houston. Not the city where he was the "unofficial Black mayor." This could not be happening in *his* city. Torey had been suspicious of his wife's behavior for some time, but this was definitely the evidence he needed to confirm his thoughts. Although Torey could be insanely jealous, he decided that he would not confront his wife until he gathered more information. Something told him that the instant messages and the liquor store receipts would only be the tip of the iceberg.

Torey heard the garage door open and quickly stashed the printed emails in his suitcase.

"Keisha is that you?"

"Oh, hey Baby. You're home early," Keisha replied.

"Yea, it was a misprint on the team itinerary. We got in a couple of hours early."

Keisha hugged her husband and kissed him as lovingly as she did the day they got married, "I'm sorry about the game."

Torey's heart ached but he loved his wife so much, that often his feelings painted over his reality.

"Oh, that's alright, I'm home with my baby now. I hope you had a better weekend than I did. What all did you do this weekend?" he inquired.

"Nothing really. I just went down to the club and had a few drinks with Sharice and D'Angelo on Saturday. He said thanks for the champagne."

"Didn't you go out Friday too? Because I called you at the house and on your cell but I kept getting the voice mail."

"Umm nah, I was probably asleep... But I did go eat with Sharice. Then I came home and drank nearly a whole bottle of wine by myself. I just didn't hear the phone ring, I guess. What time did you call?"

"Hmm, you didn't hear the phone ring? Baby you wake up if my pager vibrates. So how..."

"Look, I said I must have been asleep. I hate it when you start in on me like you don't believe me. Why the hell are you always interrogating me anyway? You don't trust me?"

"Relax baby, I was just asking a question. Are you hungry?" As much as he wanted to know the truth he didn't feel like arguing. More importantly, he was horny as hell. He knew this line of questioning would leave him not only hungry, but with a hard, neglected penis.

"No, not really. I have a headache. I'm just going to take a hot bath. Do you mind just going out and picking up something to eat?"

"Why don't I just have something delivered, and then I'll join you in the bathtub after the food arrives?" Torey suggested.

"Not tonight baby, I'm not feeling too good."

Torey had ruined what little chance he had to make love to his wife that night. And as sexual as she was, Keisha's poor little vagina couldn't handle any more pounding than it had taken the two nights prior. D'Angelo was addictive and she just couldn't get enough.

"Well I'm gone," Torey said, obviously disappointed.

"Bye, I'll probably be sleep when you get back. I love you." Keisha knew his feelings were hurt but he was a big boy. *He shouldn't have started questioning me like a child,* she thought to herself. The deeper she slid down into the hot water, the less she was concerned about her husband. The warm bubble bath was just what she needed to set her mind at ease.

13

As Keisha became less and less attentive to her husband, Torey decided to take action. Even though he had enough evidence to prove his wife's infidelity, he still wanted to salvage his relationship. Since his team was not scheduled to play a game that upcoming Sunday, Torey thought it would be a good idea to get away for the weekend with Keisha. Torey called his travel agent to plan a romantic weekend get-a-way. He figured Miami would do the trick. Keisha loved South Beach and the free-spirited culture that permeated the city. He could relax without hearing rumors about his wife or his football career, and Keisha could shop and lay out until all their problems were nowhere in sight. Best of all, they could enjoy one another's company, something they had not done for some time.

No sooner than Torey ended his call with the travel agent, the phone rang.

"Hello."

"May I speak to Torey Franklin please?" an unrecognizable voice asked.

"This is Torey Franklin. Who's calling?"

"Torey you don't know me but we've met before. My name is Teri Boyd."

"Teri Boyd?" Torey's mind began racing, attempting to recount the many escapades of his past.

"I'm sorry for calling you but I'm D'Angelo Hampton's girlfriend and I think we need to talk." D'Angelo had a harem of women, so he wasn't surprised that one would claim to be his girlfriend. However, he was certainly disturbed that he was receiving a call from one of them.

"Talk about what Teri?" he asked, hoping she had made a mistake.

"Now, what reason do you think I would call you –a married man who's wife spends more time with my man then you do?"

"I don't want to assume. So since you called me, how about you tell me what this is about?"

"Well I'll get straight to the point and then you can check it out for yourself. Your wife is fucking my man, the father of my two children. Her cell number and your home number's all over his phone bill, and at all times of the day and night. But if that's not enough, I heard them on the phone last night planning to meet in New York this weekend."

Torey's blood pressure was climbing so high he could've had a heart attack. He sat in complete silence.

"Hello… Hello… Torey are you there?"

Torey vaguely remembered that Keisha had mentioned an "all girls" trip to New York a few weeks back, but he had been so engrossed with his team that the details of the trip had slipped his mind.

"Um, yes, I'm still here. I'm just trippin' right now, that's all. Let me ask you something. Isn't D'Angelo's birthday November 8th?"

"Yeah, why?" Teri questioned.

"Because, the other day I just read some interesting exchanges on my wife's computer between her and somebody with the screen name Scorpio 1108." *Damn,*

Scorpio 1108 Torey murmured to himself, *CHECKMATE...*

"Torey, I know you probably think I'm stupid for dealing with D'Angelo, but his kids need him around. I deal with enough of D's other bitches so I sure as hell shouldn't have to deal with a woman who is married.

"No Teri, I don't think you're stupid. I know you're trying to look out for your children. You had to do what you had to do, and so do I. Listen, can you please fax those phone records to me tomorrow morning?"

The starlit evening was beautiful. Keisha was looking sexier than ever and Torey was feeling relaxed from the cognac he sipped before they left for dinner. They would dine at one of the city's most romantic rooftop restaurants. As much as Torey wanted to bring up D'Angelo, it was more important that he follow through with his initial plans.

"Baby, you know we have three days off before our game next Thursday. So, I was thinking that we could go to Miami for the weekend. What do you think?"

"Uhh, well..."

"Don't you want to spend some time with your man baby?" Torey asked calmly even though he felt himself becoming enraged.

"It's not that. You know I was supposed to be going to New York to see my girl Stacy."

"Oh yeah, that's right. Well, I'll tell you what, I'll just change the flights I had for Miami, and I'll just roll to New York with you instead. Stacy's man Robert is real cool, so

I'll just hang out with him while you and your girl do the 5th Avenue shopping thing."

"Baby you know that this is an all girls' trip. We're going to the spa, shopping, and to a couple of Broadway shows. You hate those shows," Keisha reasoned.

"I know it's a girls' trip, but I'll stay out of your way. You can hang out with your girl as much as you want, then you can have me after you're done with her each day. That's the best of both worlds. What could be better than that?"

"I don't even think Robert will be in town."

"Oh, that's okay, I'm a big boy. Plus, I have a few Psi Kappa brothers that live in New York I could hang out with instead," countered Torey.

"Torey, baby we can go somewhere during your next off-week if you want, but I just wanted to do the New York trip with my girl. We've been planning this trip for months. Why don't you go on to Miami or to Vegas? You know how much you love Vegas."

Torey was crushed. The thought of Keisha lying to him in order to meet D'Angelo in New York had his heart aching. That was the last straw for Torey. His wife had just chosen a trip with a lover instead of a romantic get-a-way with her husband. As much as he had done for Keisha, she was betraying him for another man. It was clear to Torey, that no matter what he said, his wife would not change her mind.

"Well, that's cool," a despondent Torey replied. "You've wanted to take that trip for a while. Maybe I can win us some money in Vegas. When are you leaving for New York?"

"Well, my flight is scheduled to leave early Thursday and return next Tuesday."

Torey wanted to believe that his wife was indeed traveling to New York to see Stacy only. He was hoping that D'Angelo's woman Teri had gotten it wrong. Maybe Keisha was loyal, still loved him, and just needed space. Maybe not?

Keisha was pissed at herself. She was about to miss yet another flight because she was running late. Keisha traveled often, yet she still couldn't seem to catch a flight on time, unless Torey forced her to pack the night before. If her cell phone hadn't rang she probably would have forgotten it. "Where is that damn phone?" she mumbled as it rang and rang. When she finally found the phone buried at the bottom of her Louis Vuitton suitcase, the ringing had ceased. *I hope that was my baby D'Angelo*, she thought to herself. Just as she started to check her recent calls the home phone rang.

"Damn I bet this ain't nobody but Torey's ass," she grunted aloud. "Torey, I'm leaving now…" Keisha shouted.

"Hey Keisha this is Sharice. Are you busy?"

"Oh hey girl, I thought you were Torey checking to see if I left the house yet. But I am running late, so let me call you as soon as I get in the car. The town car is outside waiting, and my slow ass still ain't ready as usual."

As she rushed to put her things outside, a strange feeling came over her. She felt as if she was going on a long trip away from home. Not being the sentimental type, the moment quickly passed. She finally got her things to the porch and as the driver loaded the car, she proceeded to return Sharice's call.

"Sharice, hey it's me. What's up?"

"Where are you and Torey going?" Sharice asked.

"Girl, Torey went to Vegas. I'm going to New York to visit my girlfriend Stacy Leeks."

"Oh, well we need to talk. You may be used to this, but I can't take being around Torey like this."

"I'm used to what?"

"Well, the other day Torey asked me if you and D'Angelo were fucking."

"And what did you say?" Keisha was getting a bit concerned.

"I said I couldn't answer that or I didn't know. Shit, I don't remember exactly what I said. The point is, I just can't take this anymore. I know you've heard about the rumors flying around about you and D'Angelo. Hell, Torey has even mentioned having a private eye follow you. He has been a good friend and employer. The bottom line is that Torey and I are close and ..."

"Bitch you weren't talking about how close you and Torey are when your tongue was all down my throat. Before you do something stupid, just remember that you were with me and D'Angelo the other night. See, I knew you might be dumb enough to open up your mouth about me and D. That's why what happened the other night in the limo was videotaped. So go ahead and start something if you want. I'll take Torey's ass for every dime he has and you, his trusted friend and confidant, will be black balled and out of a job. So you better think very carefully about

your next move. I gotta go, I'm nearly at the airport."
CLICK...

Sharice was thoroughly confused. She knew that most people that crossed Torey were usually not around long enough to apologize. *Why did I even go out with them?* She thought. Now she knew she couldn't afford to be involved. She would try her best to stay out of the middle of their mess.

Now Keisha was even more pissed off. While she was panicked about nearly missing her flight to New York, she was also furious that Torey would hire someone to follow her. *How in the hell is he going to be investigating me? I need to be investigating his slick ass*, she thought to herself.

Keisha's mind began to race. *Maybe I should cool it for a minute with D'Angelo until the heat dies down. Maybe I'll fly to Vegas instead of New York and surprise Torey so he won't be so suspicious. What if Sharice tells him about what happened the other night? After all, I don't really have a videotape of what happened. She could really mess things up if she says something.* Suddenly, Keisha's devious mind concocted the perfect plan. A plan that would let her have her cake and eat it to. All she had to do was fix it so that Torey was pissed at Sharice and then his ear would be off to anything she had to say. *But what could she say? S*he thought to herself.

Keisha pulled out her two-way pager to message Torey. *Baby when you get back you need to do something about Sharice. I heard she's been stealing from the bar and doctoring the books. I'll explain later. I think we need to let her go because it came from a very good source. Don't confront her about it until I can get some more*

*information. Let's just wait until we sort all of this BS out.
I love you. Call me when you get this message. Try not to
worry, have fun and win us some money. Miss you
already...About to board the plane.*

Keisha smiled as she walked through the airport. She
was going to make her flight, her husband was in Vegas,
the only true threat in her relationship had been eliminated,
and she would be fucking D'Angelo's brains out in a
Manhattan penthouse suite, within a matter of hours.

14

Torey slept during the entire 3-hour flight to Vegas. He always slept when his brain was overloaded. As much of a playboy as Torey had been during his lifetime, he never thought he would get played. And as bad as he was getting played, it just didn't feel right being gone with everything that was going on in his relationship. He knew in his heart that this was a crucial period in his marriage. But what could he do? His wife had chosen another man.

As the plane approached the gate his two-way began to vibrate. It was a message from Keisha. Torey read the message in disbelief. *What the hell?!* He couldn't believe what he was reading. Sharice was one of his closest friends. *Damn*, he thought. That just didn't sound like Sharice. He was always there for her and found it hard to believe that she would ever stab him in the back like this.

Torey began to calm down a bit when he remembered that his insurance policy would cover any lost revenue due to theft at the sports bar. He would put in a call to Marcus and have him stick around the bar during closing for the next few weeks. Torey figured no one would be stupid enough to blatantly steal in front of his most trusted employee and best friend, Marcus. Marcus was not only observant; he was also certified to carry a gun; just one of the reasons Torey chose him to manage his nightclub.

As he reached in his bag to get his cell phone, he felt it vibrate. *Who is this?* he wondered since he didn't recognize the number. He answered in his professional voice,

"This is Torey."

Torey didn't immediately recognize the voice but it was a female that sounded like she was crying, "Hey Torey. This is Teri Boyd. Are you busy?"

"Nah, I just landed in Vegas. What's up?"

"Is your wife with you?"

"Actually, she went to New York. Why?"

"Because that no good bastard D'Angelo just got on a plane to go to New York. He said he had business to take care of for that concert he's trying to promote. Lying muthafucka!" she wailed.

It was as if someone had turned the knife in his heart. Torey had hoped that Keisha really was going to New York just to visit her friend.

"Teri, calm down. I'll find out what the hell is going on and I will call you back later okay?" Torey was livid and had no intention of ignoring all the evidence he'd accumulated. He was so upset that he left his luggage at the baggage claim and headed straight for the ticketing counter.

"Hello Sir, may I help you?" the attendant asked.

"Yes please… I need one ticket to New York."

Torey's flight to New York was different than his sleep-filled flight to Vegas. He was wired, full of energy and anger. He paced the length of the plane several times during the four-hour flight thinking about how surprised Keisha would be when she saw his face in New York. Because of his haste to catch the flight he was not able to call his wife before take-off. However, he wasn't surprised that she hadn't left him another message since the one concerning Sharice. There would be no easy way to confront his wife, but as the plane touched down in New York, the inevitable seemed all too real.

With only a single carry-on bag, Torey was able to rush out of the airport and straight into a cab that would take him to the Trump Towers. Torey loved the privacy and luxury the Towers offered. Even though he was one of the NFL's most recognizable players, he knew he could spend a few days there in complete seclusion. After resting for a few hours he was ready to do what he came to New York to do.

The sound of the phone ringing scared Stacy out of her sleep. "Hello," she answered groggily.

"Hey Stacy, I'm sorry for calling so late. May I speak to Keisha?"

"I think she's in the bed Torey."

"I would hope so, it's four o'clock in the morning. Could you please wake her up? Her cell phone is off."

From the sound of Torey's voice, Stacy could sense that something was wrong. "Okay. I'll go get her up."

"Hello," Keisha said into the phone.

"What's going on Keisha?" asked Torey.

"Who is this?"

"Who *is* this? Who in the hell do you think it is Keisha? What other man would be calling you this late?"

"What's wrong with you? It's four in the morning Torey. I was dead sleep."

"Look, I need you to be honest with me. Are you fucking D'Angelo?"

"What?! What are you talking about Torey?"

"I'm talking about what I just asked you. Is he in New York?"

"How am I supposed to know that? You tell me if he's in New York. You seem to know something I don't know."

"Listen Keisha, if you really want this to work between us, I need you to meet me back in Houston by tomorrow. I already bought you a plane ticket."

"Look Torey, I just got to New York. I am NOT meeting you in Houston tomorrow! You're always trying to pull this shit. I'm tired of you trying to control every damn thing I do. I'm grown and if I want to visit my best friend, you shouldn't have a problem with that."

Torey calmed himself and began to plead with his wife. "Look baby, it is vital that you meet me in Houston. Don't you love me anymore? I am going to book us both flights around noonish. I will text you the confirmation number."

"What do I need to come to Houston for? We can talk now!"

"Look baby if you never trusted me before, trust me now. I NEED you to come to Houston for us. We need to talk face to face. If you don't meet me we are DONE, do you understand me?"

"Torey, don't threaten me!"

"Listen Keisha, I am VERY serious about this. I saw my attorney last week. If you don't meet me back in Houston I'm filing for legal separation."

"What the fuck is a legal separation?"

"It's time the courts give you to work things out, and if it doesn't happen in 60 days then we can just divorce under irreconcilable differences."

"Torey, what is there to work out? I'm not signing shit. All the shit you've done to me and now you want to run out on *me*. I never should have married you!"

"Look, like I said I'm done with the screaming and yelling. If this can be worked out I'm willing but..."

"Look, whatever," Keisha snapped, cutting him off.

"Keisha, I know D'Angelo is there in New York. Hell, he may be sitting right there looking at you. So please stop trying to play me."

"And what does that mean?"

"It means I'm tired. I may not be perfect, but I'd never put another woman before you."

"Torey maybe you don't have other women, but you certainly put everything else before me. Maybe it's all those fucking programs you volunteer to participate in, or maybe it's that pathetic sports bar that eats up half your salary. Have you ever thought it could be that groupie ass nightclub of yours? Hell, most of the time you can't even speak to me at the club because you're playing 'host' to all the women of Houston who want to be in my shoes. You do realize that the only reason those hoes come to the club is to get your attention?"

"Look Keisha, all that stuff is for us. It's OURS, not mine."

"Fuck that Torey. Who wants to have all that shit and be at home by themselves seventy-five percent of the time? See, the problem is that you have to always have everything your way. You're self-centered and spoiled. I guess I have your mother and the NFL to thank for that. Always me, me, me... Even with this whole thing about flying back to Houston. Why does everything have to always be on your terms??? You're intentionally trying to ruin my weekend with my girl. It's always your way or no way at all. So fuck this Torey. You do what you have to do. Oh, and don't you ever believe you're the only nigga that loves and wants to take care of me." CLICK...

"Hello... Hello... Keisha... Keisha!!! Hello?" *Damn, I can't believe she's doing me like this. All the time, energy, and money I've put into this relationship and she's up here gallivanting around New York City spending MY money on some other nigga?!!*

Before drifting off to sleep, Torey decided that he would go to Stacy's house later in the day and talk to his wife. Keisha at least owed him an explanation, and he did not intend to let her off that easy. *This shit is not going down like this. She's going to have to tell me face to face that she doesn't want to be with me anymore. And Lord help D'Angelo if he is anywhere near my wife when I track her down.*

15

Keisha wasn't overly concerned with the conversation she had with Torey earlier. He had threatened to leave before. One time he even put the house up for sale, only to take it off the market two weeks later. She knew that deep down, Torey did not believe in divorce or breaking up a family. His parents had survived similar and worse circumstances but remained committed through thick and through thin. So Keisha knew he wouldn't walk away simply because of rumors or suspicion. She figured she would just meet him back in Houston after her trip, apologize, sex him down and move on like usual.

"Keisha, don't you think you should go meet your husband? I'm not trying to tell you what to do but, I think you need to do what you need to do on this one," Stacy counseled.

"Look I wish everybody would stop telling me what to do. Everybody thinks he's so perfect. Fuck him, he can have Houston. I came here because I wanted to, and I'll go home when I want to."

"But what about your marriage Keisha? You and I have done our dirt the past couple of days, so I think you should meet him back in Houston. This is your husband we're talking about not some random nigga off the street."

"Look, he needs to know that I'm the only one who controls me. He has to understand that he can't dictate everything and everybody in my life. I don't say shit when he goes to coach those bull shit mini camps in the summer and comes home 3 days later than he said. I don't say shit when he keeps his ass out all day working out and working at the funky ass sports bar. So, now I'm going to be a few days late. Do unto others as they do to you."

"But Keisha, it's your man's JOB to go to mini camps right? That's what keeps the food on the table and the minks on your back, so you better think about this. You know you're my girl till the end, but this time I think you're wrong. Go home for your own good."

"Okay, I'll go home tomorrow. But, I'm going to kick it with D'Angelo one more night. Then I'll head home, okay?"

"Good."

Torey couldn't believe that he hadn't heard from his wife. Did she not believe that he actually visited his attorney's office before flying out to Vegas? His wife was no longer responding to him sexually or emotionally and most importantly, she was not supporting or encouraging him. He felt like all hope was lost. He thought about calling his mother but felt that she wouldn't fully understand. She had dealt with his father's infidelity, which resulted in him having an illegitimate daughter. And to make matters worse, the mother of the child had become a member of Pastor Franklin's church, forcing Torey's mother to deal with her on a weekly basis. Despite his mother's initial anger and disappointment, she adapted graciously, refusing to let the "devil" or her husband's transgressions ruin what God ultimately had in store for her family.

Mama can't help me this time. I'm going to have to deal with this my way, Torey thought. Torey was determined to go to Stacy's and raise hell. But he just couldn't bring himself to do it. He knew that seeing Keisha and D'Angelo together might trigger something in him that could cause him to do something crazy or as drastic as Jay Carson had done. "J Carson" had become the catch-phrase for NFL players who found themselves in predicaments that had them contemplating the worst revenge possible. Jay Carson, was a former NFL star that was currently serving a life sentence for taking matters into his own hands in a similar situation. Torey recalled as early as the week before, that one of his teammates used the term on the team plane: "Man," the teammate said, "I almost had to J Carson that psycho bitch. She slashed my tires man! I knew I shouldn't have given her ALL the dick." Torey hoped he wouldn't go "J Carson" on his wife and her lover, but he knew the possibility was very real.

On his way to Stacy's brownstone, Torey began to cry uncontrollably. He cried because he was failing at something he had seen work his entire life - marriage. He wanted to be the man his father was and provide his own family with everything. The fact that his wife had chosen another man over him tore him apart. But there was one thing Torey was used to and that was coping with the pains and hardships of life. He truly believed everything happened for a reason, and prayed that God would forgive him for everything he had done to Keisha. He also prayed that God would give him the strength to forgive Keisha for the things he knew about, and the things that would never be revealed to him.

After arguing and debating with himself for hours, Torey finally mustered up enough energy and nerve to continue on to Stacy's home. Torey waited in the rented town car along with his driver for nearly four hours outside Stacy's brownstone. During his stakeout he never saw Stacy, Keisha, or D'Angelo, and Keisha had not returned any of the voice mail messages he left for her on her cell phone. Growing weary of sitting in the vehicle, Torey decided he would knock on Stacy's door. Just as he was exiting the car his cell phone rang.

"Hello."

"Is this Torey?" the voice asked.

"Yes, this is Torey. Who is this?"

"Mr. Franklin this is Dr. Rondier Singh. It is imperative that you get to New York as soon as possible. Your wife was brought to the emergency room because she was in a car accident. She wasn't hurt badly. However, we conducted a blood test and found some abnormal cells in conjunction with an irregular heartbeat. But Mr. Franklin I would rather discuss this in person."

Torey wiped his eyes as tears began flow down his cheeks. As angry as he was at her, he did not want to lose her. Not like this. "Is she going to be alright?" he asked.

"Mr. Franklin please, it's important that you get to the hospital as soon as possible. Like I said, I would feel much better talking in person. I have your number in case her condition changes."

Torey pushed his anger aside and informed the doctor that he would get to the hospital as soon as possible. *At least Stacy is there with her*, he thought. Torey felt for his wife. Despite everything they had gone through, he had always been there to protect her. Now, neither his money, nor his fame could help her. He felt helpless and his heart ached more than ever. Torey vigorously dialed his wife's cell phone number, hoping that someone would answer.

"Hello," said the female voice.

"Hello, this is Torey Franklin, Keisha's husband. I was told that she was in an accident today and I'm trying to find out how she is doing? Who is this?"

"Oh, hi Torey, this is Natasha, Stacy's sister. I'm so glad you called. I wasn't able to talk to Keisha to get your number because she was unconscious for a couple of hours after the accident. She didn't have any numbers programmed into her phone. *So irresponsible* Torey thought, *I told her to always keep at least my number programmed into the phone.*

"The good news is that the doctor says she seems to be doing fine," said Natasha.

"What room is she in?" asked Torey.

"Room 823."

"Okay…"

Torey had always hated hospitals. Any time he entered one he would flash back to when his best friend Marcus was seriously injured during football practice in college. Torey quickly remembered that Keisha loved fresh flowers and decided to stop in the gift shop and get a beautiful arrangement of red, white and pink roses. As he stepped off the elevator onto the 8th floor, Torey made a bee line for the nurse's station.

"Hello Miss," he said to the nurse at the desk. "Where is room 823?"

"Room 823 is five doors down on your left Sir."

"Thank you very much."

Before entering the room Torey collected himself. He could hear several voices through the room door, one of which belonged to a male. *Good, the doctor is in there,* he thought to himself. Most importantly, he could hear his wife's voice. He had never been so glad to hear her voice in his life. *Thank God she woke up,* he thought. Torey said a small prayer of thanks to the Lord and opened the door. But just as he entered the room his knees buckled. Stacy's eyes widened as if she had seen a ghost just as Torey watched D'Angelo lean over and gently kiss his wife on the lips while stroking her hair.

"You better get well baby," D'Angelo said, not noticing that someone had entered the room.

"Torey!" his wife gasped.

Torey could've killed everyone in the room and not thought twice about it, but he was too numb to be violent. As he slammed the flowers to the ground and stormed out of the room, he nearly fell to his knees trying to cope with the pain of what he had just witnessed. Torey tried not to lose control but he just couldn't contain himself. He had to release at least *some* of his anger. The only thing in reach was a multi-level food cart that he hurled against the wall with all his might. The shattered trays startled the receptionist who quickly picked up the phone to alert security.

Keisha loved her husband and wanted him to love her back, but she knew him all too well. The only way he would even consider taking her back was if she told all. That's just the way he was, he had to know everything and control most things. And in this situation he did neither.

And as much as she wanted to start all over, telling all was just not something she thought Torey could handle.

Stacy tried to console her friend, "He'll be back. Just give him some time to clear his head. You know that boy loves you more than anything. It'll work out. I promise."

Keisha wanted to believe her friend, but the look in her husband's eyes confirmed that there were some long days ahead. "I don't think so Stacy, I don't think so." Keisha finally cried herself to sleep, detaching herself from the two people that had been watching over her. First her lover, then her best friend, tread softly out of the room to avoid waking her.

Amy Santiago aka The N.I.C.E Girl
Chapter 16

"Damn, who is *that*?" a tall, handsome honey-skinned Black man asked his colleague as they sipped on their morning coffee.

"Don't even look twice my man," his colleague responded.

"Shit, why not? Did you see her?"

"Yeah, I saw her. I also saw that 5 carat ring on her left hand."

"Well I didn't! Who is that? Baby looks familiar."

"Man, that's Amy Santiago-Wilson."

"Ohhhh. That's why she looks so familiar. She's married to Shannon Wilson right, the NFL baller."

"Yep, one in the same."

"Damn."

"Damn is right. No wonder the big dogs here do business with her. Who can say no to all that? Shit, I might sign over my next three pay checks to her if she walks too close to me."

"Slow down playa, I saw her first. Man, what does Shannon have that I don't have?"

"Hmmm... You mean besides the $20 million contract, the Bentley, the butter Pecan Rican who just strolled through here with the D-cups, and the huge mansion in the hills?"

"Okay man, I get it. I get it. A man can dream though, can't he?"

Amy Santiago was born in Puerto Rico to a mother and father of modest wealth. By the age of seven, her parents had moved the family to Florida in search of business opportunities. Her mother Lupe, was a homemaker of traditional Roman Catholic values, but feisty nonetheless. Her father was a man of few words, extremely strict and most unforgiving. When he did talk, he would yell and scream, mostly because of all the cheap wine he consumed almost daily. During his drunken rages, he would yell at his wife constantly, ranting that he never should have married her. Nothing suited him. The food Lupe cooked was never good enough; he'd say she was fat even if she lost 10 pounds; even if the house was spotless it was never clean enough.

Ever the faithful daughter, Amy attempted to run to her mother's aid, only to be scolded and hurled out of the way. She was thrown outside in her pajamas on more than one occasion when she tried to save her mother from her father's wrath. Amy grew numb to the phrase *"You're just like your stupid mother."* Lupe always pleaded with him to leave Amy alone, and to forgive her, since of course everything wrong was her fault. Eventually, Amy came to think he hated them, especially since Maria, her little sister, was the only one in the house that wasn't scolded or beaten. Although Amy thanked God that her younger sister was spared, she also envied their relationship. Amy never understood why he seemed to hold a special place in his heart for Maria. He would often sit her on his lap and pay special attention to whatever she was saying to him, and at night he would take extra time tucking her in while looking right through Amy who slept only a few feet away in a matching twin bed. Maria, would brag to Amy, (as only a little girl could) that when she got to school in the morning, she would sometimes find candy or a dollar in her backpack with a note from their father.

Both Santiago girls were absolutely beautiful just like their mother Lupe (when Lupe didn't have a black eye or fattened lip from her husband's fist). Both girls had deep and exotic eyes accentuated with long thick brown hair. Everyone took notice of their appeal, often commenting on how adorable they were or urging their parents to put them in commercials or movies. Amy was the "nice" little girl who was a straight 'A' student, did all her chores without being told, and often the caretaker of her younger sister. Maria on the other hand was extremely spoiled and rarely held accountable for things she did wrong. She was the typical adorable little sister who always got her way.

By the age of 12, Amy had grown accustomed to the distance that existed between her and her father, but still didn't understand it. Amy and Maria were extremely close, sharing everything. But when it came to Victor (as only Amy called their father, rather than Father or Papi), Maria was never willing to join in on the talk about the abuse that Amy and her mother endured. Amy soon discovered why.

During a night of one of her father's infamous, drunken escapades, Lupe escaped by running out of the house. She knew the large black frying pan she flung at her husband's head would not be met with flowers and candy once he regained his senses.

"I can't take this anymore Victor!!! I have given you everything!!! And nothing I do ever makes you happy!" Lupe yelled and sobbed while clutching her stomach.

Victor stumbled across the kitchen floor attempting to grab his wife, but the pain from the iron pan forced him to his knees.

"Then go, leave you whore! You'll be back, and when you do, that kitchen will still need to be cleaned... You live like a pig, you stinking pig!" Victor could barely stand, let alone make complete sentences. Just as Lupe ran out of the house, she dodged a plate that Victor threw in her direction.

Amy had long stopped coming to the defense of her mother, seeing that she never stood up for herself. She came to realize that no matter what he did to her mother, she would never leave him... Lupe had witnessed the abuse her own mother suffered at the hands of her stepfather and yet her mother never walked out on her family. That's just the way it was.

Both the girls quietly held each other, expecting that Victor would come for them next. Amy knew however, that she would be the only one he'd hurt. When the house fell completely silent, the girls felt safe and eventually fell asleep together. In the middle of the night, Amy awoke dazed to feel the emptiness of her tiny twin bed. *Where's Maria?* she thought to herself. Amy began searching the house for her sister. As she crept down the hallway, she could hear noises coming from her parents' bedroom.

Mommy came back just like I knew she would, Amy thought to herself.

"No Papi, that hurts me... Noooooo, please Papi," Maria's tiny muffled voice cried out in anguish.

"Stay still, be quiet... You know I would never hurt you. I love you... Ooohh, yes, I love you....You're daddy's little girl right... right?"

"Yes Papi."

As Amy peeked through the cracks of the slightly opened door, her soul ached with every moment she watched. She sat in frozen disbelief as her father raped his own daughter, only nine years old at the time. A part of her wanted to save her sister, but she was paralyzed. She could neither help nor peel her eyes away from the horror of what she was seeing. The tears streamed down her face mechanically, as she watched her father collapse disgustingly on top of her little sister. She promised herself that this would be the last time that any man, including her father, would ever hurt her or her sister again. *He's going to pay for this. I swear on my life he's going to pay*, she thought to herself.

Despite her modest upbringing, Amy was quickly establishing herself as a rising star in the world of entertainment and sports. After only a few years she made partner at one of the most established management firms in the country and became known for closing huge deals that no one else could handle. Amy's tenacity and business acumen paid off big for her firm. Her intelligence mixed with her exotic eyes, picture perfect breasts and legs, and her flawless lips made company men weak at the knees.

As much as she had accomplished in the professional world, Amy could not shake the emotional baggage of her youth. Her weakest quality was her inability to forgive. Amy held everyone in her life accountable at all times, never giving an inch. She loved hard and her word was iron clad. After her father began regularly molesting her little sister Maria, she promised that any man in her life who crossed her would pay, in blood if necessary. And when Amy and Maria tried to tell their mother about the molestation, she would apathetically dismiss them and defend her husband. It was this that made Amy realize how powerful love was; it had clouded her mother's vision so bad that her maternal instincts no longer existed. Having a husband took first place and protecting her young was no longer a basic instinct.

Although her mother couldn't win at the game of love, Amy fell hard and married an amazing man. Shannon Wilson was not only the *perfect husband* to Amy, he was also a caring and loving father. Amy met Shannon in Hawaii during a high school all-star game. As one of the nation's top college football prospects, Shannon had been selected to participate in the Hawaii Bowl High School All-Star Game while Amy was a cheerleader on one of the national AAU cheerleading squads selected for the game. Shannon's coach made him run laps after catching him staring at the beautiful cheerleader practicing on the nearby sidelines. It was a chance meeting neither of them would ever forget.

It was a match made in heaven. Shannon and Amy became the "it couple" during their tenure at the University of Northern California. Amy, a talented athlete, ditched cheerleading and accepted a full scholarship for track and field. Shannon became an All-American and Butkus Award finalist. He had become one of the nation's best linebackers during his junior and senior years at Northern and his 7 years in the league proved it was no fluke. He was the captain and franchise player of the San Francisco Quake. His NFL peers voted Shannon onto the All-Pro

144

team every year after his rookie season. He would have made the team his rookie year, but many NFL veterans simply refused to give him the honor.

The twosome practically grew up together at Northern. In addition, Amy was still battling the demons of her past. A lot of Amy's fear subsided because she found a true soul mate in Shannon. They talked about everything and kept very few, if any secrets from one another. The couple married in Belize after Shannon's rookie year in the NFL and went on to have a beautiful son named John Jeffrey, who they called "2J," a nickname the couple had absolutely nothing to do with. When 2J was one-and-a-half he would quickly remind people, "Me no J.J., me 2J!" Eventually his grandparents caved into his cuteness and continued calling him "2J" even though it drove Shannon and Amy absolutely bananas.

Shannon was a passionate man and it showed both on and off the football field. The only thing Shannon loved more than football was his family and his best friend Keith E. Yarborough, a.k.a. "Keys." Keys was Shannon's ace. They were like two kids when they were together. Keys' talent and Shannon's money helped Keys become a major hip-hop and R&B music producer. Although Keys didn't self-promote himself, Shannon took pride in telling everyone he knew that his boy had received several Grammy and American Music Award nominations. The two men shared everything. They golfed together, drank together, and smoked together, whatever. You name it they did it. They had a lot in common, from their love of music and sports to their love of the Santiago women. Keys planned to propose to Amy's sister Maria soon and Shannon was doing his best to keep this secret from his wife (not an easy thing to do since they tended to share everything).

Although Amy believed that Shannon was the perfect mate, she was unaware of his one temptation - exotic women. Of course Shannon was not the only man to succumb to his primal urges. He subscribed to a personal philosophy when dealing with his vice: he always took care of home first, then he took care of *himself*. Shannon was extremely careful not to publicly embarrass his wife and family. He always chose his "side" women cautiously. He knew that Amy was totally unforgiving. She wasn't to be played with when it came to matters of the heart and her emotional well-being. Shannon knew that carelessness could ruin his marriage, thus, he always dotted all the i's and crossed all the t's.

17

"Good Morning Mrs. S.," Amy's secretary said with her usual chipperness.

"Good morning Jackie. Do I have any messages?" Amy asked.

"Just one, Mr. Arrington from the Williams-Jones Agency said that he is looking forward to the meeting this morning."

"Just great, *he would be on time* for this meeting. The guy is usually at least 10 minutes late. "

Not only was Amy's firm the largest in San Francisco but it was one of the best in the country. She had helped sign some of the biggest names in the sports and entertainment field, in addition to managing and negotiating deals for some of their megastar client base. Although she knew many celebrities and professional athletes, her favorite client was Torey Franklin. She had met Torey at a music conference her first year with the firm. After he signed with the company he began introducing Amy to other NFL players, most of which eventually signed with her firm. Because of the firm's overwhelming success, the powers-that-be at the William-Jones Agency were very interested in merging the two companies. Amy and the other partners felt that a merger was not the direction they wanted to move in at the time, but felt compelled to at least listen to the proposal. The fact that she would be partner in the largest firm in the country with a five year guaranteed salary was enough to pique Amy's interest.

"Mrs. S, your sister is also waiting to see you. I told her you have a meeting in a few minutes."

"That's okay Jackie send her in." Amy knew that Maria only came to her office unannounced if she was troubled or if there was an emergency. *I bet Mamma needs us to pay some hospital bills again. Victor is going to send her to an early grave. She needs to leave his ass. I can't believe she's still with him* she thought to herself.

"Hey sis we need to talk?" Maria said, looking terribly disturbed.

"What's wrong Maria? What did Victor do to Mami this time?"

"Well I don't know how to say this."

"Just say it Maria. What's going on?"

"Okay, I'm just going to say it… Keys is fucking another woman."

"Excuse me?!" Amy asked incredulously, feeling her anger rise.

"Keys is fucking another woman," Maria said flatly.

"Wait, how do you know this is true?"

Jackie chimed in on the intercom, "Mrs. S., Mr. Arrington is asking if he should reschedule."

"Okay Jackie, two minutes. Maria I am truly sorry but I have a very important meeting. Can we talk about this later?"

"Okay, but there's something else you need to know."

"What's that?" Amy asked.

"Well, you know that Keys and Shannon do everything together…right?" Maria was looking for some type of reassurance, a nod or something, but her sister just stared at her blankly. "…Well, this is no different."

Amy's face turned bright red as she covered her mouth. "What do you mean by that Maria?"

"What does it sound like I mean? Yes, your husband is in on this with Keys. He's doing the same damn thing."

"Hold the fuck up... Oh Lord, please forgive me. Maria, you should be ashamed of yourself. How dare you drag my husband into your man's bullshit. I know you're upset but..."

"Look, call me when Keys picks up Shannon to go play cards tonight, and I'll come over. You can see for yourself. Trust me. I love you sis." Maria signals for Amy to call her as she grabs her purse and rushes out of her office.

Amy was thoroughly confused. She had never considered the possibility of Shannon cheating, and she definitely was not going to jump to any conclusions. He was her best friend. For her, it was almost impossible to take the thought seriously.

"Mrs. S. are you ready?" Jackie asked.

"Yes Jackie, are all the partners assembled in the conference room?"

"Yes, they're all just waiting on you."

Amy became numb as she walked towards the firm conference room. Her mind began playing tricks on her. She wanted more than anything to cancel the meeting and track down her sister to get to the bottom of the situation.

Amy didn't hear a word during the meeting, constantly looking at her Rolex wondering when the meeting would end. Not a second after the meeting concluded, Amy hastily thanked everyone for coming and sped down the hall back to her office to gather her belongings.

"Mrs. S. are you alright?" asked Jackie.

"Yes Jackie, I'm fine. I just have an urgent matter that I need to tend to. Be sure to reschedule the remainder of today's meetings. Whatever looks available for next week is fine. And please be sure to apologize to everyone for me."

"When should I expect you back?" Jackie inquired.

"Tomorrow. Thanks Jackie, I'll see you then, and don't worry, everything is fine."

Amy stormed out of the office while dialing her husband's cell phone number. She dialed Shannon's cell phone number at least 10 times but never pushed the "Send" button. Her instincts told her to just stay calm, after all, *There are always at least two sides to every story,* she thought to herself. *And his side better be damn good.*

Instead of calling Shannon, Amy called Maria, insisting that they meet immediately. As soon as Shannon left the house with Keys, Amy called Maria to let her know the coast was clear.

"Hey sis," Maria said glumly after entering the foyer of her sister's home.

"Hey lady, come on in. I hope you don't mind, I made us a couple of martinis." Amy felt that a stiff drink would prepare her for what she was about to hear.

"Oh my goodness Amy, this drink is strong! Did you use anything besides vodka?"

"Honey, desperate times call for desperate measures," Amy responded. "I've already had two of those, so you have some catching up to do."

"You're right. And after you see this tape, you'll probably drink two more yourself. But you've got to swear on grandmother's grave that you will not overreact or say something to Shannon just yet."

"Tape, you never said anything about a tape!"

"I said promise Amy Santiago!"

"Okay, I promise."

"No, promise on grandmother's grave."

"Sheeesh, okay, I promise on grandmother's grave. Now, show me the damn tape."

As the tape rolled, Amy's hands began to tremble so bad that she started spilling her drink onto the carpet. As she sat paralyzed, staring at the graphically pornographic scenes on the 60-inch monitor in front of her, tears streamed steadily down her perfectly painted cheeks. She was hoping Ashton would soon ring the doorbell and tell her that she had just been Punk'd. Since Maria had seen the tape herself, at least 10 times, she wasn't visibly shaken. Amy on the other hand, was in total shock. Shannon's unmistakable laugh filled the airwaves as the tape rolled. Amy simply couldn't believe what she was hearing... or seeing.

"Turn it up Maria." Amy didn't want to miss a word.

"Yo, Keys, man where did you get these fine ass women?"

"Boy, you know me. They're in a group I've been working with."

"Can they sing?"

"Man, can they sing? They don't just sing, they SANG playboy! Hell, they can sing, dance and a lot of other stuff you don't know anything about."

"Hey what's your name again?" Shannon asked the petite, big-bottomed, Brazilian girl slinking towards him.

As she sat half naked on his lap she responded, *"I'm Star and she's Precious."*

"Ahhh, yes she is," Shannon joked, filling the room once again with his signature laugh. *"So..."*

"To hell with this, fast forward Maria!" Amy snapped. "Let's get on with the show."

Maria knew Amy was about to explode. Her sister's fiery temper was as much a part of her as eating and breathing. She fast-forwarded the tape and poured Amy another drink.

"Ooh yea, suck it, ooh shit take it all. Damn, Keys come check this out." Shannon said within the video.

Amy started drinking the expensive vodka straight from the bottle, and then passed it to her little sister.

"I'm going to kill that mother-fucker. You know that right?" Amy asked in a surprisingly subtle tone. "I gave up a lot for that son of a bitch. Here I am, turning down opportunity after opportunity from firms in New York and Chicago to stay here, have his babies and be Mrs. Shannon Wilson. I'm going to kill him. I'm fucking going to kill him!"

"Relax Amy. You can't afford to do anything too crazy. Remember, you do have 2J and you're also too high profile to be acting the evil bitch you can be at times. Girl you are HOT out there right now. You can't afford to throw all that away over your lying, cheating husband. So calm down...PLEASE."

"Fuck that Maria! My husband, not my boyfriend, my man, or my fiancé... My HUSBAND is on a tape fucking somebody else. And now the dirty bastard is going down on another woman," she said as scene changed to reflect her sentiments. "His ass is dead!"

"Amy you promised you wouldn't do anything crazy!"

"Okay, just keep it together. Just keep it together," Amy mumbled. "Cut that off. I said cut that shit off! I can't watch anymore."

The women sat staring at each other. After a few moments of eerie, tense-filled silence, Maria wanted to know exactly what was going on in her sister's head. She visualized Amy doing something that would land her in prison for sure.

"So what are you thinking Amy? Talk to me."

"I think that if that bastard had any sense he'd know that no pussy is worth what he's getting ready to lose."

"That's for sure. He's crazy to do something like this. And Keys, I want to kill his ass too. He probably dragged Shannon into all this."

"No Maria, Shannon is a big boy. No one makes him do anything he doesn't want to do. Trust me on that. It's not Keys' fault at all. I'm not holding him responsible for my husband's actions. But Shannon is going to pay for this in every way imaginable."

"Tell me something sis," Amy said after a few more minutes of silence. "How did you get this tape anyway?"

"Well this guy that's been asking me out forever; he gave it to me. Turns out that he had a few cameras installed in his home after he got wind that his girlfriend was sexing other guys in his house. Remember the girl "Precious" on the tape? Well, that's his girlfriend."

153

"Shit, how could I forget her? She was riding my man like a rodeo star a few minutes ago. BASTARD!"

18

"Hey Amy guess what?" Maria said with excitement.

"Hmmm, let me guess… Chicken butt?"

"Nooooo! I'm not trying to trick you, THIS time. Really, guess what!"

"Okay, I'll play along. What?" Amy asked.

"Look at this!" Maria yelled as she held up her left hand to expose the 6 carat diamond ring Keys had given her the night before. "I'm engaged! Can you believe it?"

"Uhhh, well, hell no I can't believe it! Were you watching the same video tape I was watching last week? What do you mean, you're engaged? Why would you marry that cheating ass son of a bitch?"

"Because I love him Amy. I love him. Can't you be happy for me ONCE during our lifetime?"

"Maria, you and I both know that you're making a terrible mistake. Have you even thought about the things you DON'T know about Keys? The things he's done or that he's doing that you will never find out about?"

"No Amy, I'm not you, I don't think that way. All I know is that I love this man and he loves me. He makes me feel like a woman. And that's all I need. Besides, WE weren't married…I've done a bunch of shit he could've left me over. But when we get married it'll be different."

"Well, you're not the only one he makes feel like a woman…remember 'Star'?!" And sweetie, marriage doesn't change men, it only changes the repercussions of their actions. Unless you're FUCKING Victor Santiago of course!"

"Fuck you Amy. Fuck you!"

"Yeah, that's right, go ahead and curse at me while your man walks all over you. You haven't changed one bit since we were kids. You always have to be the apple of a man's eye, even when he has absolutely no respect for you."

"What are you talking about Amy?"

"You know damn well what I'm talking about Maria. Men have shit all over you your entire life and you keep going back for more. Just like with Victor. You had to be daddy's favorite all the time huh? Even though he kicked our mother's ass all the time, you still had to make sure you were his favorite little girl. But I guess you did what you had to do right?"

"To hell with you Amy! I didn't want that. I didn't want any of that. He raped me! I didn't ask for it!"

"Hmmph, you could have fooled me."

"You think I wanted our father to do that to me?" Maria was on the verge of breaking down.

"All I know is that nothing in you has changed. Always forgive and forget with you, especially with men. They use you up, fuck you, and stomp all over you, whatever. And you keep going back for more."

Maria's violent reaction startled Amy. The sting of Maria's open hand slap to her right cheek reminded her of the days they fought as teenagers.

Shannon rushed into the house to break up the catfight. "Amy! Maria! You two stop this!" Shannon yelled while stepping between the two women. Both women had a handful of the other's hair as he pried them apart.

"You Bitch!" Maria yelled.

"Get out of my house! And don't come back!" Amy yelled.

"Oh, I'll be back. And when I come back it is ON!" Maria replied.

"Ladies, ladies, please, calm down! What the hell happened ?" Shannon asked.

"Mommy, what's wrong Mommy?" a sleepy 2J asked as he climbed down the stairs.

"Come on 2J," Shannon said, "Let's get you back into bed." Shannon's piercing stares directly at the two sisters said more than any statement could.

"See, this is about ME, not you Amy," Maria exclaimed. "You always think the world revolves around you and what you think. I'm an adult now, you don't have to protect me from our father or any man for that matter."

"Whatever. Get out! And don't come running back to me when Keys shits all over your stupid ass – AGAIN!" Amy yelled, as she slammed the door nearly hitting her sister.

Amy loved Shannon more than anyone or anything except for her son 2J. But as much as she wanted to forgive her husband for what he had done, the scars from her childhood were making it very difficult. Shannon began noticing his wife's sporadic behavior. It appeared that no matter what he did for her, no matter how much he said "I love you," Amy seemed to grow angrier by the day. He could not figure out what he had done wrong, especially since Amy wasn't telling him what was bothering her. Although he didn't know what was troubling his beloved wife, Shannon was determined to right whatever wrong he had committed.

Shannon decided to treat his wife to an evening of luxury and fantasy. Not only did he have six dozen long stemmed red and white roses delivered to their home, he also paid a top local designer provide 10 dresses for Amy to view. He wanted her to choose one especially for that evening, along with any others she wanted to keep. Perhaps the biggest surprise of the evening was that Shannon would prepare a gourmet meal for the two of them. Although he was an extremely good cook, he could not remember the last time he prepared a meal for his wife. Shannon arranged for his mother to pick 2J up from pre-school while Amy was being spoiled at a nearby day spa.

The evening was going wonderfully. Shannon cooked one of Amy's favorite dishes, Arroz con Pollo and Rum Pound Cake for dessert. Amy made the pina coladas unusually strong. She wanted to escape her troubled mind, at least for tonight. Dinner was excellent and the evening was going as planned. As Shannon began kissing and caressing his wife she couldn't resist. But as they began to make love on their bedroom balcony, Amy's mind began to wander. She zoned even further from the pleasurable moans of her husband, and fell deeper into thoughts of his infidelity and betrayal. Amy's distrust for men was deeper than she had ever let on. It was about violation. It was about being violated and betrayed by the first man that she ever loved and trusted. Amy had been through things that only she and Maria knew about. They were so devastating that the two sisters swore never to discuss them with anyone. And after finding peace and sense of love and trust for so many years with her husband, the skeletons of her youth found their way back into her life, and were haunting the hell out of her.

Amy and Shannon ventured from the balcony to the bed, but for some strange reason, she felt as if she were a child again. Not unlike her father, her husband, a man that she trusted whole heartedly and loved more than anything, had hurt her in the worst way. As her mind drifted once more, she was 12 years old again, and the silence of the little girl she so desperately tried to ignore, was deafening.

Her mother had just escaped their home, and her abusive husband, leaving her two girls defenseless against the man that had nearly beaten her to death. Amy still vividly remembered stumbling quietly down the dimly lit hall searching for her sister who was not in her bed. A scene that replayed itself over and over in her dreams, but this time it was as if Amy was actually there controlling her thoughts and actions.

The sounds coming from her father's bedroom were unlike those she sometimes heard when her parents were on good terms. The noise grew louder as she approached the bedroom door.

"No Papi, that hurts me... Nooooo, please Papi." *Her sister Maria cried out in anguish.*

"Stay still, be quiet...you know I would never hurt you. I love you... Ooooh yes Papi loves you...you're daddy's little girl right...right?"

"Yes."

As Amy peeked through the cracks of the slightly opened door, her soul ached with every moment she watched. She watched in disbelief as her father violated his baby.

In her recurring dream, just as in real life, Amy did nothing but watch in horror as his father had his way with baby sister. But tonight she would get the ultimate revenge. This time she would do something.

As she silently crept to her father's gun cabinet she could hear a baby sister's muffled screams. The closer she got to the gun cabinet the angrier she became. Amy had seen Victor hide the key to the gun rack after he returned from one of his so called hunting trips. As she opened the cabinet door the only question was which gun would actually kill him. Amy walked mechanically toward the screams as though she was possessed by an unknown evil. As the door flung open, Victor continued to pummel the little girl that lay beneath him. "Victor, get off my sister!" she yelled. Before he could reach for her, multiple shots rang out with the final shot causing her little hands to burn. She dropped the gun; her father lay bloody and lifeless, having taken three bullets into his back and one directly into his right temple.

There was rarely a day when she didn't think about what her father had done. But in her mind, what was even worse was that she did absolutely nothing to rescue her sister. She wasn't a tenth as brave as she was in her daydreams.

"No! No! No!" Amy wailed.

"Baby, baby? Are you okay?" Shannon asked his wife, not realizing that she had fallen into a dreamlike delusion.

"I'm alright Shannon. Just hold me until I fall asleep, okay?"

"Anything baby. Anything," Shannon said as he held her close to him.

Amy had been distant for reasons unknown to Shannon for the past couple of weeks, so her smooth, naked, perfectly shaped body felt better than ever. For Shannon there was nothing like early morning sex. However, he didn't want to appear insensitive towards his fragile wife and he wasn't sure if Amy would take offense to his advances. Amy's peaceful sleep made it clear to him that she felt safe and protected in his arms. The more he thought about how much he truly loved his wife the more Shannon's erection grew. As he moved up against his wife's perfectly contoured buttocks, Amy too became aroused. Although she was angry with Shannon, she could not deny his amazing body or raw sexuality. She swore not to make love to him after watching the vile sex tape, but as much as she hated to admit it, she still wanted her husband.

"Shannon, you feel so good," she breathed as her husband's hands caressed her neck and back.

"You feel good too baby," Shannon whispered as he teased her nipples with his lips and tongue.

"Oh yes Papi, lower... lower" Amy whispered, while pushing his head down between her thighs. "Yeah... Yeah, that's it, right there." Amy closed her eyes as Shannon's expert tongue explored every inch of her. He gave her multiple orgasms with every erotic flick of his tongue causing her to nearly squirm off the bed. As he spread her beautiful tan lips apart he began to write a Spanish love letter with his tongue. Amy's unbridled groans were evidence that she understood every word of it.

"Ooooh, Papi, you're gonna make me," Amy whispered while biting her lip and gripping Shannon's head tightly. "You're gonna... Oh, yeahhhhh, yeahhhh, I'm gonna... Oooooohhhh." Amy bucked against her husband's face until she could no longer contain herself. Although she thoroughly enjoyed his expert tongue, it was no match for his perfectly sculpted penis.

"Shannon, take me baby. Take me now, PLEASE?!"

"Anything baby...I'll give you anything you ask for." Shannon's sexy voice whispered while pushing himself deep inside her. "Do you like that baby?"

"Oh yes Papi, you know I like that. Ohhh." Amy was on the verge of another orgasm as Shannon stroked deeper and deeper. She hated the way he could make her feel that good even when she was pissed at him. Her anger was never a match for her powerfully built husband whose sexual pleasure was the peace maker during stormy times. Amy was overcome with emotion as she grabbed her husband's muscular shoulders and bit his chest. Tears streamed down her face as both Amy and her husband erupted simultaneously. As wonderful as the love-making was, Amy began to feel the same violation that her sister must have felt during their childhood. In a split second reaction, she pushed her husband off of her and ran into the bathroom.

"What's wrong baby? What's wrong?" Shannon asked while tugging at the locked door. "Baby, please tell me what's wrong. What happened? Did I hurt you?"

Amy wanted to yell to the top of her lungs, "HELL YES YOU HURT ME! WORSE THAN YOU WILL EVER KNOW," but she held back. Now was not the time.

"I'm okay Papi. I think I had a small panic attack. I have a big meeting and I'm nervous about it. I'm alright. Just give me a few minutes."

"Are you sure you're alright? You haven't had one of those in years. Do you need some water?"

"No, I'm okay Papi. I'll be out in a few."

Shannon had no idea what was going on. Unbeknownst to him, he had broken his wife's heart. He had disrespected her in the worst way. And unlike her mother, Amy simply could not look the other way while her husband disrespected their marriage.

"Are you better now?" he asked as Amy emerged from the bathroom.

"Yes, I'm fine. All better."

"Come lay down," he said as he helped her back into bed. "I love you. Don't worry Papi's here for you."

"I know …and Shannon, no matter what, I love you."

19

Amy's wheels were spinning for days since watching the tape. Shannon had made a fool of her. Amy was not used to these types of problems. He had always been the perfect father, husband, and gentleman. She was totally confused, and didn't know what to believe. She even began to think that since Shannon had actually cheated, she must have done something to cause it. What hadn't she done? Was she not sexual enough? Had she made a mistake in choosing a career over being a full-time housewife? Had their entire marriage been one big lie? Amy knew she could have simply taken the tape of her husband's sexcapades to an attorney, but she wanted to make Shannon feel her pain. She was haunted by visions of her man doing things to another woman on tape that he would not even do to her. In order to get even she had to leave him with some memories that would make him suffer for a long, long time. Amy's mind was at work, and she wasn't certain of anything. However, the one thing she was certain of was that payback was a MUST. It was in her blood, Amy was a *N.I.C.E.* girl; *Never Intended to Cheat, but had to get... Even.* Shannon had no clue what was about to hit him.

Amy picked up her cell phone and scanned through her client list until she reached the number she wanted.

RINGGGGGGGGGGGGGGGGGGG...

"Hello," answered the male voice.

"Hello Torey, this is Amy, how are you doing?"

"I'm doing much better now," Torey said with a smile. Although both of them were married, Amy knew that Torey was very attracted to her, not to mention he was legally separated and practically divorced. But Torey had always been careful to not cross the line with his flirting. Amy didn't mind the flirting, the eye contact, or his eyes subtly wandering up and down her body when they saw each other. In fact, she actually enjoyed her interaction with him. She thought to herself many times, how she'd be all over Torey if she wasn't married to Shannon.

"How's my favorite agent doing today?" Torey asked. "Uh oh, I didn't miss an appointment with someone did I? I know how pissed you get when we miss meetings with people who want to write us checks."

"Actually, I was just calling to see how you were doing, believe it or not," Amy answered.

"You're right, I don't believe it," he joked as both of them laughed. "So what's up? What's on your mind?"

"Torey, I know you and Keisha are on the verge of splitting up," Amy said.

"Man, I sure hope you didn't call to try to convince me to stay with her for the endorsement money. I know these companies want brothas to be married with 2.5 kids and the white picket fence thing, but…"

"No, actually Torey, I wasn't calling to talk to you about that. I wanted to ask you a few questions and I want you to be completely honest with me. First, do you think I've ever cheated on my husband?"

"Huh?" Torey answered caught off guard by the question.

"Do you think I ever cheated on my husband?"

"Well, …Amy, no I don't. I mean, why would you cheat on him? I'm sure he's handling his business at home… isn't he?"

"I'm asking the questions right now Mr. Franklin," Amy responded.

"Okay, my bad. Well you said you had a few questions. So, what's the second one?" Torey asked.

"Aren't you going to be in town with your team in a few weeks?"

"Uh, let me check my schedule," Torey responded while rifling through his planner. "Yep, you're right, we'll be in Cali later this season."

"This is the last question," Amy said.

"Okay, shoot," Torey responded.

"Have you ever thought about making love to me?"

20

After the plane landed in Tampa, Shannon headed for his usual front seat, of the team charter bus. He always sat on bus #1 on the way from the airport to the team hotel so that he could quickly avoid the autograph seekers and get to his room. Although Shannon hated to fly, he actually looked forward to road trips because of the online exploits he enjoyed with his wife after hours. Usually Amy would indulge her husband by having phone sex with him or masturbating via web cam so that he could watch her.

"Thank God for technology," Shannon would exclaim after mind-blowing web cam sessions with his wife. The performances had quickly become Shannon's favorite. After rushing to find his name on the players table, Shannon quickly headed towards his room, declining offers from teammates to continue the gambling sessions that had started on the plane. He couldn't wait to get to his room. He knew his baby would be waiting online, and for some reason he was feeling hornier than ever.

Shannon anxiously connected his laptop and computer cam. While the computer was loading he removed his suit and threw on some of his easy access boxers. Like clock work his beautiful wife was already online, waiting.

"Are you watching me baby? This is for you... Amy said while kissing the screen. Shannon could barely contain himself.

Amy, who in the FUCK is that?! Shannon yelled furiously.

Who he is, doesn't matter baby, Amy replied as the masked stranger sitting behind her began fondling Amy's ripe breasts.

Don't you like this baby? I thought you were into sharing, Amy teased.

Amy, don't do this! This shit is not cool! Shannon pleaded.

Oh it's not, is it? Amy typed back while licking her lips seductively and arching her back. *His hands feel soooooo good Shannon. Even better than yours I must admit.*

This is not right Amy! Is this some kind of cruel joke?

Does it look like I'm joking Papi? The stranger's right hand wandered from her breast down to her wet opening. Amy inched closer to the screen to give Shannon his money's worth. *You see that Shannon? He has my pussy soooooo wet baby. I MUST do something to return the favor don't you think?*

HELL NO!!! Don't do it Amy! I'm warning you!

Don't do what baby? You don't want me to do THIS? She said as she kneeled before the stranger to take in his entire shaft into her mouth. The mocha skinned stranger was obviously enjoying himself. His masked face weaved from side to side as he was treated to one of the best blow jobs he'd ever experienced. Neither Shannon, nor the masked stranger could contain himself. Amy was driving both men wild simultaneously, and she was enjoying every minute of it. Just as her masked partner was about to top off, she took him deeper inside her mouth, refusing to release him until he was completely satisfied. She wanted Shannon to know just how good she was feeling. No one knew more about Amy's exceptional skills than Shannon, so the agony of watching her was clearly wounding him beyond repair. Enraged, Shannon could not bear to watch another moment. Without thinking, he snatched his laptop from the desk and flung it across the room where it crashed wildly against the wall.

A few seconds later someone was violently pounding on his suite door. "Hey man!" his teammate Greg Lamont shouted through the door, "Are you okay in there? What's going on?"

"Nothing man," Shannon said while partially cracking the door, "I just dropped my computer."

"Now I know you haven't been in there getting toasted from the mini bar, right? You better watch it playa. You know we need you tomorrow," Greg said.

"It's cool man. I'm cool. Go back to bed."

"Alright man, you better get some sleep too," Greg responded.

Shannon's repeated calls to his home and his wife's cell phone went unanswered throughout the night and into the early morning. *I can't believe this* he thought. Shannon had tossed and turned in his suite all night. When he did finally fall asleep, he'd awake from nightmares of his wife pleasing another man in *his* bed. He didn't even want to imagine what they did *after* he destroyed his computer.

Amy made sure she turned off all the ringers. She knew her husband well enough to know that he'd be blowing up the phones all night until he talked to her. She wanted to thoroughly enjoy the rest of her evening with her guest, undisguised and with no interruptions.

"Now we can finish what we started Torey," Amy said while removing his mask.

21

Shannon could barely wait until the chartered plane touched down. Absolutely distracted, he had just played the worst game of his life. He had been beaten badly by an average tight end that caught the game-winning touchdown. He was in no mood to face the ravenous media that was just waiting to tear his performance apart. As Shannon filed past his teammates and coaches to board the team bus, he noticed that hardly any of them even acknowledged him. Understandably so, he had played shoddy football and he knew it. He could still hear his coach from the sidelines, *"Where the hell is your head at, son?"* To make matters worse, he wasn't getting any younger and the buzz about him being released by the team had been swirling all year long. He dreaded going to the complex the next day. However, his future in football was not as important to him as his future with his wife. He couldn't believe she would humiliate him like that. Shannon knew he wasn't a choirboy by any stretch of the imagination, but as far as Amy knew, he was a saint. He was always careful not to screw around with local women or anyone who would threaten his family life. In Shannon's eyes, Amy had absolutely no reason to fuck another man, let alone, revel in it the way she did on the computer the evening before.

As Shannon screeched into the driveway of his home, he nearly rammed his precious canary yellow Ferrari into the oversized security gate. It was as if the gate sensed his fury and opened slower than usual, allowing him time to calm down.

"I'm going to kill that bitch. I can't believe she'd do this to me. And if I find out who that guy was, he's DEFINITELY dead. No one fucks with Shannon Wilson like this. NO ONE!" He jumped out so quickly that he left his keys in the ignition.

Damn, I left my keys in the car, he thought as he reached the doorway. Instead of going back, Shannon banged loudly on the door and psychotically rang the doorbell.

"Open this fucking door! Shannon screamed. I know you're in there! You better open this door before I kick it in! Amy!!! Amy!!! Open the goddamn door you fuckin' slut!!! I can't believe you'd do this to me! Don't you know who I am? I'm Shannon Wilson! What, you think you can make a fool out of me? Open the fucking door... NOWWWWW!!!!" Shannon pounded the door harder and harder to no avail.

As he inadvertently twisted the knob, he realized that it had been unlocked the entire time. "What the???!!!" Shannon asked incredulously. "Amy! Amy!!! 2J!!!" Shannon's irate roars echoed throughout the house. Much to his surprise, it was as barren as the day they bought it. While walking through the massive structure, Shannon became weak. The emptiness of room after room confirmed his worst fear. It was not until he reached the third floor: his beloved trophy room, that he located any parts of his life.

Amy knew how much Shannon loved that room, so despite her anger, she didn't touch a thing. The large, hand made, mahogany trophy case contained every award Shannon had ever won, dating back to little league. Nearly a hundred trophies, three-dozen game balls, and various other awards embellished the walls. It was in this room that Shannon would relive his greatest moments as an athlete. The longer he reminisced the younger he felt.

Shannon was baffled as to how Amy could've done so much, in so little time. What he didn't realize was that Amy had actually begun clearing the house only a few minutes after he left to catch the team flight to Tampa. As Shannon was driving to the airport, moving trucks were pulling up to their home. After the workers had taken all of their belongings from the home Amy sat in the middle of the trophy room with her husband's wooden bat, a memento given to him by Larry Johns, the home run hitting sensation of San Francisco's thriving Major American League Baseball franchise. Amy visualized herself going berserk in the room, smashing everything in sight. She contemplated shattering the 60-inch flat screen television, Shannon's personal favorite. The thought of Shannon finding his room covered with broken glass and dismantled trophies was tempting, but as much as she wanted to hurt him, she did not want to destroy what little he had left. Besides, he would be devastated enough.

Shannon surveyed the room to make sure that no damage had been done and that everything was in its place. His immaculate stereo system and immense CD/DVD collections were untouched.

Whew, if she had taken those, I would have had to go J. Carson on her, he thought while eyeing his prized collections. As he approached the big screen television he noticed that a white package was taped to the top of it. He quickly ripped the package open. He found a note attached to the DVD inside the package that said: *Watch this, just a little surprise.*

Shannon was not prepared for what he saw. He sat speechless before the enormous television as the action he engaged in a month prior played itself out on the screen. Mistaken identity was not an option, as it was clearly Shannon DeShaun Wilson, performing like a pro, with his co-star "Precious." Their sexual exploits were enough to make even the porn-star Naomi Mount blush. Shannon couldn't believe what he was seeing. That entire night had been a blur that began with him taking Ecstasy, and ended with him face down, butt naked on a bearskin rug. Shannon was completely devastated. He had made some mistakes before, but this was the ultimate sin in Amy's eyes and he knew it. Shannon knew Amy loved him unconditionally; however, he also knew her stance on infidelity. She had spent her entire childhood in a dysfunctional household, with an abusive father and now she had no tolerance for men who disrespected their wives. As he fought back the tears, Shannon sat motionless with his head in his hands. One of the most talented quarterback stalkers in the NFL had just been sacked himself. Shannon was so dazed he barely heard the doorbell ring. Hoping that Amy had returned, he jumped up to sprint downstairs to answer the door, flinging it open.

"Baby, I'm so sorry," Shannon's voice trailed off as a messenger sat staring at him blankly.

"Hello, are you Mr. Shannon Wilson?" asked the messenger.

"Yes."

"This is for you. You are being served by the State of California." the messenger said.

"Served for what? What did I do?"

"Sir, I just deliver the papers. But I'm pretty sure your wife has filed for a divorce. Uh, do you think I can get an autograph before I go?" asked the messenger.

Valerie Robinson aka The S.O.B.
Chapter 22

Valerie Robinson always knew she was different. Although she grew up in Birmingham, Alabama, once labeled the most racially divided city in America, she was never comfortable with the teachings of her upbringing. Both her parents were staunchly religious people who believed that "race mixing" was a sin and that biracial children were the offspring of immoral whoremongers. After all, her grandfather was a proud member of the Ku Klux Klan, so neither her father, Charlie, nor any of his seven brothers and sisters were allowed to interact with "niggers or spooks" while growing up. Linda Robinson, Valerie's mother, was the daughter of a loud talking preacher who claimed God had put him on earth to help maintain the purity of the white race. For these reasons, she wanted to attend college as far away from Birmingham as possible.

Since Val graduated as the salutatorian of her senior class, she was offered academic scholarships to several in-state institutions, and other prestigious schools like Vanderbilt and Duke University. However, in Val's mind, even Duke was much too close to her roots and to her parents as well. It was also located in the South, something she wanted to avoid at all cost. So when Stanford called, she answered without hesitation. It was her opportunity to get out of Alabama and best of all, she would only be able to return home once or twice each year, if that, because of the distance.

During the second semester of her freshman year, Val began dating Tommy Lawrence, a rich, good-looking son of a powerful Silicon Valley corporate attorney. Tommy was an intelligent, All-American white boy with tan skin, blonde hair and deep blue eyes. He was known as the "young Brad Pitt" of Southern California, a compliment that he obviously cherished. Valerie met Tommy in a math class that she absolutely hated. But, since Tommy was in the class, it was much easier for her to tolerate the 90 minutes of hell every Tuesday and Thursday morning. The two were pretty much inseparable after their first encounter. What Val liked most about Tommy was that he was a total free-spirit who hated playing by the rules. For a girl raised in an overly strict Southern household, he was a constant summer breeze, rather than just a breath of fresh air. Tommy, although a wanted man by many of the ladies on campus, was very much in love with Val and vice versa. Like many young college couples, they spent every waking moment together. Val often fantasized about the day when she'd be Mrs. Tommy Lawrence. She even believed her father would approve of Tommy, a feat in itself.

"Hey Sarah, you ready to go?" Val asked her friend as she put the finishing touches on her glossy puckered lips. *This could be the night,* she thought while taking one last look into the bathroom mirror. *Tommy has been waiting patiently, so tonight I'm going to surprise him.* Val was technically a virgin (since blow jobs "did not count" in her book), but she had been thinking of going all the way with Tommy for quite some time. They had dated for only a few months, but she was sure he was the one worthy of taking her virginity. She was falling in love with him, but also growing tired of hearing her friend Sarah, talk about all her sexual conquests. Val was tired of feeling like the outsider. She wanted to be a participant in the conversations, not only with Sarah but all of her friends.

"Okay Val," Sarah said. "I'm ready to go. But what's the rush anyway?"

"Well, tonight I'm finally going to do the dirty deed with Tommy!" Val squealed with excitement.

"You little slut! I thought you said he hadn't tried to have sex with you," shrieked Sarah.

"Well, he hasn't technically. He knows I'm a virgin, so he's been real sweet, a perfect gentleman I must admit. But I hope he doesn't want to be a gentleman tonight!"

"Just make sure he goes down on you first!" responded Sarah with a laugh.

Val asked to use Sarah's phone to call Tommy to make sure he was on his way to Ray's Pub. The plan was to meet him at Ray's, hang out for a while, then leave with her girl Sarah and meet up with Tommy later at his place. However, she planned to sneak back to Tommy's apartment to wait in his bed for him when he returned home. Val called Tommy several times before finally giving up.

"I swear, Tommy can get lost like no other," she said to Sarah.

"Well, at least you *want* him to be lost this time. It'll give you some time to get a few drinks in your system before you play hide the salami."

"You are disgusting, Sarah," Val said while laughing.

"That's not what Bill thinks….. or Wallace, or Jimmy for that matter," Sarah kidded.

"And you're calling *me* a slut?" Val asked Sarah with a wink. "Let's head to Ray's so we can pick out a good spot before the place gets too crowded. I want to be front and center when Tommy arrives."

While at Ray's , Val continuously called Tommy on his cell phone, but he still did not answer.

"Oh shit, there's Bobby Jackson Val!" Valerie's roommate Sarah exclaimed.

"Bobby who?" Val asked.

"You know Bobby! The ball player in your biology class dummy! He's only the cutest and smartest hunk of man on campus."

Bobby Jackson was a tall, dark afro-wearing cutie who arrived at Stanford as the most heralded recruit in the history of the program. A mathematical genius who also sported a wicked jump shot was the toast of Palo Alto. Whenever he touched the basketball, the crowd would chant his nickname "B-J" in unison. He fed off the crowd and usually gave them something they could remember.

As Bobby entered Ray's he could feel the eyes on him. The basketball team defeated USC by a last minute shot made by none other than BJ himself. Although he had grown accustomed to being stared at, he often wished he could just hang out like the other students who frequented Ray's or any other establishment in town, however, he did enjoy the attention at times. As usual, Bobby arrived at the pub alone. After all, he spent most of his time with one or all of his teammates.

"Heyyyyyyyy, Bobbyyyyyyyy!" yelled Ray, the son of the original owner of the popular pub. "One Philly cheese steak, hold the peppers and add a side of fries for my main man BJ!" he said loudly to one of the cooks.

"BJ special coming right up boss!" blared the cook.

"How 'bout a nice cold beer Bob?" Ray asked jokingly, knowing that Bobby was a non-drinker. Of all the students who frequented the establishment over the years, Bobby was the only non-drinker Ray could remember. Bobby had only had one drink at the bar after missing two free throws with two seconds to go in a game his team lost by one point.

"As a matter of fact Ray, I will have a beer. A *ROOT* beer," he said with a charming smile. Bobby was a picture of health, but he also didn't want to do anything to jeopardize his athletic or academic career at Stanford.

"Oh yeah, I remember Bobby," Val responded unenthusiastically while glancing at her watch. *Where is Tommy, he's 40 minutes late* she thought to herself. "Yeah, Bobby's cute I guess, but he's not my Tommy," she giggled to her friend.

"Whatever," said Sarah. "He may not be Tommy Lawrence, but you know what they say about the brothas," she continued while tossing her red hair to one side and smiling devilishly.

"Sarah!" Val said while covering her mouth.

"I've got jungle fever, I've got jungle fever," Sarah sang while swaying her shoulders. Valerie had never heard the Stevie Wonder tune from the movie *Jungle Fever,* so she was confused by the tune.

"Jungle fever?" Val asked. "What in the world is that?"

"Val, you've never heard that phrase before? Ever?" her friend inquired.

"Nope."

"I see I have to school you on more things than I thought," Sarah said with a grin. "Scientifically speaking," Sarah said while straightening up and fixing her glasses as if she was about to make a presentation in class, "Jungle fever is a connotation often applied to interracial relationships my dear," she said in a prim and proper voice.

"Oh," Val replied while turning beet red. "So you... you... you've had black boyfriends before?"

"Oh honey, I've done MUCH MORE than that."

"Oh my God Sarah!"

"White, Black, Hispanic, I don't discriminate."

"Obviously."

"Don't knock it, till you try it. Multiculturalism can be fun, and not to mention, educational!"

"So *you* say."

"Now *that* is an ass," Sarah whispered to Val as Bobby strolled by without noticing them.

Uh huh, it sure is, Val thought to herself not wanting to admit that she agreed totally.

As Bobby walked to his car, Val knew what her roommate was thinking before she said a word. "Go ahead and say it Sarah," Val said with a smirk.

"Multiculturalism!" Sarah bellowed as they both laughed aloud.

Val admired Bobby from afar but kept her distance. Although he seemed to be a very nice guy, she remembered what her father said about Blacks, "*No matter how nice*

181

they seem, when you least expect they'll turn on you like a dog!"

The two roommates stayed at the pub for about an hour before finally deciding to leave.

"Let's go. Take me by Tommy's place before I drink too much and pass out." Val said to her friend. "He hasn't called back so maybe he's doing something with his fraternity brothers tonight."

As the two friends approached Tommy's apartment, they noticed that his car was parked in its usual space. *Hmm, somebody must have picked him up,* she thought as they approached the dark apartment.

"Well, since he's not here, I'll just wait on him to return. I know where they keep an extra key."

Only seconds after entering the dark apartment, Sarah tripped over a bar bell and nearly fell flat on her face in the cluttered living room. "I swear, men are so fucking filthy!" she exclaimed while catching her balance. "Do they have anything to drink here?" she asked.

"Frat boys? Of course they have something to drink. They may be intelligent frat boys, but they're still frat boys, right? Not that either of us need anything else to drink, but check the fridge. I'll be right back; I gotta go to the little girls' room."

"Please," her roommate said while looking around in disgust, "there *definitely* isn't a little girl's room in this pig sty. Make sure you take some Lysol with you to clean off the toilet seat!"

Just as Val reached the restroom she heard manly grunts and groans coming from Tommy's room. Val's hands immediately flew to cover her mouth. *This can't be,* she thought, *he's cheating on me?* The grunts grew louder and louder as she slowly approached the door. *I bet it's one of those whorish pom pom girls! I can't believe him!* Val said to herself as she grew more and more angry. As she opened the unlocked door, Val couldn't believe her eyes. Tommy and his sex partner were so enthralled with one another that they didn't even hear her come in.

"Ohhh, that's feels so good. Please, suck it, yes, suck it, suck it... Oh yeah Steve, that's so good man! You're the best Steve, Steve, ohh Steve!!!" Tommy grunted to his male partner who was hungrily sucking his manhood.

"Oh my God Val, what are you doing here?!" Tommy screamed as his eyes opened to see his shocked girlfriend staring at him wide-eyed.

"No wonder you haven't tried to have sex with me you bastard! I hope your freakin' cock falls off!" Valerie was so drunk that the entire situation seemed like a blur. Storming her way back through the mess, she felt somewhat relieved. She was starting to think that *she* was the reason Tommy never attempted to make love to her. The six drinks that she and Sarah had at Ray's would wait no longer.

"Val! What the hell are you doing?" Sarah couldn't believe her eyes as Valerie squatted and urinated right there in the middle of the living room.

"Piss on you Tommy Lawrence, you faggot!" Valerie screamed as the ladies laughed drunkenly and ran from the apartment.

Val spent the last few weeks of her freshman year in near seclusion. She attended class of course, but decided to stay out of Ray's Pub and the other places her friends frequented. This was partly since Sarah had blabbed the story about Tommy and Steve to just about anyone who would listen and partly because she had no one she could trust. The story spread like wildfire and there was nothing Val could do to quell the rumors. Eventually, she stopped speaking to Sarah, and did everything she could to avoid her. Humiliated and ashamed, Val nearly became a total recluse. She would wake up early each morning and jog to the rec center to workout. She wore her signature Stanford hat low on her head so that no one would recognize her. The treadmills became her best friends. She would blast music into her headphones and run for hours, completely zoning out everything around her.

Tommy was also unable to escape the madness of being caught in the bed with his best friend Steve. It wasn't long before he transferred to an Ivy League school and discreetly disappeared. Val also considered transferring to another university, but she had no desire to return to Alabama or anywhere remotely close. She decided she would tough it out. She knew that a degree from Stanford would be worth any humiliation she would face during her final years of college.

23

During the first few days of her junior year, Yolanda Stevens, a student from Ft. Lauderdale, Florida, became Valerie's first official "Black friend" at Stanford. Yolanda and Val had been assigned as roommates for their full sophomore term. Although the two young ladies grew up in totally separate worlds, they seemed to have a lot in common; from their love of sports and poetry, to shoes they couldn't really afford. After meeting Yolanda, Valerie began to question her parents' philosophies even more. Yolanda wasn't the lazy, baby-making Black woman her parents often mentioned. Yolanda actually studied harder than Val, and often motivated her to stay up late at night perfecting assignments. She had also been reared in a home with both of her parents; a father who served as an officer in the Marines, and a mother who taught elementary students for the better part of two decades. Val soon realized that everything she heard about Black people from her parents couldn't have been further from the truth.

Yolanda's mother and grandmother were proud members of Delta Kappa Alpha, a historically Black sorority founded in 1909. Since Yolanda was a little girl it was drilled in her head that she too would be a member of the "pink and gray" when she attended college. Valerie attended the Delta interest meeting with Yolanda. She didn't know what to expect, however, she was excited and anxious about the meeting. She had thought about joining one of the historically White sororities on campus, but none of them appealed to her. They all seemed to be about social status versus sisterhood. She also knew that whatever sorority she pledged, she'd probably be confronted with stories of her catching her ex-boyfriend Tommy and his fraternity brother in a compromising position.

"What are you wearing to the meeting tonight Val?" asked Yolanda.

"I'm thinking about wearing this nice pink and gray outfit I picked up the other day at Lenny's," Val replied.

"Girl, you *obviously* don't know a thing about Black sororities. Those girls would probably kill *both* of us if you show up in their sorority colors. Remember, we're a long way from being members, so we don't want to do anything to piss them off."

"Do you really think I have a shot of getting in the sorority Yolanda? I mean, I would be the first White girl to pledge a Black sorority on this campus."

"Well, my mother told me that there are several White women in the sorority who pledged at universities all over the country, so I think you definitely have a shot. Plus, you know I have my mother working on things behind the scenes," she said with a wink.

"I sure hope you're right," Val sighed.

After a long "underground" pledge process, Valerie arrived back in her hometown for Christmas vacation, decked out head to toe in pink and gray, Delta Kappa Alpha paraphernalia. She had endured the wrath of her big sisters and even some of her pledge sisters who openly questioned her commitment to Delta. Therefore, she wanted to display her passion for the organization as often as possible. This was her first visit back to Birmingham since the summer, and she realized she hadn't missed her hometown one bit. As usual, her mother and sister Kathy picked her up from the airport. Val and her father hadn't seen eye to eye since she decided to attend Stanford during her senior year in high school. Once he realized he could no longer control his daughter, the relationship slowly deteriorated. He never called her while she was away, and rarely spoke to her when she called home. Val was beginning to hate her father, and it was obvious to her that the feeling was mutual.

"Hi mom!" she yelled excitedly as her mother and sister pulled curbside to the baggage claim.

"Hey Val! How's my oldest girl doing?" her mom asked.

"Great Mom, Stanford is really great. I hope you can visit me some time soon."

"We'll see sweetie, we'll see. Hey, I like your new shirt...pretty colors. Are those Greek letters like with sororities? Did you join one of those fancy sororities out there at Stanford Val?" asked her mother.

"Hey Val, isn't that a *Black* sorority?" asked her sister, obviously trying to start trouble for Val.

"A Black sorority?" asked her mother looking at her DKA shirt as if it were now disease infested.

"Well, yes ma'am, my sorority was founded by 10 Black women, but now we have members of all colors and nationalities."

"What in the hell are they teaching you out there in California girl?" asked her mother.

"Mom, please don't start," Val replied with a frown on her face.

"Your father will not approve of this Val," her mother added while looking at her daughter's shirt once more. "We probably shouldn't tell him."

Valerie's parents both grew up in rural Alabama during the height of the Civil Rights struggle. Val could not tell if they were racists simply because that was all they knew, or if they simply chose to be that way because they actually hated all Black, Asian, and Hispanic people. She had never felt any of the bad feelings her parents and grandparents felt towards Blacks and members of other races. She liked everyone. Her best friend all through elementary school was a little Black girl named Charlotte Little. However, after Val's father found out the friend his little girl wanted to invite to a slumber party was Black, she was forbidden from even talking to Charlotte anymore. She often wondered what became of her dear elementary school friend.

"Val!" her father yelled, obviously agitated about the news he'd heard from Val's mother. "Are you trying to embarrass me, embarrass this family? It's not enough that you have a nigger roommate, but now you're in a nigger sorority too?! Well I may as well start planting the watermelons, huh?"

"Well, hello to you too Daddy, and please don't use that word around me!" Val replied defensively. *I should have known mother would tell him. She never could keep a secret from him. I bet she didn't even let him sit down before she told him,* Val thought as her father continued to berate her.

"I can say any damn thing I want to, this is my house young lady! NIGGER! NIGGER! NIGGER!!! I didn't raise you to go off and start mixing with black mongrels! Hell, the next thing you know you'll have a nigger boyfriend too! And then comes the baby porch monkeys and I'll be Grandpa Coon! I'm very disappointed in you Val."

"And I'm very disappointed in you too Daddy. I just can't take this anymore! I'll be leaving in the morning."

"Why wait until the morning? I think you should leave now," replied her father.

"Daddy, I would like to spend at least one night with my sister. I'll leave in the morning like I said. I'll go stay with Auntie Jamie Lynn."

"You obviously think you're grown enough now to disrespect your father and this family. So maybe it's time for you to be out on your own. I won't allow this anymore. If you cannot play by my rules, you cannot stay under my roof, not even for another night."

"Fine Daddy," she replied as the tears welled up in her eyes. Although she was sad, Val knew it was the best thing for both of them. She made up her mind that if her father wanted to ever see her again, he would have to find his way to California. She had outgrown Birmingham, and her father's ignorant racist ways.

Valerie decided that she would spend the remainder of her college years avoiding her southern roots and backwards parents as much as possible. She had adapted to California quite well and decided that she would try something new after graduation. She had not spoken to her father directly for over six months. And as usual, her last conversation with him ended in an argument. She did however, speak to her mother every week or so, as well as her younger sister who was about to graduate from high school and head off to college herself. Val just hoped that her sister hadn't been too brainwashed by their father, and would find her own way out of Birmingham as soon as possible.

24

Although Val had seen Bobby Jackson in passing on campus from time to time, she actually met him for the first time face to face at the on-campus mall, the only on-campus shopping mall in the country. The mall had become the most popular hang out spot at Stanford. Bobby and a few of his teammates were at the mall scoping out the young ladies. Bobby spotted Valerie while she was exiting her favorite store, Nordstrom's. Although Bobby was fully aware of the pressures associated with dating a White woman, Valerie was so stunning he could care less what anyone thought about his attraction to her.

Bobby Jackson was brought up in inner city Oakland, but his upbringing was not much different from Val's. Bobby was the offspring of radical Black parents and was raised to despise "the white man." Bobby's father was a freshman at Southern Cal in Los Angeles during the riot in 1968. He loved the reaction he got from people when he told them he was Michael Jackson's nephew. Of course he had mastered the pop star's dance moves to provide what seemed to be further evidence of his association with his "uncle."

"Excuse me," Bobby said while approaching Valerie, "Is your name Valerie? You're a DKA right?"

"Yes," Valerie responded, trying not to blush, "Do I know you… I mean, how do you know my name?"

"Whoever doesn't know who you are must have been hiding under a rock the past year. You made history all across the country as the first White woman to pledge DKA at Stanford. I remember seeing your picture in the school newspaper. Didn't they also do a story about you in *Ebony*?"

"They sure did," Val responded, impressed that Bobby knew so much about her. She recognized Bobby as well. Since the night her friend Sarah pointed him out at Ray's, for some reason, Bobby was never far from her thoughts. *Whoa, he's cute,* she thought to herself, realizing that this was the first time she actually admitted being attracted to a man of color. Although she had pledged a historically Black sorority, she still had not taken the "leap" to the other side with Black men. She didn't think her mom and dad could handle the double whammy of having a daughter in a Black sorority who dated Black guys. That would kill them for sure.

"Man, you got a ton of stuff!" Bobby laughed. "You need some help getting to the car with all that?"

"Sure," Val replied, "My parking space isn't very close, so I hope you don't mind."

"Nah, I don't mind. I will have to charge you a small fee though," he replied with a chuckle.

"Oh yeah?" she replied flirtatiously, still trying to keep her composure.

"Yep. You have to give me your phone number or I'll have to leave all this stuff in the middle of the parking lot."

All at once, a million thoughts went through Val's head: *Oh my gosh, he wants my number! Should I give it to him? He is so cute. My Dad would KILL me. How would Yolanda feel if he calls me? I bet he's a great kisser. Of all the girls on campus, why does he want MY number?*

Bobby's voice startled her. "Ahem! So do I get the number or do I have to leave you here unguarded with a million dollars worth of new clothes?" he asked.

"Well, I don't really have a choice then, do I? It's 485-9807."

"Whewwwww! I was hoping you'd take door number one, I'd hate to leave a beautiful woman in distress." Bobby said grinning. *Man, she is so fly. My mother would die if she knew about this, but she'd probably kill me first,* he said to himself.

Bobby and Val's friendship blossomed over the next few months. And contrary to what her father had told her about Blacks, especially Black men, Bobby was a class act. He was hardworking, intelligent and sincere. What was so ironic was that now, two of Val's closest friends were African-American. Everyone *assumed* that Val and Bobby were more than just friends, but they both knew the truth. And though the physical attraction had always been there, they managed to keep the relationship platonic. There were many late night study sessions where Bobby would agonize over not being able to touch her. Instead, he'd have to talk to the growing erection in his basketball shorts, telling it that he and Val were only friends. They both dated other people during their last two years in college, but they often found themselves jealous of their respective mates. Val would bite her tongue when Bobby asked her to explain things to him about his girlfriend Gina, from a "woman's point of view." Val treasured her friendship with Bobby partly because he was proof that there were life lessons she had to learn for herself.

Val enjoyed being away from Alabama, but she still encountered her share of problems regarding race on campus. Although she was in California, being the only White member of a Black sorority who was also good friends with one of the most popular Black men on campus was proving to be more difficult than she thought. After the nostalgia of making history as a Delta wore off and the publicity slowed, Val had to learn to live with her sorority sisters on a daily basis.

"What's up with the White women stealing all our men Val?" her sorority sister, Lynne asked off-handedly. "I mean, you're dating Bobby Jackson, one of our most eligible brothas on the yard. What's up with *that*?"

"Lynne, I am not dating Bobby Jackson. Who started that rumor?"

"Please Valerie, don't try to act all innocent with that 'who started that rumor' bullshit!" Lynne snapped.

"Yeah, it's true that Bobby is the first Black guy I've ever been friends with, but we aren't dating. My parents are so racist that they'd die if they knew."

"Ahhh, I see, you're on some rebellious shit, sticking it to your parents, playing around with the brothas until you feel like it's time to go back and play with the White boys again."

"Damn, I thought we were supposed to be *sisters* Lynne?"

"You are *not* my sister, girlfriend. I didn't even vote for your ass. If it were up to me, you would have never got into my sorority. Believe that! Hell, my aunt was a founding member of her chapter on her campus. When I told her we were pledging a White girl, she damn near lost her mind. And I can't blame her to be honest. First we let you in, then you steal our men, and the next thing you know, you'll want to run the whole damn organization."

"Wow Lynne, I can't believe you feel like that."

"Well believe it!" Lynne said rudely. "Lil' Miss KKK, now you're all liberated and shit because you hang out with us 'Black folks'? Gimme a fuckin' break! Why don't you just admit that you want to be Black? Just say it."

"I never said I wanted to be Black, Lynne."

"You don't have to, it's obvious. I just hope I'm there when you dump Bobby and go back to lily-white land where you came from. There's no way you want him just as a friend. It's probably just like with the sorority, it's all a fad to you. You may have the other Deltas fooled, but I don't buy it. Never have, never will…"

Lynne's words cut Valerie's heart like a sharp, unapologetic knife. Why did the words hurt so bad? Was Lynne right? What would she do when the challenge of dating Bobby, if he asked her, reared its ugly head? Would she stick it out or retreat like Lynne said? As Val walked across campus from the Delta sorority house to the residence hall she suddenly felt all alone. *No one understands me,* she thought. *Bobby is my friend! I don't care what Lynne or anyone else says. Yeah, but you know you wouldn't mind more than friendship, so why haven't you told him?* A voice in her head nagged. *You're scared of your parents aren't you?* the voice continued. *I know, I know, but they would never understand. NEVER.* She continued to battle with the voices in her head until her cell phone rang suddenly.

"Hello?"

"Val, hey it's me Kathy," answered her sister.

"Oh, hey sis, what are you up to?"

"Val, I have something to tell you. It's about Daddy."

"Don't tell me. Are *your* parents giving you the business about where you're going to college again? How is our asshole of a father doing anyway?"

"Daddy… Daddy…" Kathy stuttered, trying to hold back her tears.

"Kathy, what's wrong? Are you okay? What about Daddy? What did he do? Tell me!"

"Val, he's dead. Daddy's gone, you gotta come home."

25

Valerie and Yolanda arrived in Birmingham from California on the eve of her father's funeral. Val knew that she and Yolanda would probably not be able to stay at her house. She was apprehensive about bringing her, but Yolanda was a big part of her life now and she needed the support.

Val was nervous the moment the Boeing 747 touched down. She was relieved that her sister Kathy was picking them up from the airport rather than her mother. She had told her mother that she was bringing a friend home; but failed to mention that the friend she was bringing was Black. When they arrived home, Val felt the beads of sweat swell up in her hands the same way it did when she had to give presentations in class. She had actually grown more concerned about her family's reaction to Yolanda than to the reason she was actually home in the first place, her father's funeral.

As Val entered the foyer, the familiar smell of vanilla candles mixed with southern fried chicken, filled the air. Val's mother was known for her fried chicken and catfish dinners. Family members urged her mother to take a break and relax; but Linda would do nothing of the sort. Since her husband's death, she had gone on "auto pilot;" making arrangements for the funeral, calling friends and family members, and preparing food. Everyone feared that Linda would have an emotional breakdown after the funeral or even worse, at any moment.

Val had rarely spoken to either of her parents since her run in with her father during the Christmas she was thrown out of the house. When Val first saw her mother, neither of them knew what to do. After an awkward moment of silence the two finally embraced. Val turned to introduce Yolanda to her mother.

"Mom, this is Yolanda. Yolanda, Mom."

"Pleased to meet you Mrs. Robinson," Yolanda said as she moved to hug Val's mother. The entire house came to a grinding halt and time seemed to stand still. Charlie was surely rolling over in his casket at this point

"Are you crazy bringing that nigger in this house?" Mrs. Robinson yelled.

"Mother, don't speak about my friend like that!" Val was as angry as she was embarrassed.

"You get her out of here now and I mean it!" Her mother screamed, as she stormed up the stairs.

Aunt Ruth, one of her mother's sisters, was in the kitchen fixing food for everyone. She was a large woman who obviously hadn't missed many meals.

"Here dear," Aunt Ruth said to Yolanda while handing her a plate of food. "I'm sure you like *chicken* right?" Aunt Ruth said, not realizing the stereotypical implication.

"Thanks but no thanks. I think I'll be leaving." Yolanda was offended. She was well aware of how Val had been raised but that was no excuse. "Val I'll be at the hotel, you just call me if you need anything. I'm sorry and I'll be praying for you. I love you."

As the girls hugged, tears welled up in Val's eyes. She couldn't believe the insensitive display by her mother. "Yolanda, please forgive my mother. You know how my parents are, but you also know that you're my best friend don't you?...and I love you. I'll call you after the funeral."

The funeral was the next morning, so Mrs. Robinson decided to retire early. Val didn't know if she was truly exhausted or upset about her bringing Yolanda to their home. However, it didn't matter to her. She had never been close to her father. As far as Val was concerned, Yolanda was the closest relative she never had in the Robinson family.

The funeral service lasted only a short time. Charlie was a simple man, and the service reflected just that. After the service, family members and friends returned to the Robinson house to eat yet again and to reminisce. Val's uncles told their favorite stories about them growing up on the farm in southern Alabama, while occasionally forgetting that Yolanda was nearby. The insensitive statements didn't bother Yolanda much though. No one said anything to her directly and she was just glad that she was allowed to be there for her friend during her time of need.

Later in the evening after most of their company departed, Val finally got a chance to talk more with her mother. Her mother had been distant towards her, even more distant than usual. She was hoping that her father's death would bring them closer together.

"Mom, are you okay?" Val asked.

"Of course I'm not okay Valerie. In case you didn't notice, I buried my husband today."

"Yes mother, I know. But he's in a better place now."

"A better place? You call being in a cold grave six feet in the ground a better place?!"

"Mother, you've hardly said two nice words to me since I arrived. What's going on?" Val asked.

"Val, you've always been a very difficult child. And I always tried to be a buffer between you and your father for the good of the family. But I cannot believe you disrespected him by... You know he would not approve of what you did. I cannot believe you had the nerve to bring..." her mother stopped mid-sentence.

"A nigger to Daddy's funeral? Go ahead and say it Mother. You cannot believe I brought a nigger to my father's funeral. Why don't you just go ahead and say it?! Say it mother!!! Say it!!!"

"That's right, a nigger. Your father always told you how they were, and even after one of them killed your father you still..."

"What are you talking about?" Val interrupted. "What are you talking about mother?"

"Your father was on his way home late last Thursday, from your Uncle Jeb's house and pulled over to change a tire that had blown out. Some nigger robbed him then shot him in cold blood. That nigger killed my husband in cold blood." Mrs. Robinson's heart ached like never before. As her mother wept, Val sat in complete and utter disbelief.

Val was numb. *Was her father right about Blacks? Had she misjudged Bobby? Was it just a matter of time before he turned on her?* Val was confused more than ever before.

Val was an emotional wreck after her father's death. She hated that he died without ever having a relationship with her. She hated even more that he was killed by a Black man.

When she returned to school, she told Bobby that she needed space. It was too confusing and difficult for her to retain her relationship with him, while dealing with the demons of her father's death. After all, it was a Black man that had taken her father's life. Bobby hated it but he promised to be there when she was ready to resume their friendship.

26

After receiving her B.A. degree, in Communications, Val decided to move to the Miami area, where she and Yolanda set their sights on owning a public relations and marketing firm. The friends were closer than ever especially after they were both accepted to the MBA program at Florida Atlantic University. They even worked together, both receiving internships with the Disney Corporation while working on their Master's degrees.

Val was haunted by the memory of her father, and the disappointment of her mother. She could still hear him, "Marry your own kind and have beautiful white babies!" Unfortunately, the selection seemed sparse in the area. She could barely stomach any of her colleagues, let alone date one. So it wasn't surprising that she reluctantly took a girlfriend up on an offer to be "set-up" on a blind date. Her friend promised that she wouldn't be disappointed.

Although she didn't know *what* to expect, she knew exactly *who* to expect. Her girlfriend Rhonda, an attorney at a sports firm, claimed to be helping a new client become acclimated to the city. Ultimately, Val knew she was being used. Rhonda wanted a beautiful woman to entertain a powerful client – a client by the name of Johnny Royal. Johnny was a rookie quarterback for the Miami Sharks. He was a Southern Cal graduate that had broken all the passing records during his four years there. Since Val was an avid college football enthusiast, she had followed the USC football program and Johnny's career during his last two years of college. After all, her beloved Stanford Cardinal football team just didn't have the flash and dash of the mighty USC Trojans. Tyrone Willingham had single-handedly put Stanford football on the map, but it still did not compare to the pro-style USC program.

Val arrived at Stone Crab Shack about 30 minutes before the date was scheduled. She wanted a little extra time to relax and clear her mind, a ritual she adopted before every new encounter. Not to mention, it allowed her to get a head start on the cocktails. After dinner, they planned to go to Opium; an exclusive night spot where one of Johnny's teammates was having a private party.

Val was absolutely stunning. She had taken no shortcuts in preparing for her new suitor. After all, she was meeting an NFL quarterback, a rookie who probably had more women throwing themselves at him than he could stand. She knew she had to be exceptionally sexy. She spent over two hours at the elite "Chloe Milan" salon on South Beach, getting her hair, nails and make-up perfected. Her turquoise and green Chanel dress intensified the hues of her blue eyes, and exposed every voluptuous curve on her body. Her sexy sandals were her biggest splurge, a pair of Stella McCartney's that she just had to have. She had invested two paychecks into one night, but she hoped it'd be worth every penny.

Val was fully aware that she was causing a scene, staring seductively into the eyes of all the men that were watching her while she cat-walked her way to the bar. Val was one of those women that made everyone stare, even other women. As the brothas at Stanford said, she was a White woman with a Black woman's body. White women envied her and sistas hated on her – big time. Val was the dichotomy men desired but could rarely handle; she was capable of conducting a high-powered meeting in one instance, then fucking a co-worker's brains out on the conference room table the next.

I hope this guy isn't an arrogant asshole, she thought to herself as she slowly sipped on her chocolate martini. She had dated her fair share of those and was just about fed up with dating altogether. She hoped he'd at least be able to hold a decent conversation with her before trying to take her home. But, she wasn't naive in the least. Val knew that many of the NFL players, especially the younger ones could be a handful. Most of them had access to everything they wanted, V.I.P. treatment, people kissing their asses from the time they woke up in the morning until the time they went to bed. Then of course there are the women, TONS of women in all shapes, colors, and sizes. How could a young player not get caught up in such hype?

My goodness, no wonder the ladies love this guy so much Val thought as the 6'4 blonde Adonis approached the table. Johnny's blue pin striped suit fit him perfectly. His broad muscular shoulders bulged through the expensive fabric of the suit as the aqua blue shirt he wore underneath brought out his piercing blue eyes even more. As she rose to shake Johnny's hand, he grasped her hand tightly and pulled her close to him for a friendly hug. The smell of his after-shave nearly made her forget that she was there for business.

"I don't do the handshake thing," he said as he released her from his grasp.

Johnny didn't lack confidence in the least, but there was something different about him. Although things

204

seemed to come easy for Johnny on the football field, his life off the field was quite different.

Johnny grew up in the home of a high school coach who taught each of his four sons the art of football. As the second son born into the Royal family, Johnny could throw a football farther than many boys twice his age. Johnny's father was Dan Royal. Dan Royal's Hall High Tiger football teams had become a household name, winning five straight high school championships. His own four sons starred on several of his teams, each earning a Division I football scholarship. Competition inside the household was intense as all the Royal boys spent their youth trying to please their father.

Although Johnny was the most athletically talented Royal boy, his father treated him badly. Maybe he thought Johnny underachieved athletically. Maybe it was because he was his mother's favorite child whom she doted on constantly. Whatever it was, Johnny quickly learned that he was often the victim of his father's wrath. He hated it when Hall High lost football games because he knew that would lead to Dan yelling at his mother or even worse, his father getting drunk and taking it out on him. To minimize his father's abuse, Johnny trained harder and harder each year, becoming obsessed with perfecting his game, especially when he began quarterbacking his dad's high school team. He often stayed on the practice field working on drills long after the rest of the team had showered and gone home. Johnny knew that the only way to please his father was to win and win big.

Despite his father's negativity, Johnny thrived both on and off the football field. He was not only an All-

American quarterback; he was also Academic All-American during his junior and senior years in college. He ended his college career as the MVP of the "Granddaddy of them all," the Rose Bowl in Pasadena. Although he did not win the Heisman Trophy, he was one of the five finalists who traveled to New York City for the awards ceremony. Despite his father's conspicuous absence from the ceremony (he said he had to break down film for his high school team's state semi-final game), his mother and two of his brothers were front row center.

Even though all of his brothers attended college on scholarship, Johnny was the only Royal boy to play professional football, which seemed to irk his father even more. He could still hear his father's words echoing in his head a few days after the Miami Sharks made him the 10th overall selection in the NFL Draft.

"Johnny, just remember, even though you're a big time professional, you're no better than your brothers. Hell, as a matter of fact, you might be the worst of all my sons. You just got the break, so don't think you're special. Now, your brother Eddie, *he*'s a player. Now he should've been the first rounder," his father would say.

"Thanks Dad," Johnny would respond sarcastically. "You always know just what to say. You know, it's amazing that no matter what I do, it's never enough for you, is it? If I throw three touchdown passes you'll say I should have thrown four. If I don't throw any interceptions you say it was only because the offensive line protected me well. Nothing has ever been good enough has it Dad?"

"Oh stop your whining Mr. NFL!" responded his father.

"You know I finally figured out why Mom killed herself," Johnny said as he looked intently into his father's eyes. "To get away from you." If Johnny wasn't careful, the pressure of his father's standards and the feelings of "abandonment" caused by his mother's death would prove fatal if he continued to pretend that the feelings didn't exist.

Dinner with Johnny went much better than expected. Unlike 99% of the men she dated in the past, Johnny appeared to be an open-book. He communicated well and said exactly what he felt. Val found his openness and honesty refreshing, especially compared to the Hollywood types she spent time with at work and in social settings. Johnny was not only physically attractive; but he also spoke three languages, which satisfied her need for intellectual stimulation. The fact that he knew exactly which fork to use to eat his dinner salad was also a plus. He even schooled her on the menus fancy delicacies. Val felt that he was either the perfect man or the greatest con man she had ever met. The first "business" dinner led to more dinners, which led to more meetings and dates. Val was finally opening herself up to a man again. Between her father and her ex-boyfriend Tommy, who she was sure was openly gay by now, and some low lifes she dated after college, Val's luck with men left a lot to be desired. However, Johnny Royal changed all that. Johnny was not only extremely handsome; he was charming and spontaneous as well. He helped crack the shell that seemed to surround Val. Val quickly transformed into the fantasy woman that any man would crave. Val would do anything

Johnny wanted to do. His fondest memory was of an excursion they had at a matinee.

Because the movie started around 1:00 p.m. during a weekday, the film was sparsely attended. Since Johnny's fame often led to mob-like scenes, he wore a baseball cap and sunglasses to the theater. The couple had mastered the art of showing up right after the movie previews. That way they could slip into the movie and sit in the last couple of rows without being noticed.

The movie bored both of them, so Val decided to spice things up a bit. Johnny was dozing off - a combination of him being tired from off-season mini-camp workouts and the dull flick – however; he became fully alert when he felt his wife's hand caressing the shaft of his penis. Val loved the way she could make Johnny obey her every wish when it came to sex. Like most men, the head below his waist was more than willing to oblige. Johnny could barely maintain his composure as his wife's warm lips replaced her hand.

"Oh shit Val," he whispered, "what are you doing down there?"

"You know what I'm doing down here," she answered without missing a beat. "You like that?" she asked.

"Hell yeah, you know I do," he answered while closing his eyes and allowing his wife to take total control.

Like many women, Val had mastered the art of "the blowjob" in college because it was the ultimate compromise when it came to the boys on campus. They didn't care how you got them off, as long as you got them off somehow. So Val chose the lesser of two evils. She didn't sleep with all her college suitors, but she did like to please them.

"Ohhhh Val," Johnny moaned as his orgasm peeked. Val was a pro, swallowing without hesitation. Besides, he **was** her husband, and she'd do anything for him. Johnny's body convulsed as he gripped Val's silky, dark hair with both hands. She loved it when he lost control like that.

"Now look what you've done," she whispered to her husband. "Feel this," she said as she took Johnny's hand and guided it under her sundress.

"Oh shit, you don't have any panties on!"

"Why bother?" she answered as she began to caress Johnny's penis back to life.

"So this is why you like sitting in the back row huh?" he asked as Val's hand continued to stroke him. Johnny leaned his head back to enjoy his wife's skilled hand job. Val was on fire and quickly rose to straddle Johnny's legs with her back to him, hiked up her shamelessly short dress and ease down onto him. She used the backs of the two chairs in front of them for leverage as she bounced up and down on his lap.

Johnny caressed his wife's protruding nipples gently as she rode him into ecstasy. The couple could hardly keep quiet as an older gentleman in his mid-60's turned to check out the show in the back of the theater. They hardly noticed the other couple who left in a huff, obviously offended by what was happening.

"We better get out of here," Johnny said after his second orgasm, "Somebody is going to get security if we don't stop."

"Okay sweetie, we can leave, but only if we can continue this later."

"Deal!" Johnny said as they exited through the side door of the theater.

27

After a couple years of exciting marriage to Miami's hottest sports superstar, Valerie began to grow tired of the galas and stuffy dinners she was forced to attend with Johnny. Endorsers, agents, and other people were constantly trying to wine and dine her husband, and of course he wanted his beautiful wife to be with him. Val spent much of her time shopping for designer gowns and setting up appointments to have her husband fitted for custom suits. The rest her time was spent meeting and greeting every Tom, Dick and Harry vying for her husband's attention.

I swear, I've spent half my life at these stupid parties, she thought to herself. *Why do I have to always go anyway? He's only going to leave me by myself as soon as we get there anyway.*

"Johnnnnyyyyyy!" yelled his agent as they arrived at the plush mansion of AccuSport representative Tom McDonald. "I have a ton of people I need to introduce you to. Oh, hi Val, how are you tonight, dear?"

"I'm fine Drew, how are you?" she asked as if she really cared. Just as she had predicted, Drew whisked Johnny off to meet AccuSport's "check-signers." AccuSport was quickly making a name for itself as the hottest new sports drink. Johnny was the company's first superstar endorsee, hence the *royal* treatment at all their highly publicized events.

Val knew the routine all too well. She predicted she wouldn't see her husband for at least another hour, so she made her way to the sprawling buffet. *If I eat another shrimp, I'm going to turn into one,* she joked to herself. *Where's the bar?*

"Valerie! Valerie Robinson. Is that you?" a male voice called across the room.

Oh God, I knew someone would recognize me here, she mumbled under her breath. *Can't a girl just enjoy her friggin' shrimp and cocktails in peace for God's sake?*

"Valerie!" the voice continued.

Who is this bozo who keeps calling my name? Just as she turned to address the annoying voice, her eyes met a handsome familiar face.

Oh my God, she said to herself as goose bumps began to rise on her arms.

"Bobby Jackson!" she squealed attempting to maintain her composure.

"Hey Val! What in the world are you doing here?" Bobby asked.

"I could ask you the same thing Mister," she replied as she dropped her plate on the table to hug her old friend."

"Well you know I played for the Lakers a couple of seasons, but when I became a free agent the Heat offered me a contract I couldn't refuse, and so here I am. I moved here last week."

"And tonight?"

"Oh, oh why am I *here?*" Bobby asked as he smiled boyishly. "The marketing company I'm with has been trying to get me to sign an endorsement deal with AccuSport for the past few months and I'm finally thinking about caving in."

"So, you're basically here to get some ego stroking and ass kissing?"

"Basically." The two laughed at his response.

"Their executives are persistent as hell, it's like you really don't have a choice but to sign with them," she said as she remembered their very first meeting at the mall in Palo Alto, when she lamely said that she had no *choice* but to give him her phone number. Bobby was thinking the same thing, but didn't miss a beat in filling the gaps of the exchange.

"To say the least. But it's ok, for a minute I didn't think anyone would be pursuing me, especially after my contract ended. By the way, how do you know so much about the company?"

"Well, my husband has an endorsement deal with them."

"Your husband?" Bobby said, trying not to display his disappointment.

"Johnny Royal, you know, quarterback extraordinaire," she said rolling her eyes. "I don't even know why I'm here."

"Of course I know Johnny Royal, he's the best QB in the league right now. I'm sure he's getting a lot more ego stroking and ass kissing than I am. In fact, do you see anyone trying to show me around?" Bobby said with a chuckle.

"I didn't mean to be insensitive, or to sound ungrateful, but it's like signing your soul to the devil when you sign with these big companies. They expect you to show up to everything they put their name on, and that means taking time away from your family. I mean even though we came together, I still feel like I'm here by myself."

"Yeah, I can understand how you feel.

"So what about you Bobby, where's your significant other? Didn't you end up marrying Sharrie Starks?" quizzed Val.

"Yep, married and divorced all within 18 months," he replied. "I guess being married to a guy who wasn't drafted, and barely made NBA league minimum, didn't give her the glamorous life she expected -and you know how expensive California is. Of course, now that I've gotten a fat new contract, she's ringing my phone off the hook. I guess this would be the perfect time to change all of my phone numbers."

"Bobby I'm sorry, I shouldn't have asked you about that."

"It's okay, you didn't know. Life's a trip huh?"

"It sure is," Val replied while catching a glimpse of her husband as he whizzed past her on his way to shake more hands.

Bobby and Valerie spent the next hour reminiscing on their Stanford experience. While they were obviously attracted to one another in college, neither of them were willing to put their personal demons aside to engage in anything more than a friendship. So they were stuck, admiring one another from afar, neither of them brave enough to defy what they had been taught.

"Bobby, I need to apologize. I never should have stopped talking to you. After my father was killed, I just had a lot of mixed emotions and guilt."

"Valerie I understood then and I understand now. We all have to learn to trust our heart on our own terms, and like I told you then, true friends will always be there."

Val couldn't believe how amazing he was, he was more than any woman could pray for.

Bobby was still just as infatuated with her now as he was in college. *Her eyes are still as pretty as ever,* Bobby thought to himself as he tried not to stare. *He still looks the same as he did in college. He is so gorgeous. I bet the women are all over him. I know I would be,* she said to herself as she caught Bobby gazing into her eyes.

"So, what are you thinking about Bobby? You look like you have something on your mind," Val asked.

"Oh, nothing really, I was just thinking about how pretty your eyes are," he replied without thinking. *I can't believe I just said that!*

"Oh really? Well, you haven't changed a bit since college yourself," she replied.

"I'll take that as a compliment," Bobby returned.

"You should…" she replied with a smile as Johnny interrupted their conversation.

"Hey babe, I'm sorry for leaving you alone for so long. You know how these things go," Johnny offered as he kissed her cheek.

"Honey," she said, "I want you to meet Bobby Jackson. We went to college together."

"This man needs no introduction," said Johnny, "everyone knows who the King of the court is. Welcome to Miami Bobby, we're glad to have you here. The Heat finally did something smart, I see. I hear you'll be joining the AccuSport team as well? And a little birdie told me," Johnny began to whisper, "…that you're the top basketball prospect the company is pursuing. They figure they won't have to worry about any off the court problems with a stand-up guy like you."

"Well thanks man, I'm definitely considering it," said Bobby. "Besides the contract, the stuff actually tastes pretty good, so I'm looking forward to my free supply." Johnny said jokingly.

"Just let me know if you need any info about the company. I've been doing so many damn commercials and parties I feel like a salesman."

"Will do, Johnny." "Well, I better get out of here. I have an early morning workout. It was nice meeting you Johnny, and it was nice seeing you again Val."

"Same here Bobby," replied Val as she reached to grasp his hand. As Johnny turned to walk away, Val could feel herself gripping Bobby's hand as if she could not let it go. "Maybe we'll run into each other again soon," she said.

"I'd like that," Bobby replied. "As a matter of fact, I'd like that a lot. Please stay in touch," he said as he handed her his signature Bobby Jackson business card. "Don't lose that."

"I won't."

Miami was nothing like Palo Alto. Everything about South Florida overwhelmed Val; the traffic, the multitude of people, and most of all, her husband's fame. What bothered her most wasn't the fact that he could hardly eat dinner in peace at a restaurant without being asked for his autograph, but that his fame was a total invasion of *her* privacy. Gone were the days of total anonymity where she could throw on a sweat suit, a ball cap and hit the mall with reckless abandon. These days she had to be dressed to impress just to visit the local market. She and Johnny had been unofficially crowned the new hot couple in town, and everyone wanted a piece of them. She still could not get used to opening up the tabloids and seeing her face splashed across the page. Her personal "favorite," was the tabloid that pictured her with her sister and her two best friends entering a trendy eatery. The headline read, "Princess Royal and Her Court." Although her sister seemed to enjoy the publicity, the headline made Val cringe.

"Did you see the new Empire article?" she asked her sister Kathy over the telephone.

"Yeah, I saw it. Pretty cool stuff. I just wish I had been wearing my little short skirt that the boys like so much. I'd probably have a thousand voice mail messages by now," her sister said with a laugh.

"I see that *somebody* is enjoying all this annoying attention," replied Val with a sigh.

"Dang right I'm enjoying it. And you should too," said Kathy. "Live a little will ya? You graduated from one of the top schools in the world, you're rich, you're about to have your MBA, and now you're married to the hottest, most popular quarterback in football. Did I mention that you are REE-OTCH, BEE-OTCH! What else do you want? What else could any woman want?" Kathy blurted, obviously urbanized since moving from Alabama.

"*Bobby,*" Val said under her breath to herself.

"Huh?" asked Kathy, "I didn't understand what you said."

"Oh nothing Kathy, I just lost my thought."

"Well, if you would stop clouding your mind with unnecessary stress, then you might enjoy some of what you have. Heck, you could be back there in Birmingham married to Billy Joe Hunter, the guy who chased you all the way through high school."

"Ugh!" Val replied with a laugh, "now that would be awful. Thanks for the inspiration sis!"

"Anytime, ... anytime. Just remember, whenever you get weirded out about seeing your picture in magazines and stuff, think about Billyy Joe and the six kids you guys would have out on the farm," she said with a cackle.

"Kathy you are one of a kind."

"Yes I am dear sister. Now get out there and make some more headlines!"

"Yes Ma'am!" she replied. "Bye sis, I love you."

"I love you too, Val."

"Hey, by the way, how's mom doing?"

"Why don't you call her yourself and find out?"

"I may just do that."

"You should. I think she'd like that."

"I don't know, it's been a long time since I talked to her."

"Well, your birthday is coming up. Maybe this is a good time for the two of you talk. Neither of you is getting any younger."

"I know, but Daddy's been gone a while and I think she's breaking away from some of the influence that he had on her."

"I sure hope so. She needs to find out what it is *she* stands for."

"Well, just think about calling her okay?"

"Okay, I'll do that for *you*," responded Val.

"No, don't do it for me, do it for *you* Val."

28

Val awoke on her birthday on a natural high. She had finally decided to stop dwelling on the negative things in her life; her poor relationship with her mother and deceased father, her husband's absence from their home, and instead focus on all the good things that were going on. After all, how many poor girls from Alabama were living the life she was living out in sunny South Florida?

Even though Val knew her time with her husband would be limited on her birthday, she planned the day around him.

Okay, I'll make us breakfast in bed, call work to make sure I don't have any important messages, get a manicure, meet Johnny for lunch if he can squeeze it in, shop, and then maybe get a quick massage. PERFECT, she thought as she went over her mental check-list. Johnny was still asleep, so Val threw on his favorite negligee and rushed downstairs to prepare breakfast to surprise him. Even though it was her birthday, she fixed all of Johnny's favorite foods. Val was a progressive, independent woman, but she was also a throwback Southern Belle who knew her way around the kitchen. She prepared fried chicken breasts, bacon, mushroom and cheese omelets, blueberry pancakes, and her signature coffee. She bounced around the kitchen as if she were 15 again. Life was good and she was enjoying her newfound attitude.

When the food was ready, Val prepared a tray to take up to her husband. She was hoping he was still asleep so that she could slide into the sexy pumps he loved so much. She knew that the lingerie she was wearing would lead to something after breakfast, or that breakfast would be skipped altogether. Just as she poured him a tall glass of orange juice, she was startled by her husband's presence.

"Morning Babe," said Johnny as he pulled his tight Sharks t-shirt over his sculptured chest and abs. "I'm headed to my meeting."

"Meeting? It's Tuesday. You don't have to work on Tuesdays," Val responded with a frown.

"Remember Babe? I told you last week that Coach was going to start acting crazy and sure enough, he called a special "quarterbacks only" meeting for this morning. He wanted some extra preparation since we're playing a blitzing team on Sunday. So he's making us meet him at the complex in 45 minutes. I gotta get out of here or I'll be late."

"Then be late. I'll make it worth your while," she replied seductively, and eased behind him as he opened the enormous kitchen pantry door to search for something he could eat in the car. Johnny's body was a perfect sculptured mass of muscle that any woman would love. Her hands quickly found his massive chest under his t-shirt. She knew he could not resist when she caressed his sensitive nipples and kissed the back of his neck. The smell of his freshly showered body and the aftershave he wore, drove her absolutely crazy. Val was already turned on while preparing breakfast and thinking about the possibilities afterwards. She wanted him in the worst way. It seemed like it had been ages since she and her husband had made love. At this point, making love wasn't even that important, she'd take a good fuck instead. She had grown tired of getting herself off with her favorite number two "guy," the showerhead.

"Ohh," Johnny hissed as his nipples hardened under his wife's expert touch. "You know I like that, don't you?" he asked.

"Umm hmm," she answered as her tongue licked the lower part of his earlobe. She allowed her right hand to ease into Johnny's loose-fitting black sweat pants. She loved it when he wore his sweats because of the easy access. As she cornered her husband near the pantry she remembered how naughty they had been in the movie theatre during the early days of their relationship. However, today would be much different.

"Val, Val, will you please move so I can get to work!"

Val quickly realized that on this day, however, the theater encounter was a long, distant memory. She felt like she was losing her touch, since she couldn't even distract her husband from a meeting that probably wasn't even mandatory.

"Val, I'd love to stay here and finish this," Johnny said as she continued to paw at him.

"But?" Val asked.

"But, I can't be late this time. Coach would fine me God knows how much for being late today. The guy is so anal right now, I can't chance that. Just to prove a point he would probably bench me. And I need to be in the game baby. We can't win if I'm not in there. Plus, I'm trying to wrap up my $100,000 bonus this weekend for completed passes. So, I *have* to go Babe."

"Baby, I haven't seen you in months it seems."

"Don't exaggerate Val. I'm at this house every night that I'm in town, unlike a lot of husbands we know."

"You sure are, but you go straight upstairs to watch game film or you fall asleep on me."

"There you go, complaining again. You are never satisfied."

"Don't start Johnny, just go to your stupid meeting."

"Stupid? I bet it won't be as stupid when I get the $100,000 and you go out and spend it all in a weekend," snapped Johnny.

"You bastard, how dare you!" replied Val.

"How dare *me*? How dare *you* for not being more appreciative of all I do for you!"

"All you do for me? What exactly do you do for me Johnny? Tell me something you do for me that doesn't cost money? You haven't even wished me happy birthday. It looks to me like you do a lot of things for yourself."

"What do you want from me Val?!"

"I want *you* Johnny, not the house, the cars, the trips, the money. Give me some attention. Can you do that? How about a little respect? A little affection every now and then would be good. I've always wanted *you*."

"Well, you have a fine way of showing it, starting an argument with me before I have to be at such an important meeting."

"Oh to hell with it, just go."

"That's what I was *trying* to do before you started in on me," snapped Johnny. "Don't worry about fixing dinner; I'll eat somewhere before I come home."

"Yeah, I bet you will."

"What is that supposed to mean Val?"

"You know what it's supposed to mean!"

Like many professional football stars, Johnny was not immune to the excesses of the NFL. He loved his wife, but that did not matter to all the women who were willing to ignore the fact that he was married. Johnny's good looks and visibility made him the quintessential "groupie magnet." Although he claimed to have never cheated on his wife, Val had encountered too much evidence to the contrary over the course of their two years of marriage. Everyone warned her not to marry an NFL rookie. She wished she had listened.

Val sat on her magnificent oversized bed, and rested her head on the mahogany headboard. *Bastard,* she thought.

RINGGGGGGGGGGGGGGGGGGG

"Hello?"

"Hey Val, it's me Yolanda. How are you doing today, birthday girl?!"

"Not too good. Johnny and I had a fight."

"Again?"

"Unfortunately," Val replied.

"Well, fuck that. It's your birthday...We gonna party like it's ya birthday...even though he don't give a fuck about your birthdaaaaay! Yolanda sung into the phone. And you know what it starts with?"

"Shopping," the two answered in unison.

Yolanda wasn't a big Johnny Royal fan and she didn't hide her dislike for the Sharks quarterback, from Val. She first met Johnny at a Delta alumni Christmas ball. Val could not wait for the dance so she could show off her new hubby. She was also eager for her sorority sisters to see that she had not "stolen" any of their black men away from them. Yolanda immediately had a funny feeling about Johnny. She noticed the way he stared at some of their "sisters."

White boys, she thought to herself, *they always say they wouldn't be with a black woman, but they can't seem to take their eyes off our asses when they see us.*

"Hey Val," said Patriece, an alumni Delta who Val had met recently. Patriece had arrived at the function about an hour before Val and Johnny arrived, and she had obviously helped herself to the free drinks from the bar. "Heyyyyy Johnnnyy," she said as she embraced the quarterback tightly. "I'm one of your biggest fans. I don't know a lot about football, but I do like those tight pants you wear," she whispered into his ear as her right hand slipped unnoticed onto his rear end. "If you ever get out to play, you should find me. I like to play ball too."

Johnny was glad he had worn his long tailor-made sports coat, because it hid the bulging erection Patriece's sultry body had caused when she leaned in to him to whisper to him. During the remainder of the evening, Val was oblivious to the lustful stares her husband exchanged with Patriece, but Yolanda was not fooled. She had caught them eyeing one another on several occasions. Not to mention that she knew how much of a slut Patriece was. After all, she had already slept with nearly half of the Miami Sharks already, and she seemed to like the married players even more than the single ones.

Near the end of the evening Johnny saw Patriece walking towards the back of the large restroom area and

224

decided to follow her. He had been aching to talk to her a few minutes alone and now he had his chance. Besides, the four whiskey sours and the two Heinekens he drank were talking to him loud and clear: *Go ahead and give her what she wants,* he thought, as he made a beeline towards Patriece.

Johnny waited anxiously for Patriece to exit the restroom, but she had other plans. Patriece had seen Johnny following her. Instead of coming out, she opened the restroom door slightly, motioning for him to join her.

"I thought you were going to ignore me all night," Patriece said as she grabbed Johnny's Armani tie to pull him closer.

"How could I ignore something as sexy as *you*? I just didn't want the Mrs. to catch me looking at you," he replied.

"Oh yeah, lil' Miss Thing... Tell me Mr. Royal, does she have an ass like *this*?" Patriece said as she turned around and pulled up her long, tight fitting dress to expose the roundest and most ample backside he had ever seen. "Nah, there's no way she has an ass like this."

"Hell no," Johnny murmured softly as his tongue snaked into Patriece's mouth.

"Lock the door, Johnny I have something for you that your wife can't give you."

Johnny hurriedly locked the door as his penis strained against his expensive boxer briefs. They both knew they could only stay in the restroom but so long, before they were missed by someone, so they got right down to business.

"Feel this cutie," Patriece said while sliding Johnny's hand down between her legs. "See how wet that is. It's been waiting on you all night. You better come get it while you have the chance."

For the next few minutes, Patriece gave Johnny all he could stand. It was the quickie from hell that would surely have him begging for more. He couldn't help but be hypnotized by her healthy ass bouncing, as his dick pumped into her from the back. Using her hands to brace herself against the bathroom stall door, she bounced on top of him so forcefully, he could barely stand it.

"Ooooh, yeah you like this black pussy don't you?"

"Uh huh," was all Johnny could manage as he held on as long as he could.

"Come on, give it to me. Give it to me," she mumbled as he covered her mouth with one hand to muffle the sounds of both of them erupting.

Patriece and Johnny were able to slip out of the restroom without being detected by anyone at the event, except for Yolanda. She had grown suspicious as the minutes passed with no sign of Johnny or Patriece. Val was too busy catching up with potential clients to notice that his trip to the restroom was approaching fifteen minutes in length. But, Yolanda had excused herself from the conversation in order to investigate.

Yolanda instinctively placed her ear against the door of bathroom. She could hear the erotic exchanges between the two. "Shhhh, somebody is going to hear us!" Yolanda heard Johnny warn Patriece.

That muthafucka. He thinks he is so fuckin' slick, Yolanda thought as Johnny exited the restroom about a minute after Patriece.

Yolanda knew how much Val loved her husband. She also knew that telling Val anything about what she heard would do nothing but damage her relationship with her best friend. She decided she wouldn't tell Val until she had more concrete evidence to prove that he was the two-timing, low-life son of a bitch she knew he was. She hoped that Val would one day catch him in all of his lies and deceit on her own, so *she* wouldn't have to be the reason Val left his sorry ass.

"So where do you want to meet me?" Val asked, snapping Yolanda out of her thoughts about Johnny.

"I'll meet you at the Shops of Bal Harbour in an hour and a half."

"Okay, I need to work out, then head to the dry cleaners." Val replied.

"Alright Val, I'll see you in a little while."

After exercising in their in-home gym, Val showered and began gathering clothes for the dry cleaners. She had spilled cocktail sauce on one of her favorite dresses at the AccuSport event and wanted to get it cleaned as soon as possible. Johnny had also left four of his custom-made suits to be cleaned for his next two "away" game trips.

Hmmm, what's that? She thought to herself while glancing in her closet. Val bent down to retrieve the business card that had fallen from the clothing. *Probably one of my beloved husband's women's cards.* To her surprise it was the business card that Bobby Jackson had

227

given her at the AccuSport dinner. Val had been thinking about calling Bobby since they last met and to her, this was a sign.

But like many women, she needed a co-signer so she called Yolanda back. "Yolanda, may I ask you something?"

"Can I say no? I'm just kidding, what?"

"I didn't tell you, because I knew what you would say. But I ran into Bobby Jackson at the AccuSport party Johnny took me to"

"Girl you told me that."

"Yeah, but I didn't tell you that he gave me his number and I still had butterflies when I saw him. And I was thinking about..."

"Hell yes, call him! Call him now!"

Valerie was nervous but Yolanda's approval was all the courage she needed. She immediately hung up the phone with Yolanda and dialed the number on Bobby's card.

"Hello." a sultry voice answered.

"Bobby?"

"Yes this is Bobby, whose calling?"

"This is Val. Val Rober...Royal..."

29

Val and Bobby began seeing each other shortly after their first telephone conversation. She soon learned that Bobby was a lot of things Johnny could never be. Bobby was thoughtful, remembering special days in Val's life like her birthday, the date of her college graduation and even her wedding anniversary. Bobby was a gentleman who never raised his voice when he spoke to her. He also displayed his affection towards her in many ways, even though the affection occurred most often in private. The interesting thing about their relationship was that sex was not the focus of their relationship. As a matter of fact, Bobby and Val rarely had sex, but when they did, she never felt more free. Their relationship was much more than physical. They loved each other as friends. They often found themselves curled up on Bobby's leather couch reminiscing, discussing world issues or simply giving each other advice. Their connection was semi-spiritual and inspired by their emotional dependence on each other. When they did make love, they took it to another level. With Bobby, Val could be the S.O.B she had pent up inside: Sheltered, now Out of the Box White girl, or more simply phrased, Sweet On a Brother.

Val no longer had to pretend to be the nice quiet girl she was known to be in public. She could be the wild, passionate person she always wanted to explore, with Bobby. Nor did she have to pretend to be the perfect wife, or the perfect daughter who wouldn't dare touch a Black man, let alone be intimate with one.

Bobby was the "forbidden fruit" that Val wasn't allowed to associate with growing up. Now, things were quite different. She was living for herself, not her parents nor the "Sistas" who despised her for taking their men.

Bobby also found solace in abandoning his radical, "Black Power" upbringing by doing the unthinkable: bedding with a "blue eyed devil." Val and Bobby both threw caution to the wind to explore their newfound freedom. Val loved Bobby's large hands on her smooth body. She couldn't help but to notice the contrast in skin color when they lie entangled in the sheets of his gigantic bed. This was the ultimate rebellion in her mind, and Val was enjoying every minute of it. She would never forget the first time she finally gave in to her deep lustful sexual urges and went all the way with Bobby. Val had actually made plans to meet her husband at her favorite restaurant after football practice. She arranged for a limousine to take her to dinner in case the two of them had too much to drink and could not drive back home. Val sat in the restaurant an hour before she finally received a phone call.

"Val, I know you're going to kill me for this..." Johnny began "but I'm not going to be able to make it tonight Babe."

"Johnny, this is the third time this has happened this month," Val responded flatly between sips of her martini.

"I know Babe, but I have an important meeting tonight. I'll be home as soon as I can. Order something for me and I'll eat it when I get home later okay?"

"Whatever," said Val. CLICK! *Now I hope he doesn't think I fell for that important meeting bullshit* Val thought to herself as she slurped down the remaining bit of her drink.

As she entered the limousine, tears began rolling down her cheeks. "Take me back home please," she said to the driver. "On second thought, take me to 808 23rd Street."

"Yes ma'am."

As the limousine pulled up to the high-rise condominiums on 23rd street Val hoped that Bobby was home.

"Wait here. I shouldn't be too long. And I'll pay you double," Val said to the driver. Val pressed Bobby's code on the key pad and exhaled slowly.

"Hello," Bobby answered through the intercom.

"Bobby, I'm sorry for coming over unannounced. This is Val. May I come up please?"

"Val, what in the world? I thought you had plans with Johnny tonight."

"Yeah, I thought I had plans too. May I come up please?"

"Hold on, I'll buzz you in," Bobby responded.

Val's heart pounded wildly as the elevator climbed to Bobby's floor. Bobby answered the door dressed in shorts and tight black ribbed tank top. His buttery brown skin was still glistening from the moisturizer he applied after he showered. His hair was still glistening from the steam of the shower. The strong, powerful legs that helped Bobby win the pro basketball dunk contest peeked our gloriously from his fitted shorts. Val caught herself staring at his legs the way men stare at women's breasts.

"Come on in Val, I just got out of the shower. I tried to sneak one in at half time of the game I'm watching. You want a beer?"

"I didn't come here for beer Bobby. I came for *you*," Val said as she peeled away her sheer overcoat, dropping it on the plush sofa. Val's probing hands caught Bobby off guard. They had been affectionate with one another, but she had never been so aggressive. "I want you Bobby."

"Val are you *sure* about this?"

"I've never been so sure of anything in my life. I should have done this years ago," Val said as she turned to allow Bobby to unzip her dress. "I want you to take me. I need this." Bobby's erection sprang to life as he slipped Val's dress off her shoulders. She stood in the middle of the room wearing nothing but a sheer g-string and black thigh high stockings.

"You see anything you like Bobby?" Val asked seductively while tossing her long hair and licking her lips.

"Hell yeah I do," a breathless Bobby responded. For the first time in her life she was totally uninhibited in the bedroom. Val made sure that she licked every inch of Bobby's 6'7 frame, demonstrating the oral skills she had perfected. Val loved nothing better than having a long penis in her mouth tickling the back of her throat. She felt empowered while swallowing Bobby whole as his eyes rolled to the back of his head.

"Oh Val... Mmmm... Do you like that baby? Do you like the way I taste?" Bobby mumbled.

"Mm hmmm," Val growled, still devouring Bobby's mighty erection. "I want this inside me, right now," she said as she released Bobby's penis from her mouth. Bobby certainly didn't disappoint Val. His stamina matched her enthusiasm as they moved from the bed, to the floor, back to the bed. The twosome finished their torrid love-making session with pumping away with Val's limber legs over his broad shoulders. Val could still smell Bobby's scent as she crawled into bed next to Johnny later that evening.

"Hey Babe, sorry I couldn't make dinner, did you enjoy it?" Johnny asked sleepily.

"Uh huh, I sure did," Val answered as she drifted off into a deep sleep.

The more time Val spent with Bobby, the more comfortable she felt. She even shared with him, her fantasy of making love to another woman. She knew that her husband would never even consider it, but now she was totally free to experiment without judgment. After about six months, Bobby felt so at ease with Val that he gave her a key to his condo. He was not dating anyone seriously at the time, and he knew that Val could use his home as a place of refuge away from the drama that was destroying her marriage. She had fallen in love with much more than Bobby's money, fame, power, and his perfectly sculpted penis. She had fallen in love with *him*. Val loved everything about Bobby and he loved everything about her. But there was also a wild, unrestrained side to Bobby that frightened her. He had a sexual power that took Val to places she never dreamed of with her husband. Val found herself longing for the weekends Johnny would spend on the road with the team. She loved the excitement that Bobby brought into her life; however, Val knew she couldn't go on like this. Something would have to give sooner or later.

Although Val was a good girl by nature and sometimes naïve, she was clearly capable of assessing the negative things that came with being the wife of a NFL player. Johnny's money could buy Val all the things she needed to substitute for an absent husband. When Johnny was not there to make her feel good, she sometimes found herself in a downward spiral of drugs and alcohol. Even her side lover Bobby couldn't provide the stimulation drugs could. She could always smoke a joint or two, or drink herself to sleep. She was also beginning to frequent nightclubs more and more. It was obvious that the pressure of living life on the "dark side" was killing her. She now knew what it was like to be living on the "down low." And everyday that she was forced to keep her "secret," she sank deeper and deeper into a self-destructive lifestyle.

On one of her nights out without Johnny, she sat blankly, sipping a dirty martini in the posh and secluded VIP section of one of Miami's most exclusive nightclubs. She wasn't alone however; she had found several new friends: more experienced NFL wives. Prodded by the wild wife of another Sharks player, Val was contemplating taking an ecstasy pill.

"Girl, take one of these and you will want to fuck alllllll night," teased Cindy Williams, the wife of Sharks' offensive lineman Roderick Williams. "When Rod and I do 'em, we fuck for hours at a time."

"Really?" Val asked in disbelief.

"Try it for yourself. You'll see," answered Cindy.

"But my husband isn't around."

"I know, he's with my husband somewhere in New England with the team. But, who said we have to wait on them to get back?" Cindy asked as she leaned into Val with the "X" between her lips to place into Val's mouth. As Val opened her mouth, Cindy placed the "X" on her tongue and seductively French kissed her. Val chased the small pill with a full glass of vodka and lay back in the chair as her "friend" gently caressed the small of her back.

Although Val was initially shocked by the kiss, the 'X' was making her more excited by the second, and she could feel herself becoming sexually aroused by the woman sitting next to her.

"Let's go!" Cindy said.

Val followed her lead, anxious to see what the night had to offer. She wasn't sure if she'd feel this comfortable with a woman again.

As the two jumped into the Hummer Cindy had rented, driver and all, for the evening, Cindy passed a joint to Val. Either the weed was strong, or the 'X' was in overdrive, because Val's heart was racing and every nerve ending in her body was sensitive. The beat of the music coming from the speakers in the plush Hummer released an all too invigorating vibration. As the euphoria set in, Val once again felt Cindy's lips against her own. This time she was more than willingly, as she opened her mouth allowing Cindy's tongue to tease hers.

"Ummm, you taste good Val."

"Oh yeah? You haven't tasted the best part of me," replied Val, surprised by her response.

"Well, we'll just have to do something about that, won't we?" Cindy responded, while lifting the hem of Val's skirt. Cindy, obviously skilled, licked Val's clit through her panties, causing Val to completely let go. She nearly lost it as Cindy pulled the thin material of her panties to the side and allowed her tongue to explore her.

"Oh Cindy, what are you... What are you doing?" Val softly moaned.

"I'm doing what you want me to do," Cindy answered while pushing the long hair from her face to get a better, unobstructed path to Val's clit. Val shuttered through an orgasm as she felt Cindy's soft tongue ease inside her. Lost in the moment and in the haze of her high, Val could not resist.

But as good as Cindy was making her feel Val was craving Bobby badly. Tonight she wanted to do something that would please him like never before. "Cindy you ever been with a black man?"

"No, why?"

"Would you?"

"Is that a dare?" Cindy asked.

"No, but I have a friend that I trust with my life and he's the most gorgeous black man you've ever laid eyes on. I want to surprise him. Are you game?"

"The question is: Is *he* game?" asked Cindy.

Val assumed that Bobby would be home so she directed the driver to head that way. Even if he wasn't there, Val figured that she and Cindy could get warmed up and have some fun until he arrived. The closer they got to the condo, the less high Val felt as she began to second guess herself. *Maybe I should call first,* she thought to herself.

Valerie quickly dialed his number. "Bobby are you sleep?"

"Nah, I just got in. What's up?" Bobby inquired.

"I was out with a friend and I wanted to bring her by to meet you."

"Are you high Val?"

"Don't be mad, but yes. Actually me and a friend took some 'X' and smoked a little."

"So do you want to meet her?"

"If you bring her over, then I guess I'll meet her."

"I'm serious Bobby we're on our way."

"Yeah, okay. I'll see ya soon then. I forgot to tell you that I changed the gate code. It's #102569."

Val and Cindy sexed Bobby with more intensity and passion than he had ever experienced. He didn't know what had gotten into Val, but he certainly wasn't complaining. It was like this was her last dying request. After what seemed like an eternity of multiple orgasms, Val and Cindy finally allowed Bobby to drift back off to sleep. When he awoke the next morning both ladies were gone.

30

Bobby had never felt more abandoned. Three months had passed since he last saw or heard from Valerie. She had not called and she failed to return the dozens of phone calls from him. Bobby was heartbroken. He felt that something must surely be wrong; however, he saw Johnny and Val arm in arm in a magazine that spotlighted them as one of the five hottest couples in the Miami area. Val was even quoted as saying she was the happiest woman on earth. It was obvious that she wanted out of their relationship, but he needed to hear the truth directly from Val. Before dialing her number, Bobby pressed *67 to disguise his phone number so that she would hopefully pick up.

"Hello."

"Val, its Bobby. Are you hiding from me? I haven't heard from you in nearly three months. You haven't returned any of my calls. I know I've been traveling a lot and I haven't been around. But is everything alright?"

"No Bobby everything is not alright."

"What do you mean? What's wrong?"

Val started to cry, "My husband is treating me like a queen and this is what we've been wanting. So I've got to cut this off Bobby. I'm in love with you, but we both know this can't work. I know you think I'm crazy. My husband is finally doing what he needs to do to keep me happy and I'm crying."

"Val you just said, you are in love with me."

"I know what I said, but I just can't do it. I just can't. I love you and please forgive me. I have to go Bobby."

More than anything Val wanted to fall into Bobby's strong arms and disappear with him forever. But now that she was pregnant there was no way that she could follow her heart.

"Bobby, there's something else. Johnny and I decided to have a baby. I'm pregnant."

The news hit Bobby like a ton of bricks. "Wow," Bobby responded, "I, I don't know what to say."

"There's nothing to say Bobby. I'm married, I'm pregnant, and it's time for me to do the right thing for my family."

"Yeah... Yeah, I know," Bobby answered. "Well, I don't know what to say Val. Good luck? All the best? I love you."

"Bobby, don't be mad at me please? I just need to do the right thing."

"Val when I say I love you, it's unconditional, it's infinite and it's real. So you just take care of yourself and I know you're going to be the best mother in the world."

Val dropped the phone and cried like a baby. Yolanda hung up the phone for her grieving friend and held her close, reassuring her that she had done the right thing.

Val's pregnancy went well. She managed to escape the morning sickness many new mothers-to-be experienced. She was also fortunate enough to have gained little weight throughout the pregnancy. Bobby also helped the process by remaining absent. True to form, he remained a true friend. He did not want to cause any problems for Val, even though he felt that she was making a terrible mistake. She wasn't in love with her husband, but like many women, she was prepared to spend her life with him because he offered her *security* that no other man, including Bobby, could match. After all, Johnny was one of the highest paid players, on the most popular professional sports team, in one of the most well known cities in the world. He was rich, *s*uccessful, popular, and *White*, so he was safe. In America, he was about as perfect as a man could get. And though she felt Bobby was her soul mate, she could not risk her future and the future of her child because of what *she* wanted.

Val hoped that the new addition to the family would help repair the relationship she had with her mother in the same way it helped her relationship with Johnny. Since it was determined that Val was having a little boy, Johnny was thrilled at the thought of having a Johnny Royal, Jr. to follow in his footsteps. Val agreed to let her mother join them in the delivery room while she delivered the family's first grandchild as long as she promised not to insult Yolanda. Her mother had even told her she loved her recently, something she had not done in quite some time. Everything was going perfectly. Soon there would be another Royal boy running around, another boy to claim his share of the family crown.

The pains in Val's stomach told her that her baby boy would soon arrive. Her mother had been staying with them during the week prior to the expected date, just in case her daughter went into labor. Fortunately, the doctor had already informed the couple that the baby would arrive earlier than he first projected, so no one was alarmed when she began to have contractions. However, Johnny was nowhere to be found. As Yolanda gathered Val's things she called Johnny. *Same old Johnny* Yolanda thought to herself. *He can fool Val but he can't pull that shit on me.*

"Johnny this is Yolanda. Get your ass to the hospital as soon as you get this message. Val is having contractions and they're less than six minutes apart!"

"So how does it feel to know that you're going to be a grandma?" Val asked her mother in between contractions, as Yolanda sped to the hospital.

"It feels great, it really does," her mother answered. "I just wish your dad was here to see this."

"Yeah, me too," Val replied.

Since she was the wife of Miami's most popular superstar, Val was given VIP treatment the minute she was wheeled into the hospital. After having the baby, she would rest for a day or two in the hospital's largest and most private suite. Johnny arrived with his brand new mini video camera in tow, beaming like most first time fathers and smelling just like the Jack Daniels he'd been drinking.

"Hello Mr. Royal," one of the nurses on the labor and delivery floor said as he strolled down the hallway towards his wife's room. "May I have your autograph?" the nurse begged flirtatiously.

"You sure can my dear. Do you have anything I can write on?"

"I have a lot of things you can write on, touch on, or whatever," she said while winking.

"Hold that thought my dear. I'll be back after my wife delivers this baby. What time do you get off?"

"What time do you want me to get off?" she answered.

"I like your spirit young lady. Make sure I get a card from you before I leave… I'd like to keep in touch."

"I sure will Mr. Royal. I can be a really good friend, especially while your wife is recovering."

"Oh, I can definitely see us becoming friends," Johnny responded.

After a couple of hours of labor, the baby's outcry filled the delivery room. But an eerie hush quickly filled the air, as Johnny Royal, Jr's head was emerged from his mother's womb.

"Oh my God!" yelled Val's mother as her knees buckled. Everyone in the room stood staring in disbelief at the little baby.

"Uhhhh, it's a boy," said the doctor as the light brown-skinned, curly haired baby wailed above a totally stunned audience.

Pandemonium set in as Mrs. Robinson fainted, Kathy screamed, "Oh my God, he's black! The baby is black!!!," and Yolanda just shook her head. Johnny Royal was going berserk, as he threw his camera into the wall like he was throwing a 60-yard pass. One of the male nurses quickly moved in to restrain him.

"Get your fucking hands off of me!" Johnny screamed, as he stormed out of the room.

Oddly enough, in the midst of all of the chaos, Valerie *Robinson* was at peace. She felt terrible about hurting Johnny, but she had been set free. Through all of Johnny's indiscretions, she never left; but she knew that after today, he would most certainly leave her. But that wasn't important to her, because now she no longer had to hide who she really was or what she really wanted.

After asking God to forgive her, reality began to set in. She had just given birth to the son of her soul mate. She was filled with joy as she kissed the baby that would soon be named, Bobby Jackson, Jr. Valerie couldn't wait to call Bobby. "Bobby Jackson Jr.," she said to her newborn. "Wait until you meet your daddy. You're so beautiful. You look just like him." As Val stared in amazement at her new born son, she welcomed *the beautiful struggle* that lie ahead.

Charlene Johnson aka The F.L.Y. GIRL
Chapter 31

Damn, I'm late, Darrell Ray Johnson, or "DJ," as his teammates and NFL fans around the world knew him, thought to himself as he hurried excitedly through the grocery store in search of his wife's favorite foods. He knew it was a bad idea, since he could hardly go out without everyone following him around and asking or sometimes demanding, his autograph. He couldn't count all the times he politely declined to sign autographs while he was trying to eat or spend time with his wife that a fan would yell, "I'm a season ticket holder Mr. All-Star, I pay part of your salary, and you can't give me an autograph for my kid?!" But, of course he knew that most of them would run straight to the nearest memorabilia store to hawk the autographed item, or place it up for auction on e-bay.

On this day, his wife Charlene's 30th birthday, DJ certainly wasn't interested in signing autographs while searching through the grocery store. Due to his popularity, going anywhere these days had become more than a chore. He had not visited the nearby market at all during the past three years since he had become the NFL's leading rusher. So not only did he have 20 kids following him around the store, he had no idea where to find any of the items to make his wife's favorite dishes.

"Excuse me, can you tell me where I can find the live lobster?" he asked a store employee.

"Oh my God! It's Darrell Johnson! Man, I gotta have your autograph!"

"Only if you help me find the lobster," DJ replied.

DJ and the employee spent the next 30 minutes rounding up not only lobster, but crab legs, filet mignon, jumbo shrimp and fresh vegetables. He needed to hurry home to deliver the groceries to his personal chef Charlie, so he could prepare the food for his wife Charlene's surprise birthday party. DJ had done a masterful job of planning the party without his wife finding out. He had appointed Charlene's close friend Lynnette as his partner in crime to assist him in coordinating the surprise and inviting her family and closest friends.

Charlene's mother was due to arrive any minute now, accompanied by her two sisters. He was also flying in *his* mother to partake in the festivities. Since Charlene's brother Lorenzo attended a nearby college, DJ sent a limousine to pick him and his girlfriend up. Lynnette also invited Charlene's sorority sisters and various friends from Cornell to attend. DJ wanted the event to feel like a down home family reunion. He took pride in giving his wife's family members and friend's first class treatment. He loved his wife more than anything in the world and anyone who was important to her was important to him. Since he made over $5 million a year, not including his other multi-million dollar endorsement contracts, DJ had sprung for first-class airline flights and limousine rides for over 50 people.

She is going to trip out when she sees all these people, DJ thought to himself on his way home to meet Charlie. The smell of Charlie's famous gumbo met him at the door and filled his senses as he entered their impressive 12,000 square foot mansion.

"Charlie!" he bellowed upon entering the house, "Hurry up and help me get this stuff out of the car!"

"Coming DJ!" Charlie shouted back from the spacious kitchen. "I'm putting my special touches on all the food for Ms. Charlene. You know you have to *throw down* when you have your employers' "mamas" eating your food," Charlie said as he hurried out to the car to retrieve the groceries. "DJ, you do know you could save a lot of time by sending someone else to the store for you?"

"Yeah man, I know, but I wanted this to be something I did by myself for a change. This way she'll appreciate it more."

The waiters DJ hired for the event were busy setting the large formal dining room table, while Vera Wang china, exquisite platinum plated silver ware, and Tiffany flutes adorned the enormous dining room table that sat up to 18 people. Fresh flower arrangements tastefully decorated the lower level of the home as waiters scurried around filling and refilling champagne glasses of the guests who had arrived early. Of course the magnificent marble wet bar was overloaded with all the usual suspects: cognacs, vodkas, liqueurs, and beers from around the world. DJ had also taken the time to place lavender scented candles, Charlene's favorite, throughout the house.

Although DJ was a simple man, he never spared any expense when it came to Charlene. He allowed her to build their $4.5 million dream home from top to bottom. He also allowed her to spend as much as she wanted when decorating the eight-bedroom manor. All he cared about was the basement, which he labeled as *his* part of the house. The basement was his own adult playground that featured a large plasma-screen television, a weight room, a second large wet bar, a mini kitchen, and an office. This was the only place his wife would allow him to display his childhood and college trophies. The basement was his sanctuary, his place of comfort since the remainder of the house was so fancy he was afraid to touch anything. DJ was so uncomfortable in the home's living room that he would only sit on the furniture if he were dressed for Church. It was during these times that DJ would have flashbacks to his childhood when his mother only allowed her boys to sit on the "good furniture" while waiting to be taken to Sunday school.

The previous two years DJ had been forced to miss his wife's birthday because of team travel. Since they usually traveled Friday and did not return home until Sunday night, he had been forced to miss her special birthday celebrations –one of the many sacrifices of an NFL superstar. This year was different though. There was no way he was going to miss her big day, especially since she was turning 30. Although the team had flown out earlier during the day, DJ had received permission from the Rage coaches and owner Tom Wendel to take a private flight to meet the team in Los Angeles first thing in the morning. After all, special players received special treatment. And no Rage player was more special than DJ. He led his team and league in rushing four straight years and was selected as a Pro Bowler each of those years.

DJ himself was on the verge of turning 30, which some would say is "old" for an NFL running back, but DJ never felt better. Although it was only mid-season, he was well on his way to earning yet another NFL rushing title.

Not only was he a great athlete, he was also a pillar in the community. He regularly volunteered to work with inner-city youth and made many trips to local hospitals to visit sick children and the elderly. He was particularly interested in fatherless children since he had grown up without knowing his own biological father. "Pops" as he called his father, had split when DJ was six years old. Pops got up one morning to make a "run" as he always said and never came back. His mother would often recount the story, telling people, "The nigga had to make a run and just kept on runnin' I guess." DJ owed his sensitivity indirectly to his father, he supposed. He had a soft spot in his heart for kids who had chips stacked against them. Thus, he rarely turned down an opportunity to speak to young Black children at inner city schools or youth programs. *Life just doesn't get any better than this,* he thought to himself, as he gazed out of the bay window in the living room to see the limousine that had just arrived from the airport carrying his mother.

"Boy, you know you came up with *some* idea this time," his mother said as she emerged from the silver stretched limo. "Give me a hug and get that bag baby."

"Ma, I'm saving my strength for Sunday's game, no way am I picking up *that* bag. What in the world did you bring anyway?" "Hey Sam," DJ called to the hired valet who would be parking cars for the evening. "Grab my mom's bag and take it to the first room on your right upstairs."

DJ had always promised that if he ever lived in a *real* house he would reserve one room for his mother. They had lived in an old two-bedroom apartment all his life. So he vowed that he would one day take care of the woman affectionately known as "Ma." Although Pops had left the family, his mother still managed to provide for him and his three brothers, all of whom went on to graduate from college. Although his mother did not miss any of his home football games in college, she was much too nervous to travel with him to the NFL draft in New York. She just didn't want to do anything to jinx her baby's big day. After he was drafted by the Baltimore Rage as the number five player taken overall, DJ fought through a crowd of well-wishers, including his agent who had also become a rich man that day, to find a quiet place to call his mother.

"Ma, did you see that? Were you watching TV? Did you see me?"

"Yeah baby, I saw you," she said as she fought back her crocodile tears.

"We did it Ma, we did it!"

"No baby, *God* did it!" she replied.

"You're right Ma, God did it! And guess what else God did. He told me to tell you to call your boss and quit your job right now! Retire Ma, you don't have to work another day of your life."

"Look at you," his mom said bringing him out of his daydream, "All those muscles and you can't even carry your Mama's little old bag. Can I at least get a hug from my boy, or will that hurt your arms too?" she teased.

"I don't know Ma, you know I usually make people pay me for hugs these days," he replied with a smile as he embraced her tightly.

Although the house was filling up with friends and relatives from around the country, DJ could not help but reminisce. He was the biggest star in professional football, and while no one is perfect, DJ seemed to be living the perfect life. He had an intelligent, loving, and beautiful wife, a fantastic mother and supportive family, the best friends a man could have, and over $10 million in the bank.

Although he could have any material thing in the world he wanted, his favorite thing in the world was pleasing Charlene. He had been that way since they met in college. Even though Charlene had a "reputation" when he met her, he was intrigued the first time he laid eyes on her.

Unbeknownst to DJ, Charlene had begun targeting him during his senior year at nearby Big State U. She *accidentally* bumped into him at a local nightclub, Clem's on "Ladies Night." DJ and several of his teammates had gotten to know the owner of the club quite well during the past few years. They often got the V.I.P. treatment when they went to Clem's because they were big-time ball players. The free admission, drinks, and food they enjoyed were perks that violated NCAA rules, but DJ and his boys always ignored that fact. Clem, the owner, didn't care about the rules either. All he knew was the more big time ballers he had in his place, the more the ladies came out. If the ladies were there, then the other men from campus and city would come as well. Clem only cared about the bottom line, and the bottom line was that the players from Big State brought the crowd. DJ and his crew entered the club and made a move straight for the V.I.P. area. Although he rarely drank alcohol, he enjoyed the special treatment he received beyond the infamous red ropes of the V.I.P. What he wasn't used to however, was all the unwanted attention he was receiving from the ladies.

DJ spent the first three years of college wrapping himself up in football, his fraternity, and his high school sweetheart Cynthia who was back home in Chicago. No other female on campus could take her place. He had planned to marry her soon after they both graduated from college. She had even considered transferring to Big State from the local college in their hometown after her sophomore year. Then came the telephone call that changed DJ's life forever.

RINGGGGG, RINGGGGGGG!!!! Since it was 3:00 a.m., the telephone sounded much louder and more annoying.

"Hello." DJ said incoherently.

"DJ! Wake up man, wake up!" his best friend Maurice yelled into the phone.

"Nigga what do you want?!" DJ yelled back, "Do you know what time it is?" he asked glancing wearily into the darkness of the dorm room to find the red lights on his alarm clock.

"DJ, man, I'm so sorry. I'm so sorry man!"

"Sorry for what man? What happened? Why are you calling me so late?"

"She's gone man, she's gone."

"Who's gone? Ma??? Did something happen to Mama?" DJ could hear his own heart beating in the stillness of that little room. He knew his mother hid the fact that she didn't feel well all the time. She even tried hiding the high blood pressure medicine she took daily from him.

"Maurice, did something happen to my mom man? Talk to me!"

"Nah bruh, it's Cynthia. She died a few minutes ago, over in County Hospital."

"What the..." DJ's voice trailed off as he dropped the phone and sat stone-faced in the dark.

"DJ!" Maurice yelled into the now dead telephone. "DJ! DJ! Man, answer me! DJ!!!"

Cynthia's funeral marked the saddest day of DJ's young life. Funerals are always sad, but when someone young dies, they are often much worse. Especially when it is someone with so much promise passes on. Speeches about lives lost too soon, those slow songs that were the deceased favorites and the weeping mothers, fathers ,and grandparents, are often overwhelming. *She looked like an angel in her casket, even prettier than in real life,* DJ thought to himself. As the church's most popular vocalist crooned Donny Hathaway's "Young, Gifted, and Black," DJ began to sob like an infant. He had no idea that he was capable of crying so much. How would he ever get over this, ever get over her?

Like other young people who were out having a good time, Cynthia became the victim of a drunk driver. After a late-night sorority party with her line sisters, Cynthia volunteered to drive her soror Nancy (or Big Nan as they called her) back to the dormitory. Nan was known for her drinking, so her sorors always looked after her when she started looking for the vodka, gin, tequila, or anything she could get her hands on. On this particular night, a couple of basketball players and one of her sorors helped Cynthia get Nan into the car for their drive back to the dormitory.

"Girl, as usual, your ass is too through," Cynthia said to her drunken soror.

"I may be through, but I also got that fine ass Delvin's digits baby!" Nan exclaimed in a drunken slur.

"No way girl!"

"Oh yes I did too my girl. Told you. Big Nan don't play that sista girl!" she said as she passed out.

Ten minutes later Nan awoke telling Cynthia to pull the car over so she could throw up.

"Girl, your ass better not throw up in my car!" Cynthia yelled at Nan.

"Uggghhhhh, pull over Cee Cee, please!"

Nan could hardly wait for the car to come to a complete stop before jumping out to hurl in the grass near the shoulder of the road.

"Damn girl, you alright?" Cynthia asked. By now Nan was lying face down in the grass and did not respond. "Nan, you okay??? Nan!!! Nan!!!" Cynthia did not even notice the swerving automobile racing towards her.

"Cynthia," he whispered to the large picture in front of the casket, pretending that she could hear him, "I love you girl, and I'll never forget you baby."

For weeks after the funeral DJ would awaken in a cold sweat. Seeing Cynthia's face in his dreams made him never want to fall asleep. He would often drink coffee late at night to keep himself awake for fear of seeing Cynthia again. When he would finally doze off, he would awake paranoid and tense from all the caffeine he had consumed. His coaches and teammates were obviously concerned about his well-being. After all, DJ was the man who had led them to their first football conference championship in over a decade during his sophomore season. He was well on his way to breaking all of Big State's rushing records in only three years. And finally, after a while, just as his mother said they would, the nightmares stopped. DJ dedicated the rest of his college playing days to his beloved Cynthia and he ran with a purpose that no one but him could understand. Before each game, DJ would write the words "Cee Cee" on his taped wrists, in remembrance of his fallen love.

"Yo DJ, what are you thinking about man," his Big State teammate James "Hollywood" Jackson asked, snapping him out of his reminiscent day dream. "All these honeys up in the V.I.P and you're in la la land. A few Cornell honies are up in here tonight. I can use a future doctor playa," James said with a smile. Man, let's move to the floor, so we can see who else is in here. You with me?

"And you know this," DJ answered trying to hide the sadness in his heart. *When is this feeling going to go away?* he thought to himself as he began eyeing the young women on the crowded dance floor. Despite his athletic prowess, DJ had never had much luck with women while in college. He felt that most women who approached him had ulterior motives. Did they want *him,* or what they thought he could ultimately offer them? He spent the next year pushing women away. He could not connect with any of them, and didn't want to. He didn't want to risk losing another person who was so close to him. But Charlene was different, or so he thought.

Charlene and her girl Theresa attended the club that night decked out in their hottest "catch-a-man" outfits. Charlene donned a low cut sheer shirt, a tight mini-skirt, and matching pumps. Her hair was laid, as they say, and her light eyes sparkled like flawless diamonds. She was on the prowl, looking for Mr. Right, no matter who he was. Mr. Right turned out to be DJ. Charlene saw him enter the club that evening with his teammates. All of them had strong looking bodies; arms made of granite and asses made of steel. A couple of DJ's boys looked even better than he did, but Charlene knew he was the big catch. After all, Big State had been pubbing him up since the end of his junior year, and he was the leading candidate for the Heisman Trophy going into his senior season. So she redirected her animal-like attraction from his friends, and onto the leader of the pack.

When Charlene walked near his table in the V.I.P. area at Clem's, he tried to play her off, but she noticed him staring at her. How could he not? Charlene Johnson was once known as the "groupies' groupie." She had been fascinated with football players since her days as a high school pom-pom squad captain. Since she was the girl who stood out the most while in high school, she got more than her fair share of attention from the guys at school. She stood 5'8" tall and was a classic "light-skinned" red bone with long hair and legs to match. Since she was Creole, her light eyes gave her an exotic look that set her apart from most of the other girls at her high school. Even some of the male teachers fantasized about trapping Charlene in the back of their classrooms after hours and having their way with her. As a matter of fact, she was not afraid to reciprocate some of the vibes she got from the younger male teachers. Everyone knew that she only attended Mr. Winston's class less than half the time but received an "A" for the semester.

Regardless of what anyone else thought of Charlene, she was perfect in his eyes. He was grateful to have been "caught" or "tricked," because he truly believed that *he* was the lucky one.

Ding dongggg…

"Ugh, it's her. I can't even enjoy a bit of peace and quiet before she shows up? Lord, please give me the strength to deal with this woman tonight" DJ's mother said as she looked to the ceiling located 20 feet above them.

"Be nice Ma, be nice!" DJ said to his mother as he went to answer the door.

The "her" his mother referred to was his wife's mother Veronica. For some reason the two women had never clicked and unfortunately, didn't even attempt to hide their disgust for one another.

"This is going to be one crazy night," his mother added.

"Ma!" DJ interjected.

Ding dongggg…

"Can't we just pretend we're not here baby?" his mother asked him with a smirk on her face.

"Come on Ma, this night isn't about you, and it surely isn't about my crazy mother-in-law. It's about Charlene, remember?"

"Oh, but you do admit she's crazy right?" his mother replied.

"Shhhhhhh, I'm going to answer the door," DJ said as he glanced over his shoulder to his mother.

"Hello darlings, the party can begin now, the queen has arrived!" Veronica bellowed as she entered the massive foyer. DJ instantly smelled the liquor on her breath as she announced her grand entrance. She had obviously helped herself to the complimentary beverages in the back of the limousine on her way from the airport.

"Hello Veronica," Janice said as she half-hugged her in-law.

"Oh, hello Janice. Did you just get here?"

"Yes, I did, about five minutes earlier than you did."

"And you couldn't wait for me so we could ride here together from the airport?"

"Well, I knew the 'queen' would be taken care of, so I came on without you."

"Hmmph," retorted Veronica under her breath, "Your fat ass would have taken up the whole car anyway."

"Did you say something Veronica?" DJ's mother asked pointedly.

"Hey there mother-in-law," DJ said as he embraced Veronica in an attempt to separate the two queen bees.

"Hello my son!" Veronica said as she planted a fat smooch on DJ's cheek.

Veronica had always loved DJ, after all, he was paying the mortgage on her penthouse condominium *and other things he had no idea about.*

Her mother Veronica had enhanced Charlene's survival methods. She knew Charlene would be able to use her beauty to her advantage to get ahead or to just get over, especially when it came to men. Veronica was once a long-stemmed beauty herself and could still attract men half her age. She had a penchant for low cut dresses and blouses that showed off her ample bosom and short skirts that most women her age wouldn't dream of wearing. Although most women hated Veronica (or hated on her), her male suitors were the exact opposite. The men in her life simply couldn't get enough. Hell, the men who *weren't* in her life couldn't get enough.

————————————

"Here comes the bitch ya'll," one of envious women in the salon said as Veronica parked her convertible Jaguar outside.

"Yeah," one of the other ladies chimed in, "Did you ever notice how she just gets up and leaves after she gets her hair done? Some man pays for services in advance, and she has a standing weekly appointment! He even pays for her daughter to get her hair done too."

"Damn," the first woman replied, "She must have that golden pussy!"

"Nah chile, *I* have the golden pussy, that bitch must be putting roots on niggas!!!" she squealed as the room collapsed into high-pitched giggles and laughter.

"Shhh, here she comes girl!"

"Hey girlllllll!!!" the entire hair salon congregation sang as Veronica entered the shop.

Fake bitches Veronica thought to herself. "Hey ya'll, how's everybody doing today?" Veronica knew that she was by far the least liked woman in the room. She had grown accustomed to feeling this way. But she also knew that her daughter's money was longer than everybody else's. Thus, she knew that her hair stylist Simone would keep the other women on a tight leash and out of her business if she wanted to continue to get the $250 a week she was being paid.

Veronica was quite used to being the most hated woman in the room and DJ's surprise party for her daughter was no different. *If DJ's tacky mother says anything out of the way to me, I swear I'm going to slap her back to the ghetto where she came from,* Veronica thought to herself.

Ding dongggg...

The doorbell rang and rang as guest after guest arrived to surprise Charlene for her birthday. Friends and family members who had not seen each other in years had come together to celebrate the grand occasion. It was like a mini family reunion, where food was plentiful and laughs were even more abundant. The anticipation of the surprise was mounting throughout the home as the guest of honor's arrival grew nearer.

As the magic hour approached, DJ turned off all the lights to make the house look unoccupied. He wanted Charlene to be completely surprised when she opened the door. To throw her off the surprise party trail even more, DJ had set up an appointment for Charlene to visit the lavish day spa where all of the pro ballers sent their wives for birthdays, anniversaries, and times when they messed up real bad. Since DJ was supposed to miss her third consecutive birthday, he really laid it on thick. He paid for the most expensive treatments and then arranged for a chauffeured Phantom to take her to her favorite bar for drinks with her girl Nikki. But drinks were not all Charlene would have that evening.

32

Instead of showing up at the spa for her birthday treatments, Charlene and Nikki ventured to Lance Swanson's home. Lance was a successful attorney who lived nearby in the same neighborhood. Like clockwork, Charlene pulled into Lance's four-car garage as he stood grinning inside the doorway. She was certainly not a stranger to creeping out on her husband. Despite DJ's faithfulness and commitment, Charlene was never able to shake her old ways. She was a **FLY** Girl (*Freak Like in Your* dreams). Simply put, Charlene was a woman with a man's sexual tendencies. She was very capable of taking care of all her man's desires, both inside and outside the bedroom. Yet, when her husband was not around, her "tendencies" would surface in full effect. Even when DJ was around, she would become bored quickly and was in constant search of new male conquests. Charlene's versatility enabled her to thrive in any environment. She could go from a stuffy five-star restaurant to a ghetto fabulous after-party where hoochie mamas, Hypnotiq, and weed were in abundance. Her mother raised her to use what she had to get what she wanted. Sex was no exception.

Lance quickly became Charlene's "flavor of the month," after they bumped into each other at a nightclub after a home game. DJ was extremely tired from the game, and decided to stay home and let his wife hang out with her girls. Lance's style intrigued Charlene. He was an expert when it came to surprising women, and blew her away with unexpected gifts and spontaneous, romantic rendezvous.

He also loved to please women and did anything to separate himself sexually from other men. Since it was Charlene's 30th birthday, he knew he couldn't disappoint. He knew just who to call to help him set the whole night off right – Big Luscious.

Big Luscious was a male exotic dancer. He and Lance had been friends for a long time. They crossed paths several times years ago and eventually wound up promoting several events together. Lance made the call, and like always, Big Luscious was down to entertain. After securing the entertainment, Lance rounded up the remainder of his "tools": an expensive bottle of tequila, an X-Rated version of the game "Truth or Dare," massage oil and several sex toys.

The lights were low but not too low. Lance knew that Charlene wasn't into the "romance thing" when it came to him. She wanted to be serviced, treated like a slut, and then sent home. Lance would always oblige, besides, he was thrilled to finally find a woman who left her emotions at the door. Like she always said, "I can make *love* to my husband." She wanted to FUCK her lovers. And for her birthday, Lance would give her more than she could stand; they didn't call Luscious "Big" for nothing.

As Charlene and Nikki made themselves comfortable in Lance's spacious den, Lance appeared with a sly grin.

"What can I get you ladies to drink?"

"I'll have a shot," requested Nikki.

"Make mine a double," said Charlene, who was obviously ready to celebrate her birthday.

"Hey Big Luscious, bring the ladies some Patron playboy," Lance directed his order towards the kitchen.

"Big Luscious? Who in the world is Big Luscious?" asked Nikki.

"I'm Big Luscious baby," the chiseled 6'3, 240 pound sex god said as he brought the drinks out for the ladies. His bare chest took Nikki's breath away. The silk shorts he wore could barely contain his long, thick penis, as the tip of it crept out periodically while he ran errands for the ladies.

"Lance, you have really outdone yourself this time," Charlene said while directing her eyes to the bulge between his legs.

"You just wait pretty lady," Lance replied as the devilish grin returned.

"Well what I see right now, I damn sure like," Charlene responded.

The foursome took their shots and Lance cued the music.

"Ladies," Lance said, "Sit back and relax while Big Luscious takes you there."

Charlene was feeling exactly the way Lance wanted her to feel. The sexual tension in the room was maddening, and the fine Mandingo in the sheer silk boxers didn't help the situation. Charlene became so aroused that she raised her dress to straddle Lance on the couch. Charlene began to grind on Lance to the beat of the music.

Luscious' dark chocolate skin glistened with sweat as he gyrated to the booming sounds from the state of the art stereo system. The women loved his shiny bald head but not quite as much as they loved the 10-inches he was working with. Charlene's eyes lit up as Luscious stroked himself to the beat. She began grinding harder on Lance's lap as she turned her head to watch Luscious over her shoulder. Charlene was completely turned on. She wanted to cum, but decided to hold out until later.

"I want you to dance with Luscious," Lance said to Nikki.

Charlene was getting turned on even more watching her friend stroke the longest penis she had ever seen up close and personal. Nikki could not believe what she was doing. She knew her girl Charlene was wild, but until now, she had no idea just how wild. She also couldn't believe how big and rock hard Luscious was. She knew she was going to do something freaky, and soon, as he placed her hand inside his shorts.

Charlene discarded her soaking wet, La Perla panties, and turned her back to Lance. As she slid down on his erection, she watched as Big Luscious gave Nikki all 10 inches of his massive penis while she steadied herself against the couch. Nikki could barely withstand the doggy style pounding she was getting, but she took it like a true champion. Her moans and sensual sighs were turning everyone on in the room even more.

After Big Luscious finished with Nikki he turned his attention to Charlene. Charlene had always loved having two men at her disposal. One time in college, Charlene fucked three of DJ's teammates in one day. She let them all have their way with her, in any position they desired. She loved pleasing guys on campus, especially those who had stuck up girlfriends that wouldn't do freaky things for their men. Charlene quickly developed a reputation for being the girl any decent looking man on campus could get with, especially if they caught her after she'd had a few drinks. Of course DJ heard about his girlfriend's sexual exploits while they were in college, but some of the things he heard were so far-fetched that he didn't give the rumors a second thought. After all, Charlene always had an explanation or alibi that satisfied DJ. His nose was wide open, and she took FULL advantage of that. In fact, she was still taking advantage of it.

Charlene dismounted from Lance's lap and the two men slowly removed the remainder of her clothing. Although Big Luscious was built like a machine himself, he marveled at Charlene's body, it was obvious that she worked hard to keep it so tight. He wanted to touch every inch of it, from her sculptured calf muscles to her fat, tight ass, up to her gorgeous back. Charlene enjoyed the attention her two lovers were giving her. Nikki looked on from a large leather recliner as her friend got the royal treatment from two very sexy men. Nikki instinctively spread her legs and began to please herself. Big Luscious took control of the situation commanding Charlene to stand. Lance then knelt in front of her and began tasting her pussy as Big Luscious held her hands behind her back. Charlene's body quivered uncontrollably; the feeling of restraint coupled with the sight of Lance's head between her legs sent her into another world, as she lost herself in the fantasy turned reality.

After a few moments, Big Luscious ordered Charlene to place herself on the floor on all fours. His eyes grew wider as he surveyed her nearly perfect ass. Charlene winced in pleasurable pain as Luscious entered her from behind.

"Oh yeah," Charlene hissed. "Come closer Lance, I want you in my mouth." Charlene pleased her two lovers simultaneously. She was clearly not a novice at this.

"You like that don't you big boy?" Charlene asked Luscious as he pounded away from behind her. "Give it to me! Yeahhhh…" The look on Luscious' face told Charlene all she needed to know. She could feel Lance's orgasm growing as she deep-throated him. She could tell by how he was pulsating, that he was about to cum. And though she had already had what she felt was a million orgasms, she wanted to finish him.

Luscious, who was also at the point of no return, tried to fight it but couldn't, "I'm about to…" Luscious called out. Lance exploded in her mouth as Luscious reached his own orgasm. The sight of Charlene being treated like a sex slave took Nikki over the edge. Nikki had never experienced anything like this before. However, she did know that she needed to hang out with Charlene more often in the near future. Charlene lay on the couch face down for 30 minutes to regain her composure.

"Oh my goodness, I'll drink to that," she said to her girl Nikki who was still enjoying the aftermath of her own intense orgasms.

"Girl, I knew you were out there, but you are a FUH-REAKKKK," Nikki said to her partner in crime. "This calls for champagne."

"You want Cristal or Moet?" Lance asked emerging from his bedroom draped in his signature black terry cloth robe.

"Cristal of course," answered Charlene. "And let's take a bottle to my house and go for round two. I want you to see my new Jacuzzi tub."

"Damn baby, you really are livin' on the edge aren't you? Where's your man?" asked Lance.

"He's with the team somewhere. They had an 'away' game."

"Ahhhh. Cool. I must be moving up, to be invited to the crib and all," Lance teased.

"Well now is the time handsome. Do you think you have some more to give?" Charlene asked.

"Hell yeah," Lance responded. "And if I can't, I'm sure I could call Big Luscious to pick up the slack," he said with a laugh.

33

DJ could hear the car, "She's pulling up everybody! Let's get ready," DJ announced to the guests. As they waited for Charlene to enter the house, the party guests could hear her giggling and talking to someone as she probed for her keys.

She must have brought Nikki home too. I'm glad she's looking out for her girl because Lord knows she can't handle her liquor, DJ thought as he hid in the darkness. *I can't wait to see Charlene's face when she opens this door!*

"Damn," Charlene giggled loudly to her companion, "I thought I left the lights on out here. I can't see a thing. Fuck it let's go through the garage. It'll be better if I put the car in the garage anyway," she said as she clumsily dropped her keys.

As the car started up again, DJ was overcome with curiosity, *I know she's not leaving?* He said to himself as the engine of her convertible 600SL Benz revved up. He knew if Charlene left there was no telling when she would come back. Just as he began to run out and stop her, he heard the garage door open. "Good she's just pulling into the garage." The excitement was eating him up. Pleasing Charlene was an aphrodisiac for DJ, and he knew as soon as she saw the new convertible Bentley coupe he had bought her for her birthday she would go bananas, it was her dream car.

As DJ repositioned himself, he reminded family and friends not to say a word 'til he gave the signal. The anticipation was at a ridiculous level and Charlene's scream was confirmation that her husband had done well. Being a man's man, unlike the rest of the party, DJ fought back his own tears as he watched several guests shed tears of joy.

"Oh my God! Oh my God! YES! I LOVE IT ! YES!

DJ could not wait any longer as he signaled everyone to follow him towards the house entrance of the garage. As the door creaked opened, DJ quietly counted off, "One, two, three …"

"SURPRISE!!!!!!!!" yelled the party guests in unison as DJ hit the light switch.

"Oh shit, yes right there Lance!" Charlene yelled.

DJ's heart nearly leapt from his chest as his hand stood frozen to the light switch. Time stood still and the shocked guests stood looking at Charlene and her companion. While Charlene lay on top of the hood of her new Bentley, legs spread eagle, being sent to ecstasy by the tongue of neighbor and friend, Lance Swanson, the blood in DJ's body began to boil.

As her eyes opened, Charlene saw her life flash before her. Her eyes instantly poured out a waterfall of tears, and the ill feeling in her stomach was enough to make her nearly throw up, "DJ…Wait,…I…Oh my God…No…I'm sorry!"

Before Lance could look over his shoulder, it was as if the devil was torturing his soul. As DJ delivered a vicious blow with the heel of his boot to Lance's temple he yelled with pure insanity. "Muthafucka you're gonna die tonight!" DJ ran towards his H2 Hummer, and panic spread throughout the party.

"Baby please…. Please don't, I'm sorry…Run Lance or he's going to kill you!"

Lance was still dizzy from the excruciating blow he had taken. As he struggled to gather his balance he finally got his bearings and he ran towards the door. Just as DJ reached the car, Charlene's brother grabbed him in a bear hug from the back. Normally a humble, rational man, it was obvious that DJ wasn't himself as he stomped on Lorenzo's foot and delivered a crushing elbow to his brother-in-law's jaw. Martial arts, guns and motorcycles were DJ's hobbies, all of which he was an expert, so when he pulled out a gun or his martial arts, it was *life or death* serious. As Lorenzo fell to the floor, DJ reached into his $80,000 tricked out SUV and removed "Jaws," his custom made, water-proof 9mm, from the glove compartment. DJ quickly released the safety and had it not been for his expertise with guns he may have shot his friend Jason, who was blocking his path to Lance.

"Get the fuck back Jason, unless you want to die too!"

"Come on 'D,' you don't want to do this!"

"Nigga I'm not going to say it again!"

DJ had never been so out of control. He took his close friend and fraternity brother to the ground with a powerful kick that could have broken Jason's leg if he wanted it to. The commotion was at a fever pitch and the guests began to scatter, as the possibility of a stray bullet was all too real. Lance was almost to the door when DJ turned and fired two rounds from "9mm." The shots were deafening and fear consumed the room. Screaming guests quickly hit the floor. Before DJ could get off a third round Lance fell to the floor. Sure of what he had done, DJ approached the man that had shattered his life for the second time. As he stormed to the other side of the garage, Charlene cried hysterically. DJ's mind became more and more cloudy. The more Charlene cried the more he felt she feared for Lance, and not for what she had done.

The adrenaline was running through DJ's veins like it was the first play of the World Championship. He attempted to ponder the consequences of his action, but at this point, consequences ceased to matter. Everything that he lived and worked for had been irrevocably tainted and someone had to pay. DJ had always been a good Christian, God-fearing man. It was his daily goal to become closer to the man that God would have him to be, but tonight he had laid down his spirituality and it was clear that Satan was not about to let him off the hook. All DJ could see and hear was his wife moaning and the man staring back at him, between her legs. The instructions from the voice in his head were clear. *Finish the job. That bastard disrespected you in your house and everybody saw. The Bible says, "An eye for an eye..." and "though shall not covet another man's wife..." Be a man and handle this.* DJ leaped across the hood of Charlene's Benz, where Lance laid crying, panicked and covered in his own urine. Lance feared for his life, and while he had never been in this situation before, he vowed that if God would spare his life, he would definitely never be in it again. He was already bleeding from the side of his head, but he feared the worst was yet to come.

"Turn your ass over bitch!"

Lance had never been so scared, "Please DJ, please...".

"Stop crying like a bitch and get ready to pay the price for that expensive ass pussy you just had."

"Man, I'm sorry….God knows I'm sorry."

"God? Nigga how you gon' --? Don't you say another word until I tell you to, …do you understand me?"

"Yes!" Lance said as he closed his eyes and silently begged God for mercy.

DJ's mother tried to calm him, but he quickly tuned her and all the other chaos out. He only focused on himself, Lance and Charlene. "So do you love her?"

"No man, I'm sorry it's not like that. I'm sorry. We just…"

"Shut up! Do you want to take care of her and this family?"

"No man. We just got caught up. Man you were always gone to autograph sessions, road trips, church…I was just being a friend and got caught up…I'm sorry…"

"Oh, now it's my fault. So you wanna be me? You want my responsibilities? So I'm the bad guy, huh? Can you do better?"

"NO…NO…NO!"

"Do you love Charlene? Would you give up *everything* for her?"

"NO man, NO it was sex! I got carried away…DJ please don't kill me!"

"Before I end your life I have one last question." Lance could hardly breathe; he may as well have been drowning. It was as if someone was choking him while holding him under water. "You must be willing to die for her, because you did something that people kill for all the time, right?!"

Charlene was distraught," DJ please baby it's not his fault, please don't. I made a mistake...I love you please...please!"

"So you want my wife? Say it so I can hear it... before I end this!"

"NO...NO....NO...God please no!"

As DJ's focus and the barrel of his gun closed in on Lance's head, he was reminded of the pain he had once felt by the loss of his beloved Cee-Cee, and how the loss had torn his heart and life apart.

Silence filled the room. Death was in the air, and the guests could smell it. As Charlene and the others chaotically went on, it was obvious that a higher power spoke to DJ as he was reminded that the loss of his first love was not the only thing that came with Cee Cee's death. That seemingly insurmountable valley had been turned into the beautiful life he had achieved up to this point. He had been fortunate enough to witness a glimpse of what God was capable of, even in the worst circumstances. He remembered that many of the high points in his life came after what appeared to be the lowest points in life.

As the two rationales battled in his mind, DJ gave in, "Well you know what, I wish you really did love her, 'cause now you can have her!" DJ dropped the piece of steel that had caused so much panic and looked back at Charlene with tears flowing down his face, "Happy birthday baby! Happy birthday!"

That night DJ had done plenty of things he had never done. He was acting in ways he had never acted, but he recovered just in time to show mercy to the man that had committed the ultimate sin. As he stormed out of the garage, Charlene followed behind him. DJ jumped on his Suzuki 1300 motorcycle and left the entire block filled with smoke as he burned rubber out of the neighborhood. Charlene quickly jumped in her car and gave chase. She didn't know why she was chasing him. His motorcycle was three times as fast as her car, but maybe he would stop. *"Please baby, please stop...Just stop and let me hold you!"* she mumbled.

The longer she chased, the further DJ got out of sight. They had driven 5 blocks and not one light had turned red. Charlene knew that was her only hope of stopping him. She felt like fate was not on her side as DJ sped through the next 5 lights. The tears in her eyes made her feel like she was driving through a horrible rainstorm with no windshield wipers. But just as she decided to turn back, it happened.

Charlene screamed. It was the sound of unadulterated terror. It was her worse nightmare. In the distance, Charlene could see DJ's motorcycle fly wildly into the air.

"NOOOOOOOO!!! God NOOOOOOOO!!!!"

Charlene drove as fast as her new Bentley would let her. She knew there was no way that God would let a man this good, deal with so much pain; it wasn't fair, not the God that her husband always prayed to and worshipped.

As Charlene drew closer to the intersection, she knew by the number of people standing around crying, that something terrible had happened. She quickly jumped out of her car and ran to what used to be DJ's motorcycle. It was now scrap metal and fiberglass, and it had been shattered into a 1,000 pieces upon impact. The pain in Charlene's heart was indescribable as her eyes tried to focus on a mangled body that she hoped wasn't the body of her husband. As she slowly walked towards DJ's body the chaos around her seemed to dissipate 'til her husband's fleeting breaths were all she could hear. She could feel DJ's spirit, and he needed to know that she would be o.k. He had always been the soldier, provider and protector of their family, and now she had to be all of those things for him. "Hold on baby...the ambulance is on the way, you're gonna be fine," she whispered softly.

DJ knew he was hurt bad and he knew that even if he lived he wouldn't be the man that he was. "Let you tell it," he joked.

Charlene smiled but could no longer hold back the tears, "Baby..."

"Shhh ... I know...God forgives you and I do to. I do forgive you and I love you!"

If a person could die from sorrow Charlene would've at that very moment. As she leaned to kiss him on the lips, and tell DJ how much she loved him, she fell over with grief as he took his last breath. Charlene could only hold and kiss his lifeless body as the paramedics began to swarm to the scene. Her choice to selfishly fulfill *her* needs had taken the life of the man who, ironically, would've given his life in order to save hers. Now, she had to live without him, the most precious gift God had ever given her...

Epilogue

Although Torey had finished up the best season of his career in the NFL, he was glad it had finally come to an end. His team failed to make the playoffs for the third straight year, but that was the least of his worries. His individual success on the field was about to take him to new heights as he would soon cash in on his unrestricted free agent status, but Torey was still unhappy. Fortunately for him, he was able to channel his anger and frustration from Keisha onto the football field. He found solace in the notion that he would be making more money, moving on to another city and team, and that there was still *some* hope for saving his marriage. Torey had ignored Keisha's phone calls for over four months, but was still too angry to communicate with her. A new start was just what he needed, and signing with a new team would give him just that.

As Torey packed for the third trip he would make to be wooed by interested NFL teams, he hoped that this trip would give him enough information to make a decision. He wasn't quite sure which team he wanted to be with at the time, but he did know he wanted out of Houston. The city had too many bad memories in it for him. He was trying to rid himself of everything that reminded him of what he and Keisha had gone through, and leaving Houston was just the first step.

I wonder where Marcus is. Torey thought to himself while waiting for his friend to take him to the airport. Just as Torey reached for his cell phone to call, Marcus pulled up.

"Man where the hell you been?" asked Torey. "You know I need to make this flight so I can get this money."

"My bad man, I woke up late," Marcus replied. "Hey, did you hear about DJ?"

"DJ who?" asked Torey.

"You know DJ. Darryl Johnson...plays for the Rage. He got killed in a motorcycle accident last night.

"Shuttt-up!" Man stop bullshittin'! DJ, my frat brother, the running back?" asked Torey.

"Yeah man, it's hard to believe. Supposedly he caught his wife with one of their neighbors. He was trying to throw a surprise party for her and found her in the garage ballin' some other cat. He had a house full of people. Even her moms was there! Supposedly, DJ sped off on his motorcycle and lost control of the bike or something...."

"Damn, what's up with that? I guess this is how it all goes down in the world of big time pro ball huh?" Torey asked his friend. "You know, I'm thinking about signing with Baltimore if the offer is good. I think it would be a good place for me and Keisha to work things out. It would take us away from all this mess in Houston."

"Hold on Torey. Are you saying that you're thinking about staying with that ... I mean, you seriously thinking about staying with her? The same woman that kept sleeping with that nigga after you basically begged her to stop? Tell me you're not serious."

"Yeah man, I know. She's scandalous. But you know I haven't been a saint my damn self. Doesn't matter who did it first, or last for that matter."

"Maybe, but you didn't get caught. And you damn sure didn't make a fool out of her publicly. Look 'T,' you and I both have been hearing stuff about her being in a lot of the wrong places with a lot of the wrong people. Man she's not right for you. She played you so wrong, how could you just forget about all of that? She broke your heart, remember?"

"Maybe you're right. But I'm just saying, maybe a broken heart is what I needed to understand the difference between loving somebody and being in love. Man, you know I really love Keisha... I just don't know. And I don't want to drive myself crazy trying to figure it out. The one thing I *do* know, is that I'm about to get this money," Torey said as Marcus's car pulled into the "departing flights" ramp of the airport.

"Damn right playa. We need to get started on opening up another spot. I vote for a strip club!" Marcus said with a laugh.

"At least I can count on YOU not to change," Torey said with a smile as he embraced his friend. "I appreciate the ride. I'll call you after I get settled in at the hotel."

While sitting at the gate eyeing his first class plane ticket, Torey began to think back to the past few years of his life. He was about to become a very rich man. Wasn't he supposed to be HAPPY? Life wasn't supposed to go downhill from here, was it? As people began boarding, Torey realized that he had left his briefcase in Marcus' car. *Damn, I need that case,* Torey thought to himself.

RINGGGGGGG, RINGGGGGG!!!!

I hope this is Marcus calling to tell me he's on his way back up here. But I can't miss this flight. Damn, he might just have to overnight it to me. I bet I can meet him at the airport entrance and still make this flight if I hurry, Torey said to himself as he fumbled through his jacket pocket for his cell phone.

"Hello," Torey answered, "Man, I'm glad you…"

"Hello, Torey? …This is Keisha."

"What do you want Keisha? I'm about to board a flight," Torey snapped. Deep down Torey wanted so many times to hear her sweet voice. His broken heart yearned for the side of her that loved him completely for so long.

"I want my husband back. Torey, I know you still love me. So when you get back from your trip, will you please call me? I miss you."

"I gotta go Keisha."

"Bye Torey. I love you." Keisha wasn't going to lose her husband without a fight. She was going to get her husband back. Either *she* would have him, or *no one* would…

DON'T MISS:

Part II
S.L.O.W. D.O.W.N: *Choices, Decisions, and Consequences*
Coming SPRING 2006

Acknowledgements

First and foremost, thank you to the One and Only, the Most High, my Lord and Savior. Without You, there would be no me. I praise and thank you for all the blessings you have bestowed upon me throughout my lifetime. I pray that I will soon be the man that I know you want me to be and that one day **everything** I do is according to Your will. We spent many late nights and early mornings together during this process. I thank You for never leaving my side. I will continue to represent You to the best of my ability. Lord, thank You for Your grace and mercy. Most of all, thank you for your Son, Jesus Christ.

Secondly, I would like to thank my loving soul-mate and wife Johnte for loving me unconditionally and supporting me in every endeavor, til death do us part. Every single day I look forward to the rest of my life with you. To my beautiful daughter Lauren, daddy will always be here for you. I would try but words can't express what you've meant to my life. To the best parents in the world George and Ida Harris thank you for showing me, along with telling me how people should live their life. To my siblings and in-laws, Donald/Carol, George Jr./Theresa, Rock, Cheryl and Natalie/Ernest and Buck, I love you all, can't wait to start our own family reunions. To my childhood buddy, best friend and nephew, Michael, simply put I love you. To Momma Dear and Uncle Obey I love you both. To all my nephews, nieces and cousins I love you all. To all of my God-children, Kendra, Jalissa, CJ, Jayla, Kierra, Dylan, Hanna, Bryce.

A special thanks to Dr. Derrick L. Gragg, my college roommate, teammate and fraternity brother, his wife Sanya and their three beautiful children. I couldn't have done this without you my brother. Now it's time to take this thing to another level. "Books Brothers" for life!

A special thanks to Glenda Smith, the wonderful mother of my Books Brothers partner, D. Gragg. Thanks for having such a talented son "Ma."

Special thanks to the other 9 members of "DaFellaz" - Alex, Anthony, Carlos, Clarence, D. Payne, Jason, Marcus, Oscar, and William - the most dynamic, hard-working, motivated, talented young men I have ever encountered. Now that this dissertation is done, I promise we will write our book together very soon. Our story needs to be told. So get ready! And definitely to all the wonderful women behind the men I just named, thank you for loving and taking care of my boys. To my brother Carlos Broady and "Jalissa Momma" (Angela) I love you both. Thanks for being there even after my situation caused me to act REAL FUNNY for a lil' while. To all my boys in Memphis, Heavy G, Dee, Dartell, Torry, Rod and the rest of the crew it's on and poppin' now.

To Nashville, TN, the place where so much started, it was fun while it lasted. To Timothy and Jewel Winn you've always had my back, thanks. To Samantha the Pantha, Carolina aka Lil Choppa, to my ace Cheryl Gant, you know you my girl. To my manager and friend, Jasmine Sanders, its funny the roads life takes us on to get us where we're going. Let's finish it this time, SYBE Records reincarnated. Lil' Kim (not that one) you've always supported me, looking forward to working with you (hint, hint). To Shawn Wooden and Deron Jenkins, we haven't spoke in a while but I know we still down like 4 flats. To Ngwebifor aka Gwebi aka(I mean Delta) "Ms. Network" you did it again, always lookin' out for me now go ahead and get that JD. To the rest of my Cali gang Pro Bowl is around the corner. To ARPR Marketing (Arian, Catarah, Jaire, Brian, Dana "Save the Last Dance") and the rest of the crew this is just the beginning. To Tri-Destined, "The sky is the limit". To the rest of my friends, I may have forgotten to type your name because that's just Corey Harris but I haven't forgotten you. If you truly know me you know it's not intentional and I still love you, more importantly to those that hate I accomplished this, I love you too, because without you I would have never even attempted this.

Thanks to the Brothers of Kappa Alpha Psi Fraternity, Inc., the Nu Rho Chapter of Vanderbilt University – old school and new school, and the "Magnificent 7" of Spring 1990. We've come a long way men.

Thank you Mr. E. Lynn Harris for all your support. You have been a true inspiration throughout this process. Thanks for taking time to share some of your creative wisdom with me.

Finally, to the parents that may read this book. Don't ever limit your children with negative thoughts. They can be anything they want to be. And besides, life is about the journey of dreams and half the fun is chasing those dreams. So let your kids dream, help them to dream and then show them the way. Because I'm living proof that life is more than a random stroke of luck. Dreams do come true. Life is the challenge of using every gift God has given us to its fullest and anything less than nurturing your child's gift is waste of His blessings.